Michael Henry

Life thoughts of Michael Henry

Being a reprint of papers

Michael Henry

Life thoughts of Michael Henry
Being a reprint of papers

ISBN/EAN: 9783337134433

Printed in Europe, USA, Canada, Australia, Japan

Cover: Foto ©Raphael Reischuk / pixelio.de

More available books at **www.hansebooks.com**

LIFE THOUGHTS OF MICHAEL HENRY.

LIFE THOUGHTS

OF

MICHAEL HENRY,

BEING A

REPRINT OF PAPERS CONTRIBUTED BY HIM

TO THE

"SABBATH READINGS,"

ISSUED BY

THE JEWISH ASSOCIATION FOR THE DIFFUSION OF RELIGIOUS KNOWLEDGE.

———◆———

LONDON:

P. VALLENTINE, 34, ALFRED STREET, BEDFORD SQUARE.

1876.

LONDON:

PRINTED BY WERTHEIMER, LEA AND CO.,

CIRCUS PLACE, FINSBURY CIRCUS.

INTRODUCTION.

To those of the present generation who may read this volume, it will not be necessary to say a single word about the Author. For the name of MICHAEL HENRY lives, and is likely to live, in the heart of every member of that community he loved so well.

But lest, in days to come, this book may chance to fall into the hands of any to whom its Author's name is unknown, or lest Time—often only mindful of work, and oblivious of the worker—may efface from human memory the high virtues of him, whose Life Thoughts lie embalmed in these pages, it is right that the reader should, by these few words of introduction, be introduced to the Author.

The task falls to the lot of those, who had the privilege of being among his fellow-workers, and who knew him best.

His was no ordinary life. Busy among the busiest in the world's work, he was busier still in the work of improving the world. Not with the chimeras of wild theorists, nor with the unpractical schemes of ordinary philanthropists ; but dealing singly with individuals, doing practical good *in detail* to the men and women and boys and girls with whom he came in contact, and imparting to everyone, with whom or for whom he worked, a share of his own goodness, a spark of his own fervid zeal for the cause of Religion and Progress.

Good himself, he believed in the goodness of all the world besides ; and whatever faults he possessed ·were but the faults of optimism.

No one can read these pages without being irresistibly led to the conclusion that none but a truly pious man could have penned them, and that they constitute the natural outpouring of a pure, unsullied heart.

The conclusion will be a just one. It is no exaggeration to say that the lessons the Author inculcates are those which he practised in his every-day life ; and that many of the ideals of character represented in these pages were, to no small extent, realised in himself.

His life, private and public, was one long act of self-denial. Ever working for others ; ever forgetful of his own personal interests, pleasures and ambitions ; having but one aim, but one object in life—to make his fellow-men and fellow-Jews happier, wiser and better ; worthy of the ancient glories of their race, worthy of those glories which are the Israelite's hope.

CONTENTS.

MOSES.

כִּי מָצָאתָ חֵן בְּעֵינַי :

" Thou hast found grace in my sight."—EXODUS xxxiii. 17.

ENCIRCLED by the sacred halo of Revelation, Sinai stands peculiarly distinguished among the mountains of all the world. And, like the sacred hill on which the most divine of gifts descended, the Prophet chosen to receive that gift, Moses our Master, stands pre-eminent on the face of history amidst the great names of all humanity. The circumstance that he was selected to receive and promulgate the sublime code dictated by Heaven to Earth, suffices to single him out amongst the children of men, and to stamp him with the most remarkable distinction and the most intense individuality.

To fulfil a great object—the teaching of the Law of life on earth—he received from Heaven an extra-ordinary and peculiar inspiration. But his inspiration, though it glorified his being, did not transfigure it into a more spiritual order of creation. He was a Prophet, and the greatest of Prophets;—but he was a Man, though the greatest of men.

We must not misunderstand the expression *inspiration* in its Biblical sense. There are some who misuse the term, and such misuse sometimes produces a dangerous confusion of ideas. Some amplify its application, and imagine that the inspiration of the Prophet endowed him permanently with superhuman powers, and elevated him above the ranks of ordinary mortality. Others extend its supposed import, and *mis*apply it to every description of genius. Yet in the due Biblical sense of the word "inspiration," the Prophet was only inspired within certain limits and for certain objects: and mere genius is not inspired at all. Because inspiration, in its highest and theological meaning, appears to be the direct dictation by Heaven to human hands, lips, or minds, of certain laws, truths, and behests, which Heaven desires to proclaim and promulgate for the promotion of human welfare. In the Divine policy, it has seemed best that these laws, truths, and commands, be declared by the familiar channel of the voice and pen of mortal men—creatures like those to whom they are to be announced and whom they mainly affect—rather than by astounding and supernatural manifestations which might have been used to convey to earth the will of Heaven. Inspiration is, in effect, a superhuman impulse acting through human means, for a superhuman purpose directed to human objects. And we insist on this definition, because mistaken persons, who apply to genius the word "inspiration," would elevate profane writers to a spiritual level, and consequently degrade Biblical revelation from its sublime eminence; or they imagine inspiration to affect every word, thought, action, and feeling of its recipient, and thus fail to learn the lesson derivable from the consideration of a good and graceful life—the life of a man like ourselves in all respects, save for the one circumstance that the marvel of inspiration has descended upon him.

Moses is an instance in point. It is true he was inspired. Inspired surpassingly. Inspired more distinctly and directly than any other Prophet. The impulse of inspiration glorified him for the purpose of enabling him to teach humanity that moral law by which Heaven decided to control the world which it had created. No better or wiser medium could have been selected than the lips of a man of the most noble character and a most gentle spirit; a heart ever longing for justice, and warm with love for his kind.

That Moses was inspired—and far above the calibre of all other inspired men—we need scarcely urge. There is no other instance in all history of the union of such varied elements of greatness in any one character. There is no other instance in all history of one man being at the same time a legislator so farseeing and judicious; a statesman so politic and wise; a patriot so devoted and energetic; a general so able and valiant; a leader so prudent; a priest so pious; a teacher so successful; a friend so tender; a relative so meek; a ruler so decided and yet so accessible to reason. It would be idle to compare him with any character in ancient history, even those who might have boasted the greatest combination of great qualities.

Any reflecting man must easily see and appreciate the almost immeasurable distance between Moses, *our* hero, and any hero of antiquity or of modern times. And, passing from the characters of such heroes to their careers, we shall find the distance equally great, the abyss of separation equally difficult to bridge. There is no code so original, so all-wise, so universal, so immortal, as that which Moses taught the world. Other codes are compilations. The charter of Moses was a creation. There is no social system so triumphantly true.

The revolutions of the history of society confirm the superhuman wisdom of the Mosaic dispensation. It taught the purest love in an age of rage, vengeance, and hatred. It evolved the brightest wisdom amidst clouds of ignorance and superstition—even in an era in which Knowledge was disguised in magical myths, and Faith itself shrouded in mystery. It initiated and developed institutions which have been immortal: institutions which only seemed to perish when ignorance was rampant, and which were seen to rise like the phœnix from the fires of destruction into a brighter glow of resurrection, when the torch of Knowledge throws its gleam on the world. It deduced order and law despite the tangle of misrule and chaotic disorder. The inexorable and unfailing testimony of fact and circumstance forces the minds of men to bear almost involuntary witness to the inspiration of its promulgator and to the divinity of such inspiration, as thoroughly as if indeed the old Rabbinical hyperbole be an historical fact—as if it be true that not alone the souls of all men then living, but the souls of all men evermore to be, stood around the base of Sinai, when the Commandments were delivered, amidst the thunders and lightnings and the Voice of the Trumpet from Heaven!

But we must be equally careful to avoid falling into

the error of believing that inspiration so transfigured the individuality of Moses that he stood absolutely above the possible imitation of less favoured men. Though the Law was divine; though the lawgiver was inspired; though he and his faltering voice were selected for the delivery of the Law to the world; yet let us carefully avoid the supposition that the man so favoured was himself divine. No; his inspiration was in his heart, but not always; in his words, but not in all of them: on one or two occasions it failed to control all his actions. Because he was subject to human imperfections; because he was so very human, it is the more easy to believe that the perfect and super-human Law which he proclaimed was not of mortal framing, but divine.

Yes: and because he was so very human, from this humanity we learn a wonderful lesson. The teachings of Heaven do not reside only in prophetic utterances and in Scriptural records, but in the example of the careers of men. And thus the life of Moses in its struggles, its strivings, and its sorrows; in its intrinsic beauty, standing in bright relief amid the shadows of his human imperfections, presents a model offered to us not alone for contemplation—not alone for admiration—but even for imitation. He has taught us not only by his immortal Law, but likewise by his mortal Life.

And thus he stands pre-eminent among men, not only by the majesty of his mission, but also by the almost angelic, yet fully human, beauty of his character. In that character were combined the two extreme virtues of a noble nature, meekness and manliness. His meekness was substantiated by his

sturdy manliness. His manliness was beautified by his
angelic meekness.

Placed high among men by the grandeur of his
charge, the story of his life, and the loftiness of his
character, he yet seems to move amongst us like one
of us, whom we may venture to follow, and, in a
humble fashion, to imitate. It is remarkable that,
though he lived in times so remote, and though his
destiny was so peculiar, yet his nature is thoroughly
intelligible. His aspirations, his passions, and desires,
nay, his very weaknesses—were colored with the familiar tints of those of ordinary men. His virtues, though
sanctified and spiritualised, were not unreal nor impracticable. He is indeed so very real, that it seems
he might have lived amongst us yesterday, even in our
common-place, every-day walk of life; and yet he was
so holy, that if we would permit our tutored fancies to
fashion a pattern for resemblance, he would be the
man. While, if we would allow our more etherial
flights of conception to imagine an angel upon earth—
that angel would be he!

We do not learn from the Scripture record, nor need
we inquire, whether it was from his remarkable virtue,
ability, and nobleness of character, that he was selected
for his marvellous mission; or whether the incidence
of that marvellous mission communicated to him his
especial grace of moral nature. In some respects the
man and his mission are inseparable. Yet not in all
respects. Sinai was glorified when Heaven descended
on its chosen crest: yet when the Awful Presence departed, it remained in the cold outlines of its familiar
form. Thus Moses was glorified when the fire of
inspiration burned in his bosom: but when the sacred

glow passed from him, he moved in the ranks of ordinary men, spoke human words, and thought human thoughts. Yes; though the Moses of history is essentially the Moses of the Bible; though to us the halo of Sinai seems to rest upon his brow; yet we can see him even through this glowing light; and he seems to descend, at times, from the radiant path to our every-day earth, and move amongst us. We can understand him. We can conceive that a human heart throbbed in his bosom, that human ardour glittered in his eyes; that human hopes and fears, joys and sorrows—yes, and human passions also, formed and fretted the current of his career.

May the time come when an able hand will add to the literature of England a life, written by a Jewish pen, of this extraordinary man! Such a biography would far exceed the limits of these pages—and we have not attempted one; but it would be a work for which generations yet unborn would have reason to be grateful. All that we would do here is to call attention to that which seems strangely overlooked in these modern days—the character of Moses as a man, apart from his character as a heavenly missionary. We may infer something of the inner life-story of the unparalleled Prophet from the suggestive references to that story which appear from time to time in the course of the Scripture narrative, from the hour which first introduces him to the sacred scene amid the tall water-plants that fringed the Nile, till the pathetic day when that life-story is for ever parted from the narrative, with which it is so intimately blended.

The second chapter of Exodus contains, alone, sufficient allusion to the character of Moses to render its beauty thoroughly intelligible. At once, in the few verses that compose this chapter, we ascertain that his nobleness of mind precluded his allowing his interests, as attached to the princely court and dominant race of Egypt, to interfere with his determination to fight the battle of his distressed brethren, and to identify himself with the cause of this abject people. No circumstance of Egyptian education, no self-interest or ambition, thus damped the ardour of his attachment to his fallen and enslaved race. His heart was not corrupted by courtly blandishments nor courtly favours. He imperilled position, liberty, and safety, and, in fact, became an exile, by his spirited conduct. His manliness and hatred of injustice induced him to chastise an oppressor; his love of peace and his kindliness lead him to endeavour to part two struggling Israelites. This manly spirit of hatred of tyranny appears to actuate him when he flies to the rescue of the maidens of Midian. In each case, he is treated with ingratitude— which appears to follow his every step through life. His brethren revile him (verse 14). The Midianite damsels neglect him (verse 20). Meek and placid, he does not seek to punish the former, nor to censure the latter. Careless of the charms of ambition, he is content to lead a shepherd's life in the fields of Jethro.

And now we will roughly glance through some striking instances, interspersed in the Pentateuch, of the beauty of his holy nature. Chapter III. affords a remarkable testimony to his meekness and his prudence: the language of verse 11 clearly indicates no want of faith, but the reticence of his modesty and the circumspection of calm judgment. His song in Chapter XV. proves his reluctance to attribute any glory to himself;

he carefully attributes it to the Hand from which it came. Chapter XVIII. instances the readiness with which he listened to sage advice. In Chapter XXXII. he prays for his people, and even offers—himself innocent —to be punished for their sins. From this angelic sublimity of character he descends to the ordinary pale of mortality in the wild wail of despair (Numb. xi. 12, 13) with which he pleads for aid. His gentleness and self-abnegation and the absence of envy are singularly evidenced by his earnest desire that the spirit of prophecy—the real love of virtue and most direct means to moral perfection—might descend on *all* the people. His prayer—his heart's battle—for the pardon of this rebellious people (Numb. xiv.) shows the sweetness and loving tendencies of his disposition. His forgiveness of his sister and brother, who even added their bitter dole to the national ingratitude, is one of the most touching instances of the heavenly forbearance of his nature. His prayer (Numb. xvii.) for the appointment of a successor manifests his caution, his freedom from jealousy or envy, and his earnest patriotism.

In fact, two words in Chapter XXXIV. of Deuteronomy describe his character admirably; Moses was עֶבֶד ה׳ "The *servant* of the Lord." He served Him in fulfilling His behests; he served Him in proclaiming His Law; he served Him in the beauty of his life!

But—as we all know—when his great work was nearly accomplished; when he had brought his people near to the confines of the Promised Land; when he had led them from bondage to freedom; when he had taught them the Great Law of Life, and had laid the basis of that Tower which alone resists the shocks of foes and the attacks of ages—which alone reaches from

the earth on which it stands unto the heavens by which
it is crowned;—then, he died! He did not press his
weary foot on the soil for which he fought, for which
he lived, for which he languished! Oh! Brethren of
the House of Israel, who can learn so much from the
story of his life, learn something also from the story of
his death! Brethren, who have in this life toiled so
ardently for some Promised Land that your feet shall
never touch—some Promised Land flowing with milk
and honey to be gathered for yourselves, to be stored
and garnered for your own ambition, and for the
happiness and pleasure of your own children and your
own kindred—Brethren, who perish when the borders
of the Land are reached—think of *his* grief, *his* sorrow;
he who sought and strove for the Land and its
abundance, not for his own sake, not for his children's
sake, not for the exaltation of his name and family, but
for the sake of his rebellious brethren! And you, who
can understand him better; you, who follow humbly in
his footsteps, and toil for a Promised Land and for its
milk and honey for the sake of your brethren, for the
weak, the poor, the aged, the helpless, the young; for
the generations who are to live when you shall have
perished; you can in better degree sympathize with
his sorrow, when the Land he was never more to see
and never to touch was spread out before his eyes.
But you can also sympathize with the possibility of that
most divine joy which may have comforted and animated
him at the last supreme moment; when life was
passing away; when the hopes of earth were fading
from his heart, and the prospect of the Promised Land
was fading from his dying eyes—the sublime, heavenly
joy of knowing that life's great victory was won—but

not for himself. No, not for himself—but for generations yet unborn : for a world hidden in the future : for ages that should bless his name beyond all other men !

Moses was taken from us more than three thousand years ago. But,—

> " He is not dead, whose glorious mind
>   Lifts thine on high ;
> To live in hearts we leave behind
>   Is not to die."

CAMPBELL.

He is with us still—still in the spirit. For his spirit, like the cloud by day and the pillar of fire by night, leads us on our way through life's tangled wilderness, teaching us duty in the daylight of joy, and showing us comfort in the night-time of adversity. Still may he lead us, the spirit of the Great Prophet—the servant of the Father whom we adore ! Guided by the Divine Law which he proclaimed, and by the sublime life which he led—both glorious and gracious gifts of Heaven to Earth—may we pass safely and trustfully amidst the foes that obstruct us, and through the perils that assail us in life's long wilderness. But, more faithful than our fathers, may we never doubt our leader's word ; more happy than that leader, may our feet press the Promised Land on earth,—or may we meet him—happier, immortally—in the Promised Land of Heaven !

ELIJAH.

וִיהִי־נָא פִּי־שְׁנַיִם בְּרוּחֲךָ אֵלָי :

"I pray thee, let a two-fold portion of thy Spirit be upon me."
II KINGS ii. 9.

As a brilliant comet flashes across the surface of the firmament, coming we know not whence, going we know not whither, mysterious in origin, nature, purpose, and destiny, so Elijah flashes athwart the horizon of Jewish History. He is a brilliant meteor among the personages of the Bible. The little we know of him has an absorbing, almost an awful interest. He, scarcely even excepting the unsurpassed and unparalleled Moses, or the princely Abraham, is the most majestic of all the most marvellous figures of the true and varied drama, the first scene of which opened with the outburst of Nature from Chaos, and the last scene of which closed on the sacred forms of the later prophets, dejected and dispirited—yet breathing words of hope and comfort to a fallen people.

About the time at which Homer sang his stately and graceful epics, and Lycurgus framed his stern laws in Greece, this Hebrew prophet lived in Palestine. Not a hundred years had passed since the kingdom of Israel had been rent in twain by the dissensions between the tribes. The royal house of Judah still reigned at

Jerusalem. The usurping successors of Jeroboam ruled the northern provinces.

Our knowledge of the history of Elijah, and our narratives of his utterances, do not come to us from his own hand, as is the case with many other prophets. There is no book of the Bible that bears his august name, or is transmitted to us as having been written or dictated by him. What we know of him comes chiefly from the First and Second Books of Kings, though, doubtless, tradition has helped the history in fashioning it in the way in which it is usually understood. In the character and the deeds of this prophet, we find that blending of mildness and majesty, that mingling of mercy with might, which marks every messenger, every message of Heaven, which in its most sublime and ineffably supreme form marks the attributes of the Godhead. The awful prophet, whose fiery thunders invoked the flames of just vengeance on the wicked and murderous pseudo-priests of Baal; the prophet who fearlessly, with flashing eye, denounced the impiety of tyrannic kings—Elijah, the terrible minister of divine wrath, yet bent gently and tenderly over the feeble widow's boy, and with the love of a caressing father, and the love of a comforting mother, invoked divine compassion, and prayed that the breath of renewed life might flush the pallid cheeks of the child. Yes, he, whose zealous heart was ruthless when the cause of the Lord was to be set on high, is the same hero as he, who in his heart's desolate sadness, prayed to be taken away from the struggles and sorrows of his life.

For, when we remove from the history of Elijah the mysterious halo that surrounds him, we shall find in him, in the glimpses of his inner life, the human and not the superhuman element. Notwithstanding the miraculous circumstance of his translation and the promise of his return, Elijah was not really far different in the scope of his thoughts, his feelings, even his failings, from other men, men living in his own and in modern days. How otherwise can we explain his occasional weakness, when he prayed to be relieved of his severe and painful task? How, otherwise, explain the impatient almost rebellious temper which he manifested when the widow reproached him for the supposed death of her son?

Indeed, our faith in the Bible is strengthened by our appreciation of the fallibility of character occasionally evident in those whom God selected as the vehicles of His Revelation. They were only His instruments. They were but mortals, even erring mortals. They were men like ourselves, yet men who battled with temptation, and often triumphed over it. The gentle hills of Mendip, and the rough mountain of Hecla, are alike made of dull earth, though the one lifts its silent height, clothed in pleasant verdure, and bathed in serene sunshine, while the terrible Voice of God's fiery thunder roars through the other's crest, and proclaims His Might. Nay, even immortal Sinai, on which God's awful Presence rested, is a crag undistinguishable from the dull rough peaks that surround it in the Arabian wilds.

Of Elijah's early history we know nothing. He was by birth a Gileadite, but, as the land of Gilead was divided amongst at least three tribes, it is not clear to which tribe he belonged. Gilead is a region of which very frequent mention is made in the Bible.

It was situated on the east of the Jordan, and was a mountainous territory, yet celebrated for the excellence of its pastures. These pastures, or rather the sleekness and number of the cattle bred on them, seem to have attracted the attention of two of the tribes, the sons of Reuben and of Gad, who desired to settle in the fair and fertile land, instead of seeking "pastures new" across the Jordan.* Medicinal plants grew amidst the mountains, or in the fields of Gilead. The warlike judge, Jepthah, was a Gileadite, not only by family name, but by locality.

The first call of Elijah came at a sad epoch of Jewish history. Among all the wicked successors of Jeroboam on the throne of revolted Israel, Ahab stands in shameful pre-eminence. He had a very great misfortune, the infliction of a wicked wife. The wretched queen, Jezebel, has gone down to posterity as a name or bye-word for female iniquity. It is singular, but not the less true, that women when wicked (which is very rare) are *very* wicked. Posterity has, however, done its worst for women, by adopting their names in language as personifications of the vices of which they were culpable. We talk of a Jezebel, a Xantippe, a Lucrezia Borgia, a Brinvilliers, almost as if these were common nouns instead of proper names.

Ahab was a son of king Omri, who built the capital city Samaria, and who was raised to the throne, like some of the old Roman emperors, on the shoulders of the soldiers. Ahab married, as we have said, the wicked Jezebel, daughter of the king of Sidon, a domain situated on the north-west coast of the kingdom of Israel, and celebrated, or rather infamous, for the

* Numbers xxxii.

worship of Ashtaroth, probably the same as the Cretan Astarte, or the Roman Venus. The worship of idols was in full force in the kingdom of Israel. With furious cruelty Jezebel induced Ahab to slay the priests or pious "prophets," (probably preachers) of our sacred Faith, though some of these were saved secretly by the king's chamberlain, Obadiah, and concealed, by his care, in refuges in which he provided food for them, a circumstance which was afterwards reported to Ahab. King Ahab did not, however, punish Obadiah for it with death or disgrace, a fact which leads one to imagine that Ahab had some redeeming qualities, or that he did not reveal the secret to Jezebel, for certainly she would have hounded Ahab on to slay Obadiah.

Ahab's wickedness becoming intolerable, Elijah, who now first appears on the scene, was called on to denounce the king, and to threaten him with a visitation of national famine and drought.

Elijah was then directed to escape from the wrath of Ahab. We do not propose to give in other words the details so admirably related in the Book of Kings. The story is doubtless familiar to our readers, and no pen can give it a fraction of the force and beauty which adorn the scriptural narrative.

Let us rapidly glance over the events of Elijah's career.

In his retreat the fugitive was fed by ravens, a signal proof of the miraculous care by which he was preserved, a miracle which perhaps loses its intensity when we remember how, every day of our lives, greater miracles occur ; the feeding of millions of God's creatures by His tender care, manifesting itself in the wonders of natural reproduction, and that industrial genius by which Nature becomes the comrade of Art and the servant of Utility.

But Elijah was not long to dwell secluded from human society. The tender charities of home-life were yet reserved for him. From his shelter in the glens he went, by Divine direction, to the house of a poor widow in a town in the domain of Sidon, at the foot of Lebanon. There, again by miraculous providence, the scanty store in the poor woman's home failed not. Her son fell sick, and apparently died. The mother in her anguish reproached the prophet, as if his presence had caused the loss of her child. Elijah himself feared that this might be so, and for once it would seem his faith wavered. But for a moment only. He invoked the help of God, and implored Him to revive the dead or dying child. And He who is mighty to strike, is merciful to save ! He who with His hand of Power dooms to destruction myriads of transgressors, yet with His hand of Pity stanches the widowed mother's tears. And who shall deny (though we cannot understand it or fathom it), that when His Hand deals death to thousands, it is as much fraught with Love as when that Hand gives new life to the dying child !

Meanwhile the atrocities of Ahab continued. Famine and drought blighted the land. Elijah, impelled by Divine Command, went towards Samaria, the royal residence of the wicked king. On his road he met the chamberlain, Obadiah, and commissioned him to ask Ahab to hasten to him. The officer naturally hesitated to "beard the lion in his den." But he yielded; and Ahab and Elijah met. In vain the haughty tyrant

c

endeavoured to intimidate the prophet. Elijah, conscious that he held a sublime trust, and being ever zealous in the fulfilment of his duty, disregarded Ahab's threats, reproached him boldly for his iniquities, and offered to rest his credence on a test in which he should take part on the one side, and the priests of Baal on the other. Altars were raised. The priests of Baal invoked their idol to testify his power by kindling them with superhuman fire. Their efforts were vain. They were driven to desperation by the prophet's taunts, but their impotence was manifest. Their prayers, their cries, fell powerless on the senseless ear. Then Elijah, after taking care to drench the altar with floods of water, probably lest he might be accused of obtaining fire by artificial means or trickery, called on God to vindicate His power and His prophet. The fire streamed from Heaven! Then rang forth the cry that the one Lord united in himself all powers— יְיָ הוּא הָאֱלֹהִים : יְיָ הוּא הָאֱלֹהִים that cry which in the self-same words, rings year by year from the lips of the people of Israel, when the Day of Reconciliation draws to its close, and when the fire that *they* invoke from Heaven to complete their sacrifice is the gleaming light of Pardon!

Here let us pause, and consider the extraordinary faith of Elijah, who courageously upbraided a mighty and cruel king, regardless of the dangers he incurred, regardful only of his imperious duty. He knew well that the king had already ruthlessly slain many prophets, preachers or teachers of his faith. But he looked death calmly in the face; and the heart that was full of faith in God and of zeal for His cause trembled not in the presence of the despot!

But Elijah showed a still greater proof of courage —courage, moral rather than physical. Though his bravery of spirit was clearly beyond doubt; though, as it would seem afterwards, he did not cling to life; yet when he was ordered to fly for refuge and conceal-ment, he fled and hid himself. The same soul, which did not blench before a cruel monarch's throne, bowed before the will of Heaven submissively. When ordered to imperil his life, he bravely risked it. When ordered to preserve that life, he, with equal courage, sought to save it. He "feared God and knew no other fear."

He did not cling to life, but he did not know that he was not to die. It was not the foreknowledge of translation to Heaven that emboldened him to face Ahab, and to trust to the lonely and barren fastnesses in the mountains.

For when this part of his work was done; when the wicked priests of Baal had paid the penalty of their blasphemies and their crimes; when the power of Heaven had removed the famine and the drought; there came to the prophet that which perhaps comes to many a weary worker in the world—a wish for rest and death.

He had been misunderstood and unappreciated; his labours had met with ingratitude. He had removed the burdens of affliction that rested so heavily on his country and his king, but he had been pursued with implacable vindictiveness. His life was sought; again he fled. Worn with anxieties, yet ever willing to obey, he lifted up his voice to Heaven—and asked to die!

But, even in this supreme agony of his life—an agony from which men inferior to prophets are not exempt—he did not seek death by his own hand, nor strive to hasten it by any act of his. He only humbly sought to be relieved of a burden which he felt lay too heavy on his heart.

Suicide was not a crime common to the Jews of old. Nay, it was scarcely known amongst them. Yet, the so-called noble Roman and the so-called civilized Japanese exalt that crime to the rank of a virtue. The Jew meets death with fortitude and glorified hope, *now* in these prosaic days on the quiet pillow, as he met it with like hope and fortitude at the martyr's stake, or on the battle-field, in the glorious days of old. Such is his confidence in the Life Giver, who proclaimed Himself רָהוּם וְחַנּוּן אֶרֶךְ אַפַּיִם "Merciful, gracious, and long-suffering," that he thanks Him and relies on Him for both lives; life here, life on the shores unknown. The God who takes care of us here, will surely take care of us hereafter. He is as near to us now, as He will be in the world to come! What is there to fear?

אַךְ־טוֹב וָחֶסֶד יִרְדְּפוּנִי כָּל־יְמֵי חַיָּי
וְשַׁבְתִּי בְּבֵית יְיָ לְאֹרֶךְ יָמִים :

> " As through life's shadowed vale my footsteps stray,
> Thy Mercy smiles, Thy bounties cheer my way;
> And when my spirit seeks its sacred rest,
> 'T will dwell in safety on Thy sheltering breast."

And, when in some few instances a Jew has perished by his own hand, in our historic days, how noble has been the self-sacrifice! Thus Eleazar the Maccabee doomed himself to death beneath the weight of the turreted elephant, in his heroic and supreme devotion to his country and his faith; thus the aged Rabbi of York perished in the horrors of the besieged castle. Even Samson drew death on himself, so that the enemies of his country might perish,—unless, indeed, he drew down the building in which he stood, in the frenzy of agony. And Saul—well, as to the sin of suicide involved in his sad story, let us believe that, in the touching words so familiar to us, "the recording angel dropped a tear, and blotted it out for ever!"

But Elijah was not to die in the agony of his despair. His work was not yet complete.

For the answer of God came to him. The roaring wind arose and pealed in ringing thunder through the trembling rocks; the rifted mountain fell asunder, rent by the raging storm! The earthquake cleft the plains with awful shock! The raging fire flamed beneath the lurid sky! But not in the thunder of the wind, nor the shock of the earthquake, nor the flash of the fire was the Lord! . . . . But there was the sound of a still small voice: and then came the Voice of the Lord!

Oh! marvellous type of infinite Compassion! We must bear the storm, and the shock, the alarms, the pains, the scathing griefs of life—but the Mercy comes at last; and in that Mercy is God's dwelling place. Yes! He proclaims His Might and Majesty, it is true, in the stupendous voice of Nature, the "wreck of matter and the crash of worlds," but to us, to each of us, He speaks in the "still small voice," which is only heard in each man's inmost breast; heard only by himself; the Voice of Duty borne on the wings of Conscience, called into action by the mercy and grace of God.

So the prophet was told that he had yet duties to perform, work to achieve, trusts to fulfil.

But doubtless his Master had compassion on His servant's weariness, and He promised him a successor, one to relieve him from his life's burden of work. And he was enjoined to select the loyal Elisha. Even in this brief episode appears one of those touches of "nature that make the whole world kin," and which abound in the Bible; one of those "tender charities," which bring the Bible home to the heart. Elisha, in the glory of his new mission, in the pride of his triumphant exaltation, in the awful gravity of his new duties, yet asked and was allowed "to kiss his father and mother," before he parted from them—to bid his dear ones at home a tender and a loving farewell!

When next Elijah appears on the sacred scene, he had once more to confront the fierce tyrant and to reproach him for slaying and robbing Naboth; a startling instance of the wickedness of that sin of covetousness which is denounced in the tenth commandment. Ahab dreaded Elijah, whom he idly affected to accuse of personal hostility to him; for often, indeed, had the Tishbite appeared as an embodied Conscience, a living, a speaking vengeance!

Ahab died in the battle field, and a son scarcely less guilty than himself succeeded him. Unwarned by the career and fate of his father, Ahaziah pursued the paths of idolatry. Elijah was sent to rebuke him and to advise him of his approaching death, and he was preserved miraculously for that purpose from the soldiers of Ahaziah. With this act, he seems to have accomplished his life's mission.

Elijah, being conscious of his approaching departure·

from earth, desired to spare Elisha, who loved him so
well, the pain of seeing him pass away. Or it may be
that Elijah wished not to be disturbed in that supreme
moment of his departure by the presence of a friend
and follower whom he dearly loved, and whose affection formed a tie that bound to earth the soul about to
wing its flight to heaven. For it is a custom of our
people to remove gently from the bedside of the dying,
the dear ones whom they are to quit. And this is
done either lest the sorrow of the living should be too
severe, or lest it disturb the dying: or more likely the
motive is a fear lest in that mighty moment of the
soul's farewell flight, the tender loves, the trembling
hopes and fears of earth, shall mingle with the thoughts
which *then* belong to Heaven alone. For it is not
ambition, nor fame, nor avarice, nor pleasure, but Love
the Immortal, that forms the last bond which anchors
the captive soul to earth, before it breaks from earth
for ever!

And Love is immortal. Surely, we shall meet again,
in the world beyond the grave—transfigured, purified,
but still remembered and beloved—the father, the
mother; the husband, the wife; the little child—the
child matured to the strength of manhood, and the
graces of womanhood: ah! all the dear ones—from
whom we part in agony in this valley of the shade.

The faithful follower Elisha would not leave his beloved master in the looming approach of the supreme
farewell. Wherever Elijah went, he followed him;
and as the last moment of departure neared, Elisha
asked—not for worldly wealth, or rank, or material
inheritance—but for a twofold portion of his master's
spirit. "Thou hast asked a hard thing," said Elijah,

"but if thou seest me taken from thee, it shall be so."

And then occurred that marvellous and mysterious scene, the miraculous translation of Elijah. A whirlwind or a storm (סערה) arose, and a chariot and horses of fire descended, and Elijah mounted this chariot, and was wafted in it to the sky.

Elijah passed from earth to Heaven, and he cast his mantle on Elisha, and gave him a twofold portion of his spirit. That spirit was surely the spirit of duty done in spite of drawbacks, dislike and difficulty. A grander spirit never pervaded a human heart. It speaks to us all—to all who would fain neglect duty's trumpet-call from apathy, from love of ease, from jealousy, from ill-temper, from exaggerated bashfulness, from indulgent tendencies to rest or pleasure;—the many motives which urge men to be deaf to the call of duty—motives which are varied forms of selfishness.

It is true that some men are too anxious to thrust themselves into the world of action and to undertake responsibilities for which they are unfitted, or to which they are urged by ambition. But others sin far more deeply in an opposite fashion, by disregard of, or indifference to, that "still small voice" which speaks in the recesses of the heart; which bids men take up their work and do it. Our earthly powers are given to us in trust, and our consciousness of them is the advocate of duty:

> "Arise for duties yet to do,
>   Or aims achieve, or plans pursue!
>   For labour, life is given.
>   Dream not, nor idly bind the hours
>   To earthly rest by chains of flowers;
>   Arise! and think of Heaven!"

It seems to us that the characteristic of Elijah's life was this:—He was a man of quiet modest tastes, perhaps of retiring disposition, perhaps not even an impulsively brave man, certainly not ambitious. But at the voice of duty, he was aroused. All the manliness of his nature stood forth. *Self* was obliterated. Yes, regardless of self, of self-interest, of temperament and desire of ease, or even of safety, he was "zealous," and stood forth to do his duty. *For he was strong in faith.* This was his watchword. He "committed his way" trustfully to a Hand which he felt would uphold him.

Miraculous and mysterious as was the departure of Elijah, it is not more miraculous and mysterious than the translation which we call death; the ordeal through which the millions of the past have departed, and which we all await.

Oh! happy we, if when we pass away, we leave behind us, like Elijah, a twofold portion of the spirit which those whom we love have reason to desire of us! Happy, if we lead lives of faith and duty in a spirit so righteous and strong, that those whom we leave behind —the children in the home, the children in the schools, the men and women of our own time—may pray that a twofold portion of our spirit shall rest with them. *This* is, "*not to die.*"

There are certain traditions connected with him. It is said, that he who sees him in dreams, he who salutes him in a vision and receives his greeting in return is a happy man. His original mission was, it is said, delivered to him by Moses. A beautiful story is related as to a visionary meeting between him and Rabbi Joshua ben Levi, when Elijah promised the

sage that the Messianic age would be proclaimed when
men deserved its advent. It may be observed that
Scripture makes mention but once only (Chronicles ii.)
of his prophetic powers of warning as evoked against
the kings of Judah. The wicked Jehoram was then
the object of his severe denunciations.

The promise of the re-appearance of Elijah by
Malachi—as the harbinger of the Messianic reign of
peace and love, is still fondly dwelt on by our people
—though how or what will be the nature of that
return, we cannot surmise. Elijah's return typifies
the reign of duty and unselfishness, which must
prevail ere the Messiah shall come; and he who passed
from earth in the days of yore will again return to the
haunts of men. On Sabbath nights, when the day of
joyful rest is waning, and we stand on the threshold of
the newly dawning week of work, we pray for the
return of Elijah the prophet. Every night on which
we celebrate the exit from Egypt by the ancient
service of the Hagodah, the wine-cup is set in readiness for the expected Prophet. Even, in our daily
grace after meals, the anticipation of his restoration is
not forgotten.

To dwell on this advent, and on the mode in which
we may merit it, is not within our province here. Let
us rather briefly gather our own lessons from the
prophet's life. All have duties to perform that seem
sometimes hard to us. Let us rise up, be strong,
and do what is given to us to do. Not for ambition,
not for fame, not for wealth, not for vain glory, but
for Faith. Let us be " obedient to the Master's call,"
and break for the sake of Heaven the bonds that bind
us to the ease and temptations of earth. The still

small Voice speaks to us all. All of us are fed by the bountiful Hand that supplied the fugitive Prophet. All of us are called on to "labour and to wait." All of us can so govern our spirit that others may ask us for its inheritance, when we shall pass away. Many are the tyrannies and the falsehoods with which we have to struggle. True, indeed, that when *we* shall have to pass away, we cannot anticipate a glorified translation from earth to heaven. We cannot expect the glowing chariot and horses of fire to bear us from this world to the world unknown. No! we must await the resurrection of the dead in the cold embraces of the lonely grave. We must pass away in the faintness, perhaps in the pain and struggle, of death. But, may that supreme hour of death not pass in the crash of the tempest, the throb of the earthquake, the flash of the fire. Not then may the Message come to us. But, in the still small voice of the tranquillised heart, the conscience satisfied; the voice that speaks of a life's labour of duty, fearlessly achieved by the strength of Faith triumphant over self: thus may the message come!

Yes, thus, O God of the living and the dead, may we fall asleep trustfully and quietly under the shadow of Thy protection, as a child in the arms of its mother!

JOSIAH.

History often repeats itself. We find in two countries
and two ages similar historical events, brought about
by similar circumstances, and leading to like results;
and, perhaps, more frequently we find at different
periods, and in different countries, personages pos-
sessing strongly marked points of resemblance in
their characteristics or their conduct. For instance—
and one or two examples will suffice for our present
purpose—Alexander of Macedon and Charles XII.
of Sweden, were strangely alike.   So were Talbot, the
hero of the Anglo-French war of the Plantagenets, and
Nelson, the hero of the Anglo-French war of the
present century. And a striking resemblance exists
between the early life and character of King Josiah,
and Edward VI.—though unfortunately the career of
the British boy-king was untimely closed. In the
"thoroughness" of Josiah's nature, as evidenced by
his *acts*, we find a marked analogy to the disposition of
the noble Alfred, probably, not even excepting William
III., the greatest and best man that ever wore the
British Crown. If Edward Tudor had lived to manhood, he might have resembled Alfred also—at least if
one may judge from the piety and strength of mind
he manifested, until physical suffering and the prostra-
tion resulting from failing powers led him to yield to
the pertinacity of the ambitious and astute counsellors,

who surrounded him with their cajoleries and their intrigues.

Josiah, like Edward VI., was the son and successor of an evil-minded father. A modern historian, opposing tradition, and denying the authenticity of long-recognised narratives, has represented Henry VIII. in a more amiable light than that in which earlier historians have depicted him; though even Shakespeare, notwithstanding his anxiety to please Queen Elizabeth, cannot avoid leaving an impression that the "bluff king Harry" was a very disagreeable personage. However, as to the wickedness of Amon, the father of Josiah, there *can* be no doubt. The Bible expresses itself in terms of strong reprobation of Amon's career; and certainly, Josiah came to the throne under a black cloud—under inauspicious circumstances—because he succeeded a father deservedly execrated.

The virtues of Amon's ancestor, the good king Hezekiah, had unhappily left no enduring harvest; for all that he had done with the view of restoring the ancient and holy worship of Israel had been undone by the atrocious and audacious wickedness of his immediate successors. History does not record from what source Josiah received his good impressions, nor how it came to pass, whether from divine, or as it is called "innate," impulse, or from early education, or from wise surroundings, that he became attached to the principles of morality and religion which his father and his people had ruthlessly abandoned. But as the Bible makes special mention of the name of his mother, Jedidah, the daughter of Adaiah, it may be possible that Josiah, like other good and great men, owed to his mother the inculcation of the virtues that took root in his young heart. The sacred influence of a good mother, "unseen but not unfelt," is the hallowed source whence flows the golden stream of many a noble life!

It is probable that the undisturbed accession of Josiah to his father's throne was facilitated by the attachment of the Jews of Southern Palestine to the dynasty of Judah—the line of their ancient kings—or, perhaps, by their loyal attachment to fixed and duly constituted monarchical authority. Their character was more akin to that of the Englishman than to the disposition of the Frenchman of the present day. We are told that, notwithstanding the wickedness of Amon, which led to his being assassinated by some members of his own household, his murderers were duly punished, and his son succeeded him. Amon perished very much after the fashion of the Czar Paul, of Russia. He was, like him, slain in his own palace by persons of his own establishment, and his violent death was the result of a conspiracy—just as in the case of the Emperor Paul. But the regicides were seized and put to death, and the hereditary succession was secured by the immediate elevation of his little son, Josiah, to the vacant throne. From these facts, brief as is their record, one may gather a fair idea of the political status of the land at this epoch, and of the national characteristics of the Jewish people. There was no prevailing lawlessness, no anarchy, no change of dynasty, no violent revolution.

Had such events occurred in modern days, or in other climes, the chances are that the result of the conspiracy would not have been the tranquil elevation of a young child to his murdered father's throne. We find, for instance, that the overthrow of Charles I. and James II. in England, and of the first Napoleon and Louis Philippe in France, all of whom left youthful heirs, was followed by the overthrow of the dynasty to which those ill-fated monarchs respectively belonged. The crown taken from the father was not given to the son. Even in cases in which an infant heir succeeded, there have usually been anarchy and usurpation. We need not ransack English and French history for parallels or analogies. In Poland, when the young Boleslas succeeded the virtuous Lesko, the White; in Holland, when the great William, afterwards King of England, succeeded his father as Prince of Orange, disturbances ensued. In Judea, however, it seems that no revolution, no intrigue, interfered with the hereditary transmission—at least, none is recorded. The salutary and judicious constitutional influences of the Mosaic code of political government prevailed, even though wicked monarchs had overthrown, or at least abandoned, that code of religious government. The liberties and laws of the country were maintained under circumstances of exceptional difficulty, and the boy-king, Josiah, succeeded peacefully to the throne which his father had disgraced, but not enfeebled. This result materially speaking, seems due to the steady temper of the people. אַשְׁרֵי הָעָם שֶׁכָּכָה לּוֹ "Happy is the people whose portion is such." One is disposed to believe that at this period of Jewish history, the nation itself would not have been prone to idolatry, if it had not been under the influence of idolatrous kings. Anyhow, it would seem clear that the counsellors, who surrounded the youthful Josiah, led him to religious courses, and the infliction of the *lex talionis* on the murderers of his

father, is a testimony of attachment to the established
principles of Jewish law.

It is not unlikely that the character and career of
another royal youth, Josiah's remote ancestor, David,
the minstrel king, influenced the young monarch.
Might not Josiah, fired by David's example, have taken
his progenitor as his model? Having once adopted
the right course for his line of conduct, he pursued it
with steadfast consistency and earnestness. We may
even infer from the language of the Bible that adverse
influences were not wanting to divert him from the
straight path which he had chosen. "He turned not
aside to the right hand nor to the left." Certainly,
the wonderful steadfastness of his character presents a
marked contrast to the vacillation of many monarchs
of his line. Even David and Solomon were not steadfast in the pursuit of virtue throughout their chequered
careers. Hezekiah had his weak moments; Manasseh
was *not* unchangeable even in his wickedness. Josiah,
even from this point of view, was a remarkable personage and prince.

Josiah was nearly of the age at which Edward
Tudor died, when he took the great work of reforma-
tion in hand—he was a boy of fifteen. At this period
it would seem that the strength of his character began
to develop itself. One of his biographers described him
as an " amiable prince." We confess that amiability
does not seem to be one of the specially prominent
traits of his disposition, though in common experience
we *do* find that amiability and strength of character
are often combined. Superficial observers and epigram-
matic talkers indulge in the hackneyed notion that
good temper and firmness are incompatible. This

sententious diagnosis is faulty. Its error arises from mistaking weakness for amiability, and grimness or obstinacy for firmness.

Josiah was very young when he assumed the reins of government in Judea and, like Louis XIV. the motto of his reign was at once, "*L'état c'est moi.*" His first step—and this was the great object of his whole career—was to make war against the idolatrous practices of his people. The task was protracted and difficult; idolatry was no new importation; it was the besetting sin of the nation.

The idolatrous practices of the two preceding reigns had caused this heinous sin to sink so deeply into the popular mind, that it was not easy to root it out.

Idols, heathen temples, and other monuments of pagan rites were teeming — to use a recognised modern expression—from end to end of the land. The ignorant populace clung to a personal deity; the people were satisfied with an image or a picture. They were, it would seem, unable to satisfy themselves with the grand conception of an unseen, an impersonal, an intangible deity. Debased as they were, they were unable to grasp and adopt the sublime idea taught by the great Prophet of God.

Possibly in those days, as in ours, there were scholars who fancied that Faith must be subservient to Reason —or, at least, to what they mistook (honestly enough, no doubt) for Reason—and who declined to believe what they could not understand, nay, what they could not touch or see: who considered their own opinions paramount, and who, like some philosophers, and even some clergymen in our own days, set up idols of their own manufacture or adoption under various names, and worshipped them; so their prototypes in those byegone times chose to set up their idols, and worship them, rather than join in paying glorious homage to the unseen God of Faith. Many religions, however, are overthrown, enfeebled, even forgotten; but the philosophers, and the graduates, and the sages of the new school, have not succeeded in overthrowing even the most minute particle of influence of the one Religion which has lasted through all the ages, and which bears its elements of strength in itself.

Possibly another circumstance may account for the extraordinary spread of idolatry. It is true that nearly three hundred and fifty years before the accession of Josiah the separation between the tribes had been effected by a revolution, or rather a civil war, and South Judea remained under the sacred dynasty of Judah, while a recreant kingdom established itself in North Judea, under the mutinous usurper, Jeroboam. The northern kingdom succumbed to the invasion of the Assyrian king, Shalmaneser, possibly the father of the celebrated Sennacherib. Many of the Israelites were deported wholesale after the fashion of the forced emigrants of the highly civilized Russian empire. It is said that their lands were for the most part expropriated, and given to non-Jews, or to neighbouring people who followed a certain perverted Judaism. These transplanted nations followed certain Jewish customs, even though they were likewise addicted to idolatry. Their religion was a curious mixture of Judaism and heathenism, and it is just this description of mongrel creed which may have had some effect in importing idolatry into the neighbouring districts of the kingdom of Judah, as well as among the Jews remaining in the kingdom of Israel.

The conquest of Shalmaneser occurred about a century before Josiah succeeded to the throne of Judah. Then the kingdom of Israel, as it is historically called, came to an ignominious and utterly inglorious end. In those days national iniquity was punished by almost immediate retribution. This is scarcely the case now-a-days.

Now it is probable that either the conquered Jews had returned to the northern provinces of Judea in the days of Josiah, or that his sway, or at least his influence, extended over the new settlers, or that he had some delegation or suzerainty, tributary or otherwise, from the Assyrian king, for it would seem certain that Josiah exerted monarchical authority over the severed provinces of Israel, as well as over the hereditary kingdom of Judah.

Josiah set to his work right zealously. His was a policy of "THOROUGH," resembling in its *manner*, though not in its *matter*, the policy associated with the name and career of the ill-fated Wentworth, Lord Strafford.

Henry VIII.'s hearty warfare against the monasteries and conventual establishments of the Church of Rome, was a faint shadow of Josiah's expeditions against the idolatrous edifices, practices, and priests that disgraced the land. He gave no quarter. He lifted a vigorous and unsparing hand against the various forms of pagan worship then prevailing in Palestine, and which do not seem to have been confined to its borders, but either (as is probable) to have been imported thither by foreign settlers, or gathered from intercourse with neighbouring nations. Many of these forms appear to have had their prototypes in other climes and ages, and among other races. Josiah, the great iconoclast, was the Julian of an earlier day. An examination of the various forms of idolatry is curious; and though these seem to have been assailed at various portions of Josiah's reign, we may mention (and dismiss) them here. Paramount seems to have been that Sabean worship, or adoration of the heavenly host (צבא, perhaps connected with צבי, splendour) which existed in Mesopotamia in the days of Abraham, and which, in the form of the Parsee creed, exists in India and Persia to the present day. This is, perhaps, the most explicable form of idolatry among ignorant men, which quality may perhaps explain its long endurance and its wide diffusion. It spread into the Cretan mythology of Greece and Rome, in the worship of Helios or Apollo, and of Selene or Diana; it spread into the Teutonic or Saxon mythology, where Sun and Moon were adored. It was akin to the fire-worship of the Guebres among the ancient Persians; it was found among the gentle Peruvians, under the Incas, when they were conquered by the cruel Spaniards; it found its most foolish form in the Moloch worship of Canaan, and the Vestal worship of Greece and Rome. A possible verbal connection between the roots of the words, Par-see, Per-u, Per-sia, and the Greek *Pür* (whence our English word *fire*, through the Teutonic *Feuer*) has attracted attention, just as the association between Inca and Ign-is. There was then the worship of Baal, the Bel, and Belus of other countries, possibly the Vulcan of Crete. There was also the grove-worship, known to the pagans of Northern Scandinavia, and which, perhaps, was akin to the worship of Pan and the sylvan deities, and the worship of the *Dryads* of Rome and the *Druids* of Britain—the horrid and pestilent phallic worship, which seems linked, through Moloch, to the idolatry in which human sacrifices played a prominent part, as even now in the Polynesian and Melanesian islands. Then there was a worship connected with sepulchres, or *tumuli*, or heaps of stones, or "barrows," with which the Druidical worship, if Stonehenge be any proof, was also connected. There was the worship of Astoreth or Ashtoresh, said to be the Isis or Osiris of the Egyptians, the Astarte of the Greeks, and the Venus, or possibly the Vesta, of the Romans; of Chemosh, who we are disposed to believe was the Mars of Rome, and the Odin of the Teutons, the warlike character of the Moabites offering some grounds for this supposition; and in Jeremiah, chap. xlviii., verses 7, 13, and 46, special reference is made to Chemosh, of the Moabites, and one of the places in which the idol was worshipped was Aroer, a word, perhaps, akin to Ares, the Hellenic name of Mars; and lastly of Milcom, the idol of Ammon, possibly the Jupiter of the Greeks.

But the fire-worship had been audaciously introduced into the very precincts of the Temple itself. Josiah's first work was to purify the Temple or what remained of it, to rebuild what had fallen into ruins, to restore it for purposes of divine worship, to furnish it anew with the vessels and appliances used in its sacred service.

For this sublime object, a suitable system of labour, duly divided, was carefully organised. Doubtless these were not forced *corvées*, such as a tyrannical sovereign might institute, but the free work of a free people:

such as in later days was established by the noble
satrap, Nehemiah, for a similar object, and such as
Paris witnessed for a less sacred but not less patriotic
purpose in days in which patriotism had not fled from
that dejected city. Even the Levites were called on
for their share of the work—not by manual labour,
with hod, chisel, hatchet, or plane, but by acting as
clerks of the works, overseers, accountants, &c.; there
were no drones in Josiah's hive. Josiah seems to have
been a frugal and judicious prince, and in this respect
Edward VI. did not resemble him. Edward's econo-
mical grandfather, Henry VII., had a touch of him.
He did not lavishly spend the money of the State,
nor the revenues of the Crown (if it had any) for
the requisite purposes of renovation and restoration.
Possibly the national exchequer was empty, and the
financial condition of a perhaps impoverished country
would not have justified the imposition of heavy
burdens. But collectors were set to work. Money
was gathered in, not only from the inhabitants of
Judah itself, but from the tribes that had formed the
shattered kingdom of Israel. So Josiah not only re-
established the neglected national worship, but took
care that those who had destroyed it should pay for its
restoration.

In the course of the repairs, the Scroll of the Law,
which had been preserved in the Temple, but which
had been lost or neglected during the reigns of
Manasseh and Amon, was found and brought to the
king. Shaphan, the royal scribe or secretary, read
it to the monarch, whose excellent intentions were
confirmed by it. He resolved to carry out its ordinances persistently, and proceeded to act on the pre-

scriptions of royal duty as laid down in the book of Deuteronomy. The law was solemnly read to the people; but when the king heard the awful denunciations of the inspired law-giver against national disobedience—the curses hurled on the recusants—his strong heart quailed. Fearless in the sight of man, he trembled beneath the frown of angry Heaven. For indeed, Heaven's just indignation threatened his people. A thousand years ago that law had been given, those anathemas had been launched, those terrible but sublime warnings—terrible and sublime as the welkin thunder—had been uttered. Those menaces were spread over the serenity and sweetness of the Religion of Love and Compassion, as the angry storm-cloud darkens the bright face of the soft summer sky.

The echoes of the tempests of Sinai resounded in the ear of the alarmed and patriot king; for his people had sinned grievously. They had incurred the fearful penalties of the outraged Law. For himself, he had little to fear; he had done his duty. He had followed the divine behest. But the people in his own time —in the time of his father and grandfather, three generations, had committed the fatal iniquities, which, by the unerring voice of Heaven, were to be visited with the appalling chastisements revealed to the prophet Moses.

Under these impressions, he still felt some doubt as to whether those penalties might be averted, or whether he had removed all danger of their incidence by his own restoration of the ancestral worship. He called his council together; and they decided on consulting a woman, who was celebrated at that time for what is termed "prophecy." Her name was Huldah.

Here let us pause a moment, to refer to two errors that seem to prevail, even amongst Jews themselves, in respect to, first, the meaning of the word prophet, and secondly, the position of women in the Jewish system. Both these considerations are applicable to the episode of Huldah.

As regards prophecy, a notion seems to prevail that a prophet is primarily, a revealer of the future. This we doubt. The English word prophet is derived from the Greek προφημί, probably meaning, one who speaks out or proclaims, rather than one who predicts. The prefix *pro* in Greek commonly means *before*, in point of *place*, nearly corresponding to the French *devant*. The Hebrew word נביא seems to have a like meaning. Its *radix* is doubtless the stem-word, נוב, meaning, to sprout out, to bear fruit, (of course spontaneously, by innate power, as does the tree or plant) and, thence, to speak *out*, to speak eloquently (*e-loquor*). (This נוב by the way has, perhaps, travelled west-ward in such forms as *knopf, knop, knob,* the bud or the button of a tree.) Thus the French word, derived from *predico*, is *Predicateur*, a preacher—one who speaks out; one who speaks eloquently—or at least, *ought* to do so. A prophet seems to be a man, from whom the fruit bursts forth without an effort of his own will; one inspired with the divine afflatus, so that he may speak *pro-ductively*, not necessarily one who foretells. The old English sooth-sayer, or truth-speaker, is akin to this. Even the English seer, which corresponds with the Hebrew הזה, does not necessarily mean a foreteller. Indeed, many so-called prophecies are not foretellings. They are utterances, springing forth to be culled, like fruit. If this were well understood we should, perhaps, cease to hear statements of Christological writers, as to the application of certain "prophetic" passages in Isaiah, Jeremiah, and Ezekiel.

The so-called prophecies are either codes (Moses), recommendations (Samuel), denunciations (Isaiah), exhortations (Micah), visions (Ezekiel), narratives (Jonah), elegies and dirges (Jeremiah), or lastly fore-tellings (Isaiah).

Eloquence directed to such objects as denunciations, exhortations, and lamentations, often assumes the aspect of prophecy ; and indeed, much of what is commonly designated prophecy is blended with other writings or utterances of the inspired poets and preachers of the Bible. The prophets certainly spoke from "lips touched by hallowed fire," and poured out the words that were given to them ; words that might often be the out-risings of a knowledge of the past, and the clear comprehension of the present, by an intelligent and cultivated mind. They may sometimes have been the setting-forth in clear language of inferences drawn from a just and palpable appreciation of passing events, of the action and character of existing personages, and from a similar appreciation of the past and fore-judgment of the future. Yet prophecy as recorded in the Bible differed from such intellectual manifestations as above set forth, in this respect; that Prophecy was inspired, breathed into, and impelling heart, brain, lip, and hand, by the Divine Will, for the carrying out of purposes necessary in the divine scheme in its relation to man. A prophet was no ordinary man. His thoughts and utterances, his sentiments and his writings, were controlled by the Heavenly fiat. All that the prophet had to say or to write, and even all that he thought, was bounded by the limits defined by hallowed intention for the achievement of some important and, of course, sacred purpose.

Another lesson is taught by the history of Josiah. It is the fashion of superficial observers to state that women were disregarded in the Jewish commonwealth, and held as of no account. It was the interest of Christians to promulgate and proclaim this view, as it afforded them an opportunity of offering Christianity to the world, as a necessary agent for the placing of women in their proper position in humanity.

Superficial observers and writers confounded the treatment of women among the Jews with that which they met with among Moslems and heathen nations of the East. This is a mistake. Women held a high position in the Jewish commonwealth. Of this there can be no doubt. The Jews exalted the household virtues in womankind; and, in one of the most esteemed of the Jewish Scripture books, a homely matron is described as the most blessed of women. Work, it is true, is always held in high repute among the Jews. And, in intellectual and spiritual rank, the women of Israel had the same chance of obtaining distinction. We had, it is true, no "screaming sisterhood," but we had amongst us the poetess Miriam, the judge Deborah, the prophetess Huldah. It is clear that Huldah is held in high repute. She lived, according to the Authorised Version, in the "College," and according to Dr. Benisch's rendering, in the "second quarter," perhaps, the arrondissement designated as No. 2, in the topographical description of the city. She was the wife of the Keeper of the Wardrobe.

The King's council, on hearing the doubts and

difficulties that exercised the royal mind, decided on applying to this celebrated woman. She gave a reply to the question submitted to her in plain, explicit, forcible, and telling language. In vain did the King in his strong-minded goodness hope that his virtues would save his iniquitous people. O no! Vicarious atonement forms no portion of God's system. The Almighty Himself told His chosen prophet, Moses, that even *he*, good and self-denying as he was, could not save others from the consequences of their sin.

Throughout scripture, there is perhaps no prophecy or utterance delivered in terms more forcible and more touching than those in which Huldah expressed herself when appealed to by the ministers of Josiah, on behalf of this earnest and anxious king.

She cries with terrible strength, yet with serene calmness that gives point to every word of her enthusiastic reply, that the chastisement ordained by God *shall* fall on the guilty people who had forsaken the One Lord, and had provoked Him. His anger would be kindled against them; and it would not be quenched. We can imagine the fire of denunciation and menace flashing from Huldah's eyes; flashing and then fading —as those fiery eyes became filled with a woman's tender tears—when she tells the King's envoys that, since Josiah's heart was humble and gentle; since he had sought divine compassion by *his* life's obedience; *she* knew that God would save him from seeing the misery and terrible punishment of the people whom he loved. This trouble would not fall on him; Josiah would be gathered to his grave in peace! And to those who work and struggle for a good purpose, what greater reward can there be than—Peace!

Still, the good monarch made one effort to avoid the impending wrath. He gathered the people together and read the law to them, while standing on a raised platform or pulpit.

Here, Josiah solemnly promised to obey the divine law as revealed by Moses. The priests, the prophets, and the people surrounded him in vast multitude, as he stood prominently forward in the wide courts of the Temple. There, amongst rich and poor, noble and humble, the King set forth his solemn compact with the King of Kings!

He passed through the land resolved to root out idolatry; and after having performed his work in his hereditary provinces of Judah, he passed on to the kingdom of Israel. A curious incident and a prophecy, in the sense in which the word is commonly understood, are narrated in the First Book of Kings, when the rebellious Jeroboam built idolatrous altars, and was rebuked by a prophet, who himself having sinned, perished, and was buried by a second prophet, whose remains, at his own desire, were afterwards laid in the tomb of his friend. The destruction of the idolatrous altar and the advent of the good Josiah were then foretold.

The prophet prayed that his bones might not be disturbed; and one is forcibly reminded of the curious distich engraved on Shakespeare's tomb in Stratford-on-Avon church, which runs something like this:—

> "Blessed be he who guards these stones,
> And curst be he who moves my bones."

Well, centuries afterwards, Josiah in the course of his expedition northward, came to this very place.

He saw the altar, which he destroyed, and which, or near which, was a sepulchre built on a hill somewhat after the fashion of a beacon. He asked what it meant; and the story was related to him, for it would seem that he knew little of the history of his own race. The King refused to disturb the bones of the prophet.

Here, by the way, occurs another of the oft-recurring instances of the faultiness of the so-called Authorised Version, according to which Josiah, on beholding the building, is made to ask, absurdly enough, "what is this title?" Now צִיּוּן is the Hebrew word used, and it means a monument, or signal, (perhaps, the stem-word of the Latin *sign-um* whence English *sign* and *signal*, and probably it is akin to the Teutonic *zeichen*, whence our English "*token*," and also to "*zeuge*.") It is possible that the translator mistook the word monumentum for munimentum, and hence rendered it "title." Dr. Benisch puts the word in its proper meaning. צִיּוּן or צִיּוּן, is used for a sepulchral monument in Jeremiah xxxi. 21, and Ezekiel xxxix. 15.

Josiah either went or sent to Samariah, the capital of the revolted and subdued tribes, and here he destroyed the apparatus of idolatrous worship, and condemned its wicked priesthood to capital punishment.

Throughout the length and breadth of the land, the feast of Passover was solemnly celebrated. Never since the days of the Judges had the festival been held so satisfactorily. The bondage of idolatry had been broken, there was a new redemption in the land, and it was indeed fitting that it should be sanctified by the memorial of the old redemption. Ah! if the old man who died alone and untended by human hand on solitary Nebo, could have seen, with prophetic eye, the king of

his race carry out the precepts of his law, the blessed
vision may have soothed his heart, as he sank to rest
in sight of the promised land his foot should never
tread !

> "Ah ! If the fading eye, with conscious gaze.
> In the last hour that ends our earthly days.
> Could catch the vision of our hopes fulfilled.
> The spirit's farewell shriek would sure be stilled."

The prescribed ordinances of the Passover were
carried out with due precision. Josiah's powers of
organization would seem to have developed; for some
time before, when he carried out the work of renovating
the Temple, it would appear that the royal administra-
tion must have been at a low ebb, seeing that no
accounts were kept of the monies expended in the work,
implicit confidence being placed in the honesty and
economy of the persons charged with the undertaking.
But now Josiah was in the vigour of his young manhood. He was about 26 or 27 years of age. He re-
organized the ancient Temple-service with care and
order. The priests, the Levites, the singers, all had
their assigned duties; even the porters at the gates
(for there was the grand institution of שמש even in
those days) had their parts set forth. The poor were
not forgotten; ample provision was made for them.
Men of rank and wealth came forward liberally with
the contributions required of them. Judah and Israel,
long separated, were again united in this solemn assembly.
It is sublime to dwell for one moment on this grand
scene, the climax of Josiah's glory—the crowning joy
of his reign—the golden harvest of his labours. There,
in the restored Temple, stood the scion of the most

truly royal house of all the world—for Heaven had
made it royal. There stood he, surrounded by the
princes and the priests, the sages and the saints.
Round him pressed the throng of his own subjects: and
the scattered and subdued remnants of the rebellious
tribes.

Thousands of bleating sheep, hundreds of lowing
oxen, wreathed with their myrtle garlands, were led
to the altar. The songs of David resounded from the
lips of the hallowed choir. The spirit of the Minstrel
King, the spirit of the wise Solomon and the sainted
Hezekiah, lived with beatified life in the solemn
enclosure. Surely, as the song of welcome rose on
high, above the hushed murmurs of the people and
the cries of the cattle, the voices of the dead must
have whispered at the king's heart! But no. His
heart might have been proud and peaceful, but it could
not have been joyful. There was a shadow on the
sunshine. The pious and resolute king had made his
peace with Heaven, but he knew that on the mighty
throng before him the just wrath of that outraged
Heaven must fall. Yes; fall sooner or later with
unerring, even though tardy hand. Hush! Beyond
the clashing of the cymbals and the braying of the
trumpets; beyond the choral songs of the Levites and
the psalmody of the people; *he* heard the distant roar
of the thunder. It reached his heart; he felt the
whisper of the coming storm—though before its blast
should burst on his people, *he* would be at rest in the
peaceful grave.

* * * * * *

And now a new scene opens. Life's hey-day has
been reached. Noon has shone in its meridian glory,

and the day begins to wane. Josiah has passed from
boyhood to manhood. He is advancing to life's prime,
and the darkness is closing around him.

*   *   *   *   *

In those days, no such theory as the balance of power
existed. In our days it is only a theory, a name for lust
of power, and greed of annexation.

Josiah was the sovereign of a small state, wedged in
between two powerful and ambitious empires. It had
something of the position of the Netherlands in our
own days, wedged in between Prussia and France.
These powerful ancient empires on the borders of
Palestine, were Egypt on the south-west, Assyria, or
rather Babylon, on the east. These jealous rivals were
at war, just as France was in our own days, and in the
days of our fathers. Egypt attacked Assyria. The
then king of Egypt was called Necho. He was of the
dynasty called Pharaoh, and is also known in history
as Necao and Nechos. He is celebrated not only for
his battles with Assyria, but also for an unsuccessful
attempt made by him to unite the Mediterranean, the
Nile and the Red Sea, by means of a canal, a sort of
foreshadowing of Lesseps' famous Suez Canal. King
Josiah decided on endeavouring to prevent Necho from
passing through his territories, to attack the Assyrian
king at Charchemish. It seems the fashion in histories
based on the Bible to blame him for this procedure,
and the chief grounds for this censure, appear to be
that the Egyptian king, in endeavouring to prevent
Josiah from allying himself with his enemy, used
scriptural warnings, couched in scriptural language.
He invoked the divine name to prevent Josiah's inter-
ference. It appears that Necho did this unjustifiably,

for he was eventually defeated by the Assyrians, as we learn from Jeremiah.

It was clearly the interest of Necho, that Josiah should take no part in the quarrel, for had he been neutral, he could have passed through Josiah's dominions without molestation, and thus reached the Euphrates which was to the east of the Assyrian king's territory. If Necho invaded Assyria from the south, and Josiah were hostile, he would have been in a perilous position. Necho sought to obtain not his alliance, but his neutrality.

Josiah might have considered himself bound to fight for Assyria from ties of gratitude if, as we conjecture, Assyria had permitted Josiah the privilege of spreading Judaism and destroying idolatry among the provinces of Israel, which had been conquered by the Assyrians. This conjecture would account for Josiah's friendliness to the Assyrian king, and for the influence he had in rooting out idol worship in the ten northern tribes, which he could scarcely have effected without Assyria's sanction.

It may seem strange that so many thousand years after Josiah's death, one should endeavour to find out good reasons for his course of action. But there is a justification for this. We are anxious to vindicate his character, and show him in the light of a patriot king, so that he may serve, as we believe he should, as a great example for after ages.

The Egyptian army met the Jewish army at a place called Megiddo, which was in a valley to the east of the range of mountains, known as Carmel, in the province of Issachar, a district afterwards forming part of the Roman province of Galilee. Near the valley was a river, which is the waters of Megiddo, mentioned in the song of Deborah. This place was situated to the north-west of Jerusalem, and would probably lie in the way of Necho, who in passing through the Holy Land to invade Assyria, would be anxious to have a sea-board in his flank, so that he might be protected in his march by the parallel course of the Egyptian navy, a plan pursued in after ages by a modern general, and somewhat similar to that of the Duke of Wellington in the Peninsula.

This Megiddo is probably the Magdolum mentioned by Herodotus as the site of a battle.

The patriot king, actuated by no sordid ambition, as we believe, went like a hero into the thick of the battle. He disguised himself, so that he might take active part in the fight, and share the fortunes of his soldiers— and he died—died striving to do his duty to the country he loved.

So Judas Maccabeus died—so our own English Nelson died. So have perished the army of heroes that have lived since the world began, almost in every age, in every race, in every clime.

> "Whether it be on scaffold high,
>   Or in the battle's van,
>   The noblest death for man to die,
>   Is when he dies for man."

It seems that Josiah was shot by an archer, and he knew that his wound was severe, perhaps mortal. Probably, fearing that the sight of his death would operate unfavourably on his army, and produce dis-comfiture, he desired his attendants to take him from his chariot, and place him in another, possibly one not bearing signs of his royal dignity, so that he might not be known. "Take me away,"* said the dying king, "for I am sorely wounded."

It seems that he died on the field of battle: for the apparent discrepancy between II. Kings xxiii., and II. Chronicles xxvi., 24, is explicable, the latter which is probably only a record, may be thus translated: "They brought him to Jerusalem, *for* he was dead," or it even may be *when* he was dead. Josephus and one or two other writers state that he did not die till he reached Jerusalem. It matters not. He died like a hero, wherever he died.

This is the end of his life's story, though that life-story cannot be said ever to end, when its recollection still lives for a purpose:

> "To live in hearts we leave behind,
> Is not to die."

He was "mourned" by the great poet, patriot, and prophet, Jeremiah, who was a son of the Hilkiah, mentioned in an earlier part of this narrative as the high priest. Jeremiah's elegy has not been identified, though possibly it may be the celebrated "Lamentations," or it may form a portion of these. The 10th verse of the 12th chapter of Zechariah, is also an elegy on the good king:

> "And tears by bards and heroes shed,
> Alike immortalise the dead!"

His people wept for him, as well they might: and the conquering Egyptian paid respect to his memory or

---

* Probably the correct translation, judging from the use of the word עבר in the next verse, is "remove me, let me be changed from one chariot to another."

to the popular feeling, by placing his son on the vacant throne.

He perished in the 39th year of his age, and the thirty-second of his glorious reign. The period of history is cotemporaneous with that in which Draco gave laws to Athens, and in which the regal government existed in Rome, about the epoch of the reigns of the kings Ancus Martius, and Tarquinius Priscus. Archidamus was reigning in Lacedæmon.

The story is long: let the moral be short.

From the history of Josiah, young and old may learn that this king, the most manly king of Judah, was also the most religious; that he who was not afraid of crushing the old idolatries, and acknowledging his own faith, and who scrupulously observed its institutions, was also not afraid to risk his life in battle, for what he believed to be his duty. He was earnest, he was straightforward, he was thorough. Earnestness, piety, and courage, are virtues that all may imitate; and after the lapse of twenty-five centuries, the history of Josiah speaks to us from the grave where he was laid, when he perished at Megiddo—perished, on *that* battlefield; to be a signal and a beacon on life's great battlefield for ever!

NEHEMIAH.

THERE is an evil, a crying evil, in our community.
We disregard the great men of our own race. Not
the great men of modern times, of whom both
absolutely and relatively there are but few; but the
great men of ancient times—men who have left behind
them their work, the enduring record of their lives
and their labours,—so that for our neglect of them,
while we profit by what they achieved, we have no
excuse. A people that ceases to honour its great men,
ceases to regard its past with befitting reverence, and
risks its own chance of greatness. It is no small part
of the work done by the heroes of other days, that
their lives are examples to be followed by generations
yet unborn.

But we Jews allow the dull cold waters of indifference
to wash over the footprints of the men of our race.
We follow, it may be, their guiding lights, but we
forget—oh, we utterly forget the hands that kindled
them. In the upper classes of life, we Jews are familiar
with the mythological and historical heroes of Greece
and Rome, and with the shining luminaries of our
European orbit. In the lower classes these names may
be but little known, but the heroes of the drama and
the romance are thoroughly appreciated. Thus in our
public schools our boys are able to talk glibly of the
beauty of Homer's verse, the magnanimity of Leonidas'

heroism—the humour of Terence, and the bravery of Scipio, and the statesmanship of Pitt and the vigour of Wellington. In our humble schools, doubtless, the deeds of Nelson and the exploits of Napoleon are not unknown : and the fanciful performances of Jack Sheppard and Dick Turpin are familiar as household words. But how often do we hear of those men whose lives were of themselves sufficient to dignify—to ennoble—nay even to consecrate, a nation?—men who like Joshua the dauntless general, David the sublime poet, Ezra the zealous champion, and Judas the heroic patriot,—and these are but few of the immortal many —have set on the face of the ages a glowing stamp of lustrous light, in whose rays we bask : though we carelessly cast aside the line that would lead the eyes of grateful and reflecting men to the source whence the radiance flows ?

The consequences of this evil are perilous. We, as Jews, cease, and have long ceased, to entertain a due pride in ourselves—a pride which is important and perhaps necessary to the maintenance of that dignity, with which we, as true soldiers of the Faith, should rally round the banner which is our sacred heirloom. We are not proud of our race; we who are the world's most ancient nobility; whose blood is the bluest of all the life streams of the races of the earth; we whose pedigree dates from those to whom was given the most glorious patent of aristocracy—the most sublime heritage of humanity—the Revelation of God—as understood by Heaven—to be a gift to man for evermore.

There are, in the rolls of renown which we, though utterly unworthy of them, are still permitted to retain,

some names around which there shines a halo of so
sacred a glory that one scarcely ventures to approach
them; still less to deal with them so as to try to draw
them from the sublimity of their own age and its
solemn surroundings, to the more dense and less pure
atmosphere of our commonplace and unsentimental
(which means unfeeling) age. To this grave category
belong such men as Moses our Master; David our
Minstrel; Elijah our mysterious Prophet. But on
the other hand, there are other men who, though their
associations are connected with the loftiest conditions
of humanity, and their careers are hallowed with
purposes and occurrences of a sacred character, are yet
so comprehensible to our ordinary understandings, and
so legible to the reading of our hearts, that we can
feel a thorough sympathy with them, and gather a
ready lesson from their lives, their works, and their
ways.

To this class of men belongs the prophet Nehemiah,
one of the most remarkable men of his, or of any, age.
He was a peculiarly useful man: one of those personages
in whose character were intimately combined the fervour
of passionate thought and the serenity of practical
action. In certain minds, and those are very noble
minds, the powers of sentiment are found intermingled
with the powers of work. Such men are formed to be
leaders. They excite with the voice or the pen, while
they incite with the mighty force of example. In them
precept and practice find their impulses blended. And
when these conditions of being are exerted for a high,
a noble, a religious object—for the happiness of humanity and the service of the Maker—such men as
these are blest with the holiest of blessings—the

assurance that one is fulfilling a career which leads straightway from earth to Heaven, and lifts the soul on the wings of a divine influence from a human to an angelic sphere of being. Such a man was Nehemiah. He lived at a critical period of our history: a period at which such a person was wanted for the carrying out of a great object. Let the carping critics of Biblical literature say what they will, and dig out new-fangled theories from their thin soil of learning, no discrepancy that they can discover, or fancy they can discover, in the historical portions of the hagiographa-narrative can affect a fact clear to the unprejudiced investigator, the fact that Nehemiah, his writings, his character, and his recorded thoughts and deeds, fitted in most perfectly with the time in which he lived.

That time was a remarkable one. Some knowledge of it has come down to us from history. The Jews, after a long captivity, had been permitted to return to their own land. They had undergone great vicissitudes. The Chaldean or rather Babylonian sovereign Nebuchadnezzar had destroyed their city and their temple; he had overthrown their throne, and had endeavoured to crush out their nationality. Of course in this last attempt he could not succeed; for the fire smouldered in the ashes—that fire which was kindled from a heavenly fount of light; and which was, and is, and will be, imperishable. Belshazzar, the successor of the Babylonian king, had been conquered by the victorious Mede. The empire of the great and good Cyrus was established on this side of the Caspian sea, and that excellent potentate had ameliorated the condition of his Jewish subjects and had made arrangements for their restoration to their ancient land. Cyrus was a prince

whom modern monarchs would do well to imitate. He
was wise, temperate and brave; a model prince in the
age in which he lived. We all know how, under the
edict of the Medo-Persian king, our ancestors, led by
Zerubbabel, the son of Shealtiel, lineal descendant of
the anointed David, returned to their beloved land. It
was this Zerubbabel, called in the Persian history
Shesh-Bazzar, who is commemorated in our familiar
חנוכה song commencing מעוז צור ישועתי. The nation
was restored. The first stone of the temple was laid.
And here let us pause and listen to the grand record of
Scripture.

"And all the people shouted with a great shout
when they praised the Lord, because the foundation of
the house of the Lord was laid.

"But many of the Priests and Levites, and the
chiefs of the fathers, old men who had seen the *first*
house, wept with a loud voice when the foundation of
this new house was laid before their eyes."*

We can picture to ourselves, even in this cold un-
enthusiastic age, the mingled tears and smiles : how,
while the memories of the past bid the old men weep ;
the joys of the present, and the hopes of the future
shone like summer sunlight, struggling for mastery
through the shadows of lost glories and all

"The tender grace of a day that is dead."†

But though under the gracious permission and with
the generous assistance of the noble Persian monarch
our fathers were restored to their ancient land where
they could "sing the songs of Zion" once more ;
though in the sacred city and on its holy mount they

° Ezra iii. 11, 12.　　　† Tennyson.

were allowed to rebuild the temple of their worship; many of the glories of the past had fled, and could not be restored. The Jews were no longer a powerful, a prosperous, or a dominant people. Their national banner was tarnished, their renown was sullied, their *prestige* was gone; their commerce, once so splendid, was reduced to a mere second-rate condition. Their spirit was broken by captivity, and, unhappily, the pure descent of some of their ancient families was tainted by intermarriage with inferior races.

It was not wonderful then that the restoration was not at first a success. The weakness of the Jews made itself felt. They unwisely and ungraciously refused the proffered assistance of the Samaritan Jews, and they were exposed not only to their hatred but to the enmity of neighbouring non-Jewish tribes.

Ezra, or as the Apocrypha, Josephus, and the Greeks call him, Esdras, went either with the permission, or, as we are inclined to believe, with a special commission from the Persian Sovereign, and organised the nation. He re-established our religion on its former defined basis, and he even arranged a constitution, evidently of a religious, and possibly even of a political character, which afforded a settlement for the restored people. It would seem, however, that after Ezra's death or retirement, misfortunes ensued. The city of Jerusalem was not defended by walls. It was unprovided with fortifications. The condition of the city of the people and of all that they held dear became pitiable. And as news did not travel fast in those days, some time appears to have elapsed before intelligence of these misfortunes reached the Jews who remained in Persia.

In those days a king named Artaxerxes reigned in

Persia, and his sway extended from the confines of India to the shores of the Levant. He was, probably, the successor of that Xerxes who was defeated by the Greeks. But whether he or his predecessor was the Ahasuerus of Scripture seems somewhat doubtful.

When persons, in books or lectures or elsewhere, pretend to know all about these ancient kings, without giving a single fact as an authority for their statements, one need not believe them. Notwithstanding the researches of such great men as Rollin and Prideaux, there is great doubt as to the identity of the eastern kings; and historians are even now doubtful as to the monarch mentioned in Scripture History as having conquered the luxurious Belshazzar.

Things must have gone very wrong at Jerusalem; for news came to Susa, the Persian capital, of the misfortunes under which the Jews were suffering. There was then residing in Susa a very distinguished Jew named Nehemiah. It would seem that he had been carried away in captivity at a very early age, when Nebuchadnezzar conquered Jerusalem. He had risen somewhat after the fashion of Joseph, to great eminence in the court of the Persian monarch; for the great oriental satraps, more wise than those modern Christian kings who refused to emancipate the Jews, and preferred to oppress them, thought it wise to avail themselves of the signal talents, sincere patriotism, earnestness and integrity of their Jewish subjects; and as Joseph rose to distinction in the court of Pharaoh, and Daniel in that of Belshazzar, so Nehemiah obtained a post of high distinction in the court of the Medo-Persian sovereigns. He was called the royal cup-bearer. Such an office was till quite recently even a post of honour in the imperial court of Germany; an elector of the Empire, himself a sovereign prince in his own dominions, holding a similar office in the palace of the Kaiser.

The word used in scripture for the description of Nehemiah's office is the *Tirshatha*, and this word seems to be usually translated *Cupbearer*. Others, however, translate it Governor. A great authority is of opinion that the word is of uncertain etymology. It seems probable, however, notwithstanding the occurrence of the letter ת instead of ט the expression may be derived from שׂטר meaning *governor* or *ruler;* or it may be some Chaldaic compound of טר *palace* and שׂטר *governor*, the letters ת and ט being often interchangeable. Be this, however, as it may, there can be no doubt that Nehemiah filled a position of very great dignity in the court of the Asiatic monarch. But in his case, as in that of his great predecessor Joseph, the old love of nationality, and the old attachment to his country and his faith prevailed over the attractions of his exalted position in the land of exile.

When Nehemiah heard of the misfortunes of his brethren; when the sound of their sufferings reached him; when he knew that the land of his birth, the land of his race, the land in which his fathers were buried, and in which was his childhood's home, was exposed to the tread of an insulting invader, he resolved on abandoning the comforts of his home, the hopes of ambition, the pleasures of his high position, the associations of personal friendship; and he determined on casting his lot with his unhappy, his endangered, his degraded brethren.

If we wish to understand what really he did resign,

let us imagine for instance, a nobleman of Polish descent such as Count Walewski, who is so recently dead that we can all remember him, resigning the splendour of his position at the then magnificent court of Paris, where he was the intimate of the Emperor, and the cynosure of the courtiers' eyes, in order to blend his fate with that of his unhappy countrymen in subjugated Poland.

However, regardless of personal comfort and public ambition, Nehemiah left Susa, the Persian capital, and hurried to Jerusalem. It is true that the favour of his sovereign furnished, it may even be said armed, him with credentials likely to keep in awe those troublesome hordes who, whatever might have been their hatred towards the Jews, would necessarily be deterred from annoying them by fear of the anger of the great monarch who reigned at Susa.

Nehemiah arrived at Jerusalem, and almost immediately on his arrival went to inspect the city. Josephus thinks he was accompanied by a number of exiled Jews from Babylon; but this is not quite clear; indeed it is not important. Nehemiah found the Holy City in a very sad condition. The walls were in a state of dilapidation. They had never been rebuilt. He saw the danger of an unwalled city, containing treasures, and situated in a region surrounded by hostile tribes. It is not likely that persons would resort thither with a feeling of security, or that the city would be likely to attain a reputation for, or condition of, dignity, so long as it remained unfortified. Nehemiah then at once resolved to rebuild the walls. It was here that the remarkable energy of his character manifested itself. No sooner had he decided, than he at once determined on action. He hardly lost a moment; waiting only three days either for necessary rest, or possibly for religious purification after his journey. He neither exaggerated the importance of his undertaking nor the necessity of hurrying it. To use a common English expression, and a very forcible one, Nehemiah at once put his shoulder to the wheel. Hard to work he went, and wisely he made others work too. In reading the Biblical account of the building of the walls, one is reminded of an episode in the early days of the French Revolution, when a fortification was thrown up by the combined labours of persons of all classes and all ages, and both sexes. Then noblemen and priests laboured cheerfully at the earthworks. In like manner, priests, nobles, merchants, and people laboured strenuously at the rebuilding of the walls of Jerusalem. Of course there were exceptions to the general ardour. The nobles of the Tekoites, Nehemiah tells us with noble simplicity, "put not their necks to the work of their Lord." There are drones in all communities; and the idleness or pride (often interchangeable terms) of the Tekoite hidalgos has thus gone down to posterity.

The detail of the work and the division of labour are graphically and carefully described by the great writer. One could almost draw a plan of the wall and its gates from the Biblical explanation. Among the many interesting facts to be gathered from this description, two may be especially mentioned. First, it is clear that at this period there were manufactures carried on in the holy city, for the goldsmiths are specially alluded to as performing a great portion of the work; and there were furnaces, the tower—probably the high shaft or chimney—of which was repaired by two of the workers. The expression " tower of the furnaces " would lead one to infer that there were a number of fires, hearths, or furnaces discharging their products of combustion into a common shaft. If so, economy of furnace construction was not unknown to our forefathers, who may have been in an advanced condition of industrial progress. And this indeed is likely, when we consider how rapidly the wall was built.

Nor was Nehemiah content with merely throwing up the masonry of the fortifications. He took care to provide gates and fit them with the necessary furniture, so that the city boundary might be as complete for purpose of peaceable ingress and egress as for purposes of defence in case of war.

The work went on, but not unmolested. Certain foreigners—we mean men not of Jewish race—subjected Nehemiah to constant menace and annoyance, being possibly actuated by jealousy of the Jews, and apprehension of the power that might accrue to them, if their city were in a state of security from the nomadic and plundering tribes that dwelt around Jerusalem and its vicinity. First they laughed at the Jews; but when they found that Nehemiah, regardless of their mockery, pursued the work, they grew angry, and the energetic Tirshatha found it necessary to divide his band into two parties—one to work at the wall, and the other to cover them; he armed the latter so that they might be ready to protect those who laboured at the fortification in the event of their being attacked by their enemies. Indeed, he took the precaution of arming those that were actually engaged in building, or in carrying building materials, or removing *débris* and rubbish; each man, builder, and bearer had his weapon ready, and as the necessities of the work kept them apart at intervals on the fortification, Nehemiah arranged that there should be a signal in case of danger—that is to say, when a trumpet was sounded, all were to hurry to the spot whence the sound came, and thus close their ranks. By this excellent plan the risk was avoided of their being cut off in detail in case of a sudden surprise.

Imagine the grave responsibilities that pressed on this great man. He, with his brethren and his own immediate followers—his guards and servants—were in constant vigil: "Never," says he in that homely language which seems to us so strikingly forcible, "Never did we put off our clothes, save for our ablutions."

It may be incidentally mentioned that the name Nehemiah was probably not an uncommon name, as amongst the builders of the wall a Nehemiah is mentioned who is evidently not the hero of our paper, but a man who—or whose father—was a satrap of a portion of a district called Beth-zur.*

Then, while the wall was being partially built, Nehemiah met with a new annoyance. The Jews disputed among themselves, and evidently endeavoured to profit by the misfortunes of those who had necessarily raised money on their lands and houses in order to pay the taxes levied by the Persian King. No doubt the Monarch and his governors were as exacting in the matter of tribute as are the Pashas of our time in the East. To raise the necessary tribute some of the Jews had mortgaged their landed property; but

---

* The present Bassorah is the בָּצְרָה of Scripture.

Nehemiah, who seems to have had marvellous powers of persuasion, managed to set this matter right. He induced the mortgagees to promise to restore the property, and—with his usual shrewd foresight—called the priests and caused the mortgagees to seal their promises by a solemn vow; for possibly they might have repented at leisure of what they had promised in haste, under the captivating influences of Nehemiah's persuasion or the fear of his indignation. It is satisfactory to learn that the promises thus made and ratified were faithfully kept.

Nehemiah, as we think we have before mentioned, had been appointed Governor by Artaxerxes, the Persian monarch. He shewed the greatest generosity and self-denial in the exercise of his high office, and evidently presented a great contrast to the former governors. He, unlike them, exacted no tax or tribute from the people. Instead of taking from them he gave to them. He maintained a sumptuous table, at which he not only received and feasted 150 Jews, but even heathen guests. He refused to take tribute from the people, because the bondage was heavy on them. And when he tells us this, he breaks off his narrative, and, with singular pathos, that strikes home to the heart, he exclaims,—

"Think of me, my God, for good, according to all that I have done for this people!"

Sanballat was the name of the chief instigator of the opposition to Nehemiah's plans. He attacked Nehemiah with bitter words, alleging that he had treasonable motives in fortifying Jerusalem. He calumniated him by declaring that his object was to rebel against the Persian King and to make himself King in Jerusalem.

F

This was a perilous scandal, but Sanballat did not venture, it would seem, to publish this foul accusation at Susa. He endeavoured to intimidate Nehemiah, whose friends took fright and urged him to take shelter in the Temple, which was strongly fortified; for they evidently apprehended a resort to physical force on the part of Nehemiah's enemies. But Nehemiah was too courageous, too strong in his moral convictions of right, to fear the cowardly calumniator. He dauntlessly refused to exhibit the least fear of Sanballat, and—to use a homely phrase—"would not show the white feather."

Like Nelson, when his work was done, he gave all the glory to God.

We have neither time nor space to describe step by step the history told in the Book of Nehemiah. In some respects it is a repetition of certain chapters of Ezra—the fact probably being that the chapters were at some time added to the earlier book; and we believe that the Book of Nehemiah has been called in certain canons the second book of Ezra. We have been mainly desirous to urge those points of the story that bear most forcibly on the characteristics of the great Jew, and indicate the sterling beauties of his noble disposition.

One of his first acts of rule, after he found himself released from the labour of building the wall, was to take a census of the people, and to ascertain and register their genealogies. The census even extended to the cattle.

And now the worship of old was restored. The Scroll of the Law—the divine heirloom of our race, again appeared before the eyes of the congregation.

No doubt the people wept when they heard it. The feast of Tabernacles was kept with due observance for the first time since the days of Joshua.

Nehemiah organized various matters of high importance, and returned for a brief time to the king's court. For he had evidently a divided duty. But his heart seems to have yearned for his own people; for he again obtained the king's permission to set out for Jerusalem, and went thither. He found that a part of his work had been undone in his absence, and therefore he had to make various administrative arrangements.

He found, moreover, to his great disgust, that the Sabbath-day was violated in the most shameless manner. Field work and trading were carried on, but he zealously put an immediate stop to this iniquitous practice. He was no middle-course man. His was the policy of "thorough"—the only policy that succeeds in this world: and he put down Sabbath-breaking with a strong hand. He closed the gates of the city during the Sabbath, and had them guarded so that no merchandize or produce should be brought in from the commencement till the conclusion of the Sabbath. Finding that some traders had established themselves just outside the wall in the hope of carrying on business unobserved or unmolested on the day of rest, he pounced on them too, and vowed he would visit them with condign punishment if he caught them a second time at their nefarious practices. They took care not to repeat them, however. And the next abuse he stopped was the sin of mixed marriages. He forbade intermarriage of the Jews with any of the women of other nations, a practice that had apparently grown up in Jerusalem, but which he loudly denounced ; and he purified the priesthood by ejecting from the sacerdotal office a man who had married a daughter of Sanballat.

And this is all he tells us of his work. And he ends his narrative with these plaintive words, "Remember me for good, oh God!"

Yes: these not unfrequent interjaculatory supplications of his convince us, that though it is himself who has drawn the narrative of his works and thoughts, whence we infer the beauty of his character; yet that narrative is true, and not overmuch coloured or too highly wrought. It seems that he lays the story of his life and deeds, and his thoughts and hopes, not before man, but before God. It is not man whom he seeks to please. It is the Heavenly Father whom he tries to conciliate in tremulous apprehension, scarcely with the confidence one might anticipate. Yes, the Book of Nehemiah seems to us to have been written by the sacred author not to convince man of the goodness and greatness of his labours, but to plead his own cause at the Throne of the Almighty.

Nehemiah was, indeed, a great and good man. His character seems to be unfolded before us by the story of his life. His indomitable energy and his firm and "thorough" policy cannot fail to strike us with admiration. His love for his people and for the Holy City was so strong that he sacrificed, on more occasions than one, the ease, comfort and luxury of a high position in the court, and about the person of the proudest monarch of the age. He sacrificed royal favour, courtly splendour, luxurious ease—for what? To re-build the walls, to re-establish the glory of the Sacred City, the home of his fathers and his Faith. He breasted the wicked jealousies and false machinations of treacherous enemies, to risk his life for Jerusalem and his brethren. He grappled with the thousand difficulties incidental to the re-modelling of a small community, exposed to external and internecine jealousies.

We learn a great lesson from his life—a lesson not easily to be forgotten. Around himself, around his noble character, clusters the main interest of his book. The introduction of his narrative into the Canon of Scripture affords more advantage than is derivable from its historic passages, from the additions it offers to the annals of our ancient days. It serves another purpose. It is a lesson taught by a life of action. The book contains no precept of morality, no revelation of doctrine, no narration of miracles. It is the story of a life, the story of a hero; the story of a man of ordinary condition of life, which apart from the incidental surroundings of the age in which he lived, and the circumstances which signalised that age, was a condition of life of an almost common-place character. He acted in the round of his life as many of us could act if we would. But what was most remarkable about him was this. He made his duties for himself. He grooved a channel of action for himself. He set himself work to do, and he did it manfully. Oh! you who live idle lives, and declare that your position unfortunately obliges you to no duty—ridiculous assertion!—learn a lesson from this man, who finding there was work to be done, wrong to redress, good to accomplish, went out of his easy way of life to effect what had to be effected. You who complain of life's hardships, learn your lesson from this hero, who breasted *his* hardships and trials with a stout heart, and never was cast down. And through all his exertions, all his trials, all his troubles, all his struggles; he had but one thought—"Remember me, oh God!"

The walls that he built with so much care and energy exist no longer. The ramparts which he raised have been beaten down. The work which he laboured at so painfully with hand, and heart, and brain, is all undone. The enemy besieged the city and crushed the fruit of his life's labour. Is this quite true? No. The work of his life, the fruit of his life is not destroyed, and never can be. The effect of a virtuous and manly life is immortal. No enemy can break down *that* fortification. It lives on; it lives for ever.

The character of Nehemiah may be written in a few words. It was a combination of manliness and holiness. Like him, may we learn to be manly and holy; to find out the work to be done and to do it, despite obstacle and evil report, and enmity and trial; relying only on Heaven. Like him, let us be self-sacrificing, and earnest; and above all things, let us sanctify the labour of our hands, the thought of our minds, nay, the very passion of our hearts. Then we may confidently hope that " God will remember us for good ! "

———

רֵאשִׁית חָכְמָה יִרְאַת ה' :

" The fear of the Lord is the beginning of wisdom."—Ps. cxi. 10.

MANY and varied are the modes by which Heaven in-
structs mankind in the great lessons of life. We may,
indeed, suppose that the Bible, which is replete with
precept, doctrine, narrative, and example, and which
appeals with equal force to the understanding, the
imagination, and the heart, is, in itself, all-sufficient
for the moral education of humanity.

Yet the Divine scheme, which is always lavish in
its bounties, does not content itself with granting to
man the means of instruction which Scripture affords,
but graciously offers other beacons for his guidance.
Brilliant as are the lights which the revelations of
Scripture shed on the world, the Holy Hand has
mercifully kindled other lamps, to indicate and to
illuminate the road, which leads through the circumstances and conditions of life, to that earthly happiness which consists of hope and endeavour, and beyond
it, to that heavenly happiness in which hope is fulfilled
and endeavour triumphant.

The world teems with these lessons, and glows with
these lights. There are indeed, "tongues in trees,
sermons in stones, books in the running brooks, and
good in everything."

And, among the many methods by which men learn

to be good and happy, there are, excepting religion,
no aids so forcible and no systems of guidance so
effective as those involved in the examples and the
memorials of great and good men. The story of their
lives strikes home to us all. For, in all lives, however
distinct and different in circumstance and aspect, there
is, at least, some one condition of similarity, some one
element of affinity, some one connecting link. There
is a kinship in humanity. We may never know how
great or how small a thing may have kept the worst
of us from being virtuous, or may have saved the best
of us from doing wrong. But if, when we read the
records of some great and good life, we are touched by
its example and awakened to its merit and honour, do
we not all feel that we have within us the capability,
which, had we trained it wisely, directed it duly, or
seen it in time, might have made us as great or as
good as he whom we admire, or brought us to the performance of actions as heroic, or to the leading of a
life as true, as his? Do not

> " Lives of great men all remind us,
>   We may make our lives sublime ! "

For even though it may not be within the competency
of all of us to imitate every or any great action, we
may all of us, in some respect, imitate every or any
good life.

It was said by a man of genius, who not long since
rose from a comparatively humble origin to an eminent
position, " The question is not so much *what you do*, as
what manner of man you are." Indeed, the matter at
issue with all of us really is the manner of our manhood. The character of a career is not involved in an

individual action, or in isolated actions, but in the sum of one's actions, in their combined and blended effect ; or, rather, in the influence which dominates, directs, and actuates them. The loveliness and power of light do not reside in the separate elementary colours into which the prism resolves it, but in their combined effect when fused into one glittering ray ; or, better still, in the influence which, when these hues—some bright, some gloomy—are intimately blended, merges the individuality and effect of each, and strikes out from their union a new, a strong, a brilliant and harmonious, an almost immortal beauty.

The pencil of light is an emblem of what a true life should be. When analysed the every phase of one should present—like every tint of the other—a certain if not a perfect charm ; and its darker shadows becoming cleared, and its brighter glows subdued in the harmony of union, its ultimate effect should be a beauty and a glory and a blessing.

Of the many careers which serve to

"Point a moral or adorn a tale,"

there are some which are useful only as warnings, while others are useful as examples. It is of these latter that we would speak. To find such lives as these we need not travel out of the records of our own race. It is, unhappily, not the practice of our people, even on occasions, to exalt or quote the heroes of our own history, or to assert their merits or eulogise their fame. We cite instances of ancient greatness from the pages of Plutarch and Nepos, and yet Greece, Rome, and Carthage never produced more illustrious examples than did the Palestine of our ancestors. And

no modern career in the whole range on which a
Carlyle descants, or from which a Smiles draws his
didactic inferences, shines with a brighter, a steadier,
or a purer light, than does that of our Jewish sage and
philosopher, Moses Mendelssohn.

It is not so long since he was taken from us but that
we can call him a man of our own times, and appreciate
him better from our capability of understanding the
condition of society in which he lived; for its features
do not differ widely from those of our own contemporary
social system.   His station and external fashion of life
were not far removed from—perhaps the same as—
those of our readers.   Indeed, such differences as there
are between the age and conditions in which he lived
and those in which we live, are just such as rendered
the accomplishment of his greatness more difficult to
himself, and as render the possibility of imitating it
more easy to ourselves.

Moses Mendelssohn was born at Dessau (in Germany)
in 1729; his father was a schoolmaster and scribe or
Sopher, (copyist of the תורה ספר), and was so very
poor that the young Mendelssohn determined on leaving
home at fourteen to seek his fortune and relieve his
father from the burden of supporting him.   He arrived
at Berlin without the means of purchasing food, but by
the intercession of a Rabbi Fränkel, who had taught
him at Dessau, he obtained shelter in a garret and an
occasional meal.

It will not detract from the benevolence of this act,
if we mention that it was at that time customary for
the wealthy — and, indeed, for those whose means
scarcely raised them above poverty—to contribute
weekly allowances, called *wochengeld*, to students, to

supply them with the means of maintenance, in order to enable them to pursue their studies. The contributors paid these sums in turn. The custom still prevails in Poland, and among the more ancient congregations of Germany. In those old-fashioned days, intellect was not only honoured, but supported also.

Mendelssohn now applied himself sedulously to the attainment of knowledge; and his thirst for wisdom, as well as his aptitude for acquiring it—or, perhaps we should say, his energy and diligence in acquiring it, were marvellous.

At Dessau he had at first received the meagre instruction commonly imparted to Jewish boys at that time; he had learned to repeat by rote a number of rabbinical texts, the meanings of which were beyond a child's comprehension; but his gigantic mind, even while yet held in his boyish frame, greedily sought other and higher food. He determined on studying Hebrew grammatically, though in his day boys of his class did not thus learn it. He was aided in his efforts by Rabbi Fränkel. At Berlin, he became acquainted with an eminent Pole named Israel Moses, and with a young medical man named Kisch, and from these he obtained an immense amount of knowledge. His acquaintance with these friends was due to one of his numerous acts of charity. The difficulties which he had to surmount to obtain knowledge were as great as the stores of knowledge which he at length acquired. Notwithstanding the defects of early education and the drawbacks of class, clique, and poverty, he gained a profound acquaintance with Hebrew and German, a knowledge of other languages, of natural philosophy, general literature, and mathematics. He wrote twenty-one works, full of erudition and literary beauty; works which are models of style, no less than treasures of wisdom. For, though he was born of a class whose vernacular was a corrupt mixture of distorted German and Hebrew, he acquired so pure and elegant a style in the German language, that his writings are cited as having effected an improvement in the language, and as having, so to speak, formed a great step of progress in the literature of his native land.

While he was lodging with his friend at Berlin, a Jewish manufacturer, named Bernard, having heard of his peculiar abilities and attainments, appointed him tutor to his children, and afterwards clerk in his manufactory. Mendelssohn's mind, though capable of soaring to the noblest heights of literature and science, was not incapable of descending to the material details of a business career. From the position of clerk in Bernard's house, he rose to be manager, and eventually partner.

He married in 1762 and enjoyed great domestic happiness. He fell a victim to the intensity of study, mental labour, and meditation, and died in 1787 at the comparatively early age of fifty-seven.

Having given this cold sketch of his life, let us enquire a little into the "manner of his manhood."

The "accidents of birth" were, in a social point of view, wholly against him. He was born of a race despised and maligned in the age and country in which he flourished, yet he lived till that age and that country were proud of him, and glad of him. He was, as we have said, the son of poor parents, but he "broke his birth's invidious bar," and attained honourably-earned wealth, and a respectable worldly position. He was but feebly educated in his childhood; but by arduous, diligent, sustained, strenuous, nay, extraordinary exertions, he acquired marvellous knowledge, and became a very monument of learning, a model of literary taste, a bold pioneer of new paths of wisdom. He had none of those personal advantages, which even among men, exert a certain fascination, command a hearing, dignify presence, or produce effect; yet to use the words of his biographer, "he won every heart at first sight." He had not even the advantage of strong health, yet he laboured far more energetically and thoroughly than the stalwart and robust.

Immense and varied as were his acquirements, he was not in the position of life in which he could devote himself wholly to literature or study, for he supported his family mainly by mercantile pursuits; yet he was a great and an industrious writer, and he has left to posterity treasures of authorship, which perhaps a generation less material than our own will appreciate as they deserve.

In his day, every obstruction was offered to the advance and improvement of the race to which he belonged, and it held no recognised place in society; yet he lived down obstacle and impediment, and he became the central star of an admiring group of disciples, friends, and adherents. Though the wisest of his day sought his companionship and his friendship; though trusting pupils and delighted auditors surrounded him; and contemporary fame sounded his renown throughout Germany, and, indeed, throughout Europe, he never, never forgot the beauty of humility, and was as modest when he had reached the pinnacle of his fame as while he was engaged in attaining it.

He moved at first in an unenlightened and a pre-

judiced society, and was virulently opposed even by
his co-religionists ; but he was neither discouraged nor
disgusted, as a man of feebler mind, or even ordinary
temper, would have been; he only waited and perse-
vered.   He had learnt

> "—— to labour—and to wait."

And thus readily seeing evils, of which men of inferior
capacities had no glimpse, he did not dash into wild
projects of reform, but he strove to pierce prejudice
and habit with the light of truth—not with the sword
of violence—and he triumphed over hostility as much
by his meekness as by his merit.

But, above all things—and this was his greatest
glory—his life was, in its morality and its piety, a
striking and a shining illustration of the beauty and
strength of Judaism.   For high above his position, his
philosophy, his attainments, his intellectual fame, his
wordly condition, he placed the Judaism in which he
gloried.   It was the master-key to the music of his
life.   He was a Jew above all things and through all
things.   His religion was to him not only the sun that
shone high in the sky, over the earth beneath, but the
sunshine that permeated everything on the face and in
the depths of Nature.   He discovered that he could be
a good citizen, and yet a Jew; a great literate, a
companion of sages and philosophers of other creeds,
and yet a Jew; a striving, and eventually a prosperous,
merchant—and yet a professing, a practising, and a
persistent Jew.

There was no way of his life in which he failed to
shine.   Though he spiritualized his existence by intensity of meditation, and lifted his soul continually to

the contemplation of the objects which float in the regions of thought, he did not soar above worldly ties and duties, nor in any wise break from the home feelings, without which no life, however finely cast, can be completely beautiful. He was an excellent father; he was no ascetic, but enjoyed the charms of society; he was a hearty friend; and, when his frame was decaying, and the hand of death near him, he sacrificed his love of tranquillity and his natural need of repose to the duty of defending a deceased friend. Though warmly attached to his religion, he was no fanatic, but supported controversy with amiability, and endured difference of opinion with toleration. He followed the maxim of the Psalmist, he "sought peace and pursued it."

Study and knowledge sealed in his heart the great truths of religion. His was the faith which is clothed in wisdom; his the wisdom which is hallowed by faith. His faith was to him, as it should be to all of us, an *armed angel.* For faith, however firm her tread, is too ethereal to walk on earth, unless shielded by the armour of knowledge from the weapons of earthly learning. His faith presented to the world a breastplate of wisdom, against which the blows of sophistry and casuistry rang in vain; and yet, had it been otherwise, had artifice pierced the joints and shattered the almost invulnerable mail, his faith would have spread her angel pinions, and soared high above earth, and far beyond defeat!

We do not propose to enter here into the details of his life, but will content ourselves with quoting three instances to exemplify what "manner of man" he was.

While yet a boy, and very poor, he was so reluctant to become a burden to others, that he would purchase a loaf of bread, and notch it in such a manner, as to apportion it into a certain number of meals corresponding with the state of his means.

Though a profound, assiduous, and successful student of the highest branches of learning, he sedulously cultivated and acquired an elegant handwriting; because he deemed that it would help him to maintain a family respectably. And, indeed, it was partly owing to this accomplishment, that he obtained so much worldly success.

He lost his eldest child, a babe of eleven months old. Every heart to which young children are dear can conceive the heaviness of such a blow to his tender spirit. He felt it—but he did not repine or despair. No; he thanked heaven for having granted his lost little one a happy life, while she was yet on earth.

Indeed, his affectionate heart not only throbbed with love for his own kindred, but was alive to sympathy with those who needed it; he was benevolent and singularly gentle.

But these gentle spirits are often those that strive most strongly and work most bravely. He taught the world that the Jew, hitherto despised, must be despised no more: he conquered a place in society, in the highest society—the intellectual circle—for the people of his faith. And this victory he won, not by dint of clamour, or falsehood, or obtrusive self-assertion, but by the force of his own intellectual powers, his unsullied integrity, his admirable character.

His great contemporary, Lessing, having learnt from

his experience of Mendelssohn, the true beauty of the character of a good Jew, stamped that experience on the face of contemporary literature, and strove to teach it to the million, by means of his famous and popular drama, "Nathan der Weise;" and it is said that under the disguise of the hero of the piece, he paid a tribute to his friend—and to truth, by painting the character of Mendelssohn.

When, at length, Mendelssohn fell ill, broken beneath the weight of thought and labour—which while they uplift the mind bear down the body—he was bidden to desist from all mental occupation. Those to whom such work is life's main interest, vocation, and enjoyment, can conceive the penalty involved in such an abstinence. He knew that his life was a gift and a trust of precious value, which it was a duty to preserve. He made every needful sacrifice; quailed before no effort, but met disease just as a brave man meets an enemy, grappled with it, and, with the blessing of Heaven, threw his foe.

Threw him for a time only; for at length the day came when no courage, no care, no effort, could avert the blow which was to take him from the world of living men. He died, as he had lived, calmly, serenely.

It is said that while Addison was expiring, he called his pupil to his bedside, in order that he "might see," said the sinking philosopher, "how a Christian can die." But Mendelssohn gave mankind a more useful lesson, a more touching example, a more glorious spectacle; he showed—without ostentatiously proclaiming it—how a Jew should live!

The career of Mendelssohn may in certain respects be summed up in a few words—the few words inscribed

on his bust in the Berlin Jews' Free School, and
written by Karl Wilhelm Ramler,—one of the poets
by whom truth is none the less substantially told because clothed in spiritual language :

> "Weise wie Sokrates,
> Treu dem Glauben seiner Väter,
> Wie er, die Unsterblichkeit lehrend,
> Und sich unsterblich machend wie er."

> "As wise as Socrates,
> True to the faith of his fathers,
> Like him, he taught immortality,
> And, like him, rendered himself immortal."

At this day, when we hear around us complacent
ignorance questioning the solemn truths of ages, it is
some satisfaction to learn from the history of this great
man that, after he had spent a life-time in thought and
study, the glow of faith which had lighted the birth of
his labours shone on their summit with undiminished
sheen.   And it is refreshing to turn from the troubled
stories of kings, warriors, and statesmen, to the record
of this calm, pure life, in which, as in the religion he
followed, peace, love, and wisdom are harmoniously
combined.

The wisest of men, favoured with natural genius,
rich in acquired knowledge, admit that at the acme of
their renown, or at the end of their work, they have,
after all, only attained the beginning of wisdom.
Even Mendelssohn, profound as was his learning, great
and varied as were his acquirements, fruitful as were
his meditations, doubtlessly never arrived beyond the
beginning of wisdom.   But he had arrived at the
beginning of wisdom in another and a better sense,

for, on that beginning, he built the beauty of his life. His knowledge was the altar on which he stood to worship his God. For his history confirms the truth, which the Psalmist whose music he loved, taught mankind, ages ago—

רֵאשִׁית חָכְמָה יִרְאַת ה׳

" The beginning of wisdom is—the fear of the Lord."

BAR-MITZVAH.*

כָּל הַמִּצְוָה אֲשֶׁר אָנֹכִי מְצַוְּךָ הַיּוֹם תִּשְׁמְרוּן לַעֲשׂוֹת :

"All the commandments which I command thee this day shall ye observe to do."—DEUT. viii. 1.

"WORDS have wings" is an old aphorism, capable of a higher interpretation than a hackneyed reference to the rapid travel of rumour. Words have wings which not only bear them through and about the world, but spread for loftier flights, and soar for regions far beyond earth and its connections, urged not only by the cold force of intellect, but by the glowing power of the heart, being laden with the influence by which they are impelled. The winged word, like the winged horse of yore, strikes through the valleys of earth and their low-lying mists, and rises to the tall summit of a Parnassus, round whose base lie the fields of duty and every-day action, and about whose peak, high above cloud-land, gleams the warm light of an ever sunny sky. And higher still, higher than the realms of matter and nature, higher than the proudest form that matter takes, or the most majestic throne which nature rears, words wing their upward flight, and bear on their pinions our hearts and our hopes to the golden gates of heaven.

These are the winged words of which we are now

* Initiation into the duties of a Jew.

thinking ; words which, in the shape of prayer, hymn,
or blessing, carry our thoughts from the visible to the
invisible, from the known to the unknown, from time
and space to the Infinite and the Eternal.

Supernatural manifestations of an ever-present Deity
no longer arouse the senses to a supernatural awe ; the
glory of the Presence shines no more within the veil
of the sanctuary, and the fire of prophecy no longer
lingers on the lips of our poets and sages ; but prayer,
psalm, and blessing still remain to hallow our materialism, and to bind our earth to heaven. They are our
messengers. Needing no miraculous mediation, no
vicarious interposition, to bear and guide them on
their way, they soar, direct from the lips of man to
the Power which is so immeasurably distant, and the
Love which is so marvellously near. And, as they
leave us, to rise heavenward, they purify the spirit
and light the lips from which they pass, as we may
fancy that an angel, rising to the skies, leaves a glow
and a blessing in its track.

To no words do these thoughts more forcibly apply
than to the blessing which we pronounce, when bidden
to the hearing or the reading of the Law. If ever
there be a signal fitness in things, it rests assuredly in
the language of this benediction. As the heavenly
message was the most sublime of gifts, it is well that
the blessing which acknowledges it should be adapted
to its sublimity. Its frequent repetition may, in some
unreflecting minds, deprive it of its external solemnity,
but cannot affect its intrinsic sanctity. It is difficult
to imagine any combination of words for the purpose
more telling, more appropriate, and more suggestive;
and never is it more fitting and impressive than when

pronounced publicly, for the first time, by the fresh
lips of a young boy, who stands forth in the congregation of Israel, to take on himself the "yoke of the
law," and who withdraws from his father's side, and
in some respect from his authority, to yield and bind
himself by lip, heart, and soul, to the Father of us all,
whose authority he that day acknowledges, not for that
day only, but for life and immortality!

Many as are the solemn moments of a Jewish life,
there are few more solemn than this. It is a foreshadowing of a still more awful moment—a moment
not reckoned on the dials of time—when, if the vision
of the prophet and the dream of the poet be rightly
read, the soul depending on no human care, aided by
no earthly strength, shall stand forth in a greater
congregation, on the threshold of a world still more
unknown, to give an account of the fulfilment of the
duty taken in charge this day!

The boy seems to us like a traveller, who has climbed
to a ridge beneath which a valley lies outspread as if
in a dream; a valley lighted with the dawn of hope
and promise, warm and cheery in its early glow. How
cold will the landscape seem when the rosy tinge is
withdrawn, and clouds of care and mists of doubt
overshadow it! How different will it be when the
traveller goes down into the vale, and strays through
the dream's reality, till at length the night falls! But
well shall it be if the wanderer bear in his hand the
lamp which shall withstand the storm, and pierce the
darkness and the mist:

$$\text{נֵר לְרַגְלִי דְבָרֶיךָ וְאוֹר לִנְתִיבָתִי}$$

"Thy word is a lamp unto my feet, and a light unto

my path." The everlasting light of the Law he shall forsake at his peril! It shall be a signal that shall never fail—a beacon that shall never grow dim. It shall be his "cloud by day;" his "pillar of fire by night."

Nor is it only to the parents, or even to the near kindred, that the ceremony is of grave interest. Not only is it the father or the mother whose heart on that day beats with a quicker throb. For these young boys are heirs to all of us! They will inherit the world when we shall have passed away from it. But, let us not forget, the world which they will inherit will be such as we bequeath it to them. If by our misdoings, or our short-comings, we impair or scathe the inheritance, the generation which shall follow us will reap a blighted harvest. If by our struggles, our cares, our endeavours—perhaps by our vigils and our tears—we sow a healthy crop, and rear a fruitful growth—the golden yield will be gathered by our heirs in the hour of their manhood. The heirloom is theirs. The responsibility and the trust are ours. For them, spring and summer will smile, when autumn shall have fallen on us, and winter shall have laid us low. The snow which shall lie cold on our dull breasts will be lighted with the rainbow smiles of their prime. True, they may not be the children of our blood. The story of our lives may never have been rendered beautiful by the love of young children—a love which purifies and sanctifies the love of earth, and links it with the love of heaven. The voices of the young may not sound cheerily in our homes, nor whisper to our hearts. There, these tender sounds may have never been, or thence they may have passed away—

passed into the hard strife of the world, or into the
soft shelter of heaven. But not for these things shall
our hearts be closed to the voices of these children
of all Israel, when they call on, and bless, the name
of their Father and ours. They are near to us and
dear to us; for they are henceforth our brothers, and
their hands shall touch ours in upholding and bearing
down through ages the Law and the Mission which
were given to us. So, let us aid their hands and strive
to strengthen them. Let us enrich and beautify the
heritage which we shall leave to them, when we go to
sleep in the dust. And, though we may have none so
near to us as to bless our Father through their tears for
us, yet they will keep our memory green, and think of
us tenderly, lovingly and prayerfully, when, for us, the
" silver cord is loosed " for ever!

Some, listening to the law of expediency, and looking so steadfastly down on earth that they never see
the heavenly lights which tinge it, would tell us that
the prescribed age of a boy's becoming *bar-mitzvah*,
though adapted to a more fervid clime, is unfitted for
our cold and tardy zone. We cannot think it. Better
is it when the heart is fresh and young, unsullied by
the taint of wrong, unscathed by the fire of passion;
that *then* that heart should be offered as a free-will
offering, as a young lamb without blemish, on the
altar! Better, then, when the field is fresh to sow it.
Better then to take on the eager shoulders, and into
the plastic mind, the yoke of the Law, which we were
chosen to receive and to transmit—and in which is the
germ of that eternal life which, with that Law, we
inherit!

The world is in a transition age, and much affecting

it depends on this transition period of human life. It
was a selfish atheist who said, "After me the deluge!"
The believer, the man of feeling, is free from such cold
complacency. It behoves us to give a sheer temper to
the instruments which shall do the world's work when
we shall be rusted and broken. We are too apt to
regard in a boy's career in the world the world's effect
on him. Let us reverse this, and consider the world's
career, and the boy's effect on it. Great results are in
man's hands; each generation gives its complexion to
its own age; and its shadow falls before it on the ages
which are to follow. How shall we deal with these
young boys to fit them for their task?

Perhaps not quite as we are doing now. Our treatment of boys is an inconsistency; for while we talk to
them as if they were sages, we deal with them as
if they were babes. We talk to them as if their
judgments were as mature, their experience as ex-
tensive, their knowledge as ample as our own; but we
treat them as if they had no hearts, no sensibility, no
affections. Yet, a little consideration will convince us
that though wisdom and experience grow with time, the
feelings of a boy are as quick, his affections as warm, as
those of manly years.

Judaism is a faith of the heart, even more than of
the intellect. The dread proclamation of the Unity,
on which our creed is built, is closely followed by the
declaration, that man's duty to his Maker is a service
of love. It will not be more difficult for the teacher
to teach, or for the student to learn, if the lesson is to
be a lesson of love, taught through the heart as well as
through the mind.

And the mission of Judaism is perhaps on the eve

of a broader development. The doubts, disturbance and difficulties which beset the age can best be resolved by an appeal to the steady and constant principles of right and justice, taught in the Bible and transmitted by the Jews. Only but the other day, we Jews held it our duty to fight the battle of faith against astute sophisms and cunning scepticism, not the less serious because ascribed to a Zulu, nor less perilous because urged by a bishop. While infidelity shoots its random arrows, and casuistry raises its empirical mists, it is for those, who are the living witnesses of the Law of truth, to be its living lights also. It is for those who indicate the road, to cast on it the rays of knowledge. But the guide on the mountain side must not only point to the path—he must also be habituated to tread it.

Hence we must train the guides who are to follow us to be surefooted in the way; to be examples of the trusty precepts which they preach; for in this example will be the strength of their pilotage. And this is true for rich and poor. In this thing he only shall be rich who enriches the fields of his heritage; he only shall be poor who impoverishes the land.

And you, young boys, who are on the platform of the *Almemmar*; who are about to mount its steps or who have but just descended them, with the excitement of the day still fresh on your brows! to you, we your brothers who have grown old in the service, and have had aching and heavy hearts since they beat in their gay hope on our *bar-mitzvah* day, we welcome you to our brotherhood, and we do not hear unmoved the blessing in which you call on our Father's name, and thank Him for having chosen Israel for his earthly

mission and his heavenly destiny. But do not you
forget, even if some amongst us have forgotten it, that
the glow of hope shall fade, while the glow of duty
shall endure; that resolve is not truly sanctified until
it grow into accomplishment; that the excitement of
an hour is but a meteor, and plays no true part in your
life unless its consequences pervade your nature with
an even flow, as light saturates the atmosphere. Life
is an illusion, unless shaped to good purpose; a fitful
dream, unless substantiated by duty; a wavering flight,
unless it point upward ever.

> "The world is all a fleeting show,
>   For man's illusion given;
> The smiles of joy, the tears of woe,
> Deceptive gleam, deceptive flow,
>   There's nothing true but heaven."*

For, by earnestness of aim and pursuit; by solemn
fore-thought of responsibility; by imitation, not of the
frivolous ephemera whose gay plumage flutters at
random about you, but imitation of good, great and
true men; by steadfast reliance on the grace which
virtue alone can hope to win, the work shall be done,
and well done, and " triumph crown the toil."

We welcome you, as you stand before the Law, which
is to be your guide and your delight. We welcome
you as you come down amongst us, perhaps with a
resolve in your breast to sacrifice to the service many
an hour of ease and pleasure. And, with the joyous
welcome with which we greeted you in your innocent
infancy when you were first bound to the covenant,
and with which our fathers of old greeted those who

* Moore.

brought the myrtle-bound sacrifice to the altar; so may
men welcome you when you pass among them on your
way on earth—keeping the Law and the commandments.
So may angels welcome you, to your reward, at the
portals of the life eternal in heaven, when your life on
earth is passed.

ALL men are not poets; but the spirit of poetry dwells in many things, and tells its unexpressed tale to the heart. Men, incapable of penning a line of verse, almost incapable of reading a page of a poem, may yet be not insensible to the spiritualizing influence of the unseen, but penetrating, poetry which rises from material things, and strikes through the awakened senses of the heart.

The poetry of which we speak is not the metrical or musical expression in which language embodies spiritual thoughts, but rather the music of the thought extracted from the music of the language. It is the perfume, not the colour of the flower; the influence which, though it seems to spring from worldly things, wakes, from hidden chords, sounds which are not of the world, and which proclaim the presence of a sense, not wholly material, not of the matter which we can analyze, combine, transform, and regulate; but partaking of, and tending towards a higher nature, beyond the world's control.

Judaism is a poem in itself; a great, true, divine poem; the supreme poetry of the world—to the world, what other poetry is to matter—a grand, solemn, spiritual teacher, sublime in its heavenly origin, glorious in its high nature, lovely in its earthly dress.

Judaism is a poem in the hallowed grandeur of its

revelation; in the majesty of its history; in the teachings and testimonies of its existence and its career;
in the grief of its fallen state; in the mystic glories
of its aspirations; in the tender charities of its loving
precepts,—a poem in its being, its belongings, its
associations, its destinies and its hopes. Its literature,
its story, its very liturgies are poems from beginning
to end. Its ceremonies, especially, are fraught with
the holiest poetry.

Cold must be the heart of the worshipper who sees
nothing but waving verdure when the palm branches
are borne aloft; or hears nothing but a chant when the
כֹּהֲנִים bless their brethren.

The ceremonies of the synagogue are, to the intellectual witness, alive with poetry,—the divine poetry
which unchains the spirit from worldly influences,
touches the throbbing breast, fills the eyes with tears,
and lifts the yearning soul to God.

When the lithe, myrtle-bound branches wave in all
their tremulous grace; when the descendants of Aaron
stand on the steps of the Ark; when the scrolls,
hidden by their gorgeous robes and crowned with
their glittering bells, are carried amid our ranks; the
eye speaks to the heart, and the material beauty which
we see is spiritualized into a beauty which we feel.
Yet, not only in these public displays of a hallowed
pomp does the spirit of unearthly poetry dwell; but
also in the humbler ceremonies, the modest rites, which
mark, and grace, and bless the Jewish home.

For it is an especial privilege of the Jew that his
house may be a place of holy worship. As he himself
is by birthright a priest—one of a nation of priests,—
so is his house, when hallowed by the מְזוּזָה on his

door post, a house where his Lord may be worshipped
and his rites practised. We need no tower, no spire,
no glowing painted window; but in our homes—the
homes in which we dwell and follow the bent of our
every day career; in which we spent our childhood
or grew to manhood; in which our holy loves were
sanctified, our little ones first brought to our hopeful
arms, our dead taken from our tearful eyes; our homes
endeared to us by our joys, hallowed by our sorrows
and our struggles,—*there* may we worship our Heavenly
Father!

There are acts of religion, pertaining to recurring
periods of the year, month, or week, which are special
acts of the home. They are landmarks which define
the bounds or intervals of time; signals which indicate
the consecrated days and seasons; but they also serve
as beacons to which man may lift his eyes, as he pauses
in life's battles, to think of better things, and higher
hopes; beacons which lift their steady light over the
throbbing troubled seas of the world, to which one may
look back in life's varied phases with hopeful heart,
because they point from earth to heaven.

The narration of the Exodus in the service of the
הַגָּדָה; the dedication of our houses; the sanctifying
of the Sabbath; the blessings of the הַבְדָּלָה; the
lighting of the lamps at חֲנֻכָּה; these and many more,
do we all practise at home? Have we grown unmind-
ful of, or indifferent to them? Are we fully sensible
of their import and their influence?

And yet, through life, can we ever forget the impression of the home service of the Passover? Let other
people celebrate the anniversaries of their freedom by
public jousts and games, laurel wreaths and glowing

illuminations. We, in our quiet homes, round the familiar board, about which our dear ones gather, never so thickly but that a place and a cup are left for the stranger, tell again and again, year by year, the story which never grows old: the story of our great deliverance (wrought not by our own, or our fathers' prowess, but by the Divine Hand !)—a deliverance from a miserable bondage to a sublime destiny—a deliverance by which a people was brought amid the waves and carried across the wilderness, to be the enduring witnesses of a truth that cannot fail and a hope that cannot die.

A tender light shines in the Jew's home on the Sabbath eve. Blessed are the rays of the Sabbath lamp as they fall on the table round which the household gathers on the eve of rest;—the father, worn with the week's toil and struggles ; the mother, weary with the past household cares; the schoolboy tired with the exertion of mind ; the child to whom rest is only rest from noisy play. The Sabbath has been welcomed abroad by hymns and psalms. Let us welcome its presence at home by that simple but wonderful record of the origin of the Day of Rest, and by a blessing of thanks for the grateful wine, which is its type, for, like the Sabbath, it infuses renewed vigour, strength, and energy into the wearied frame.

A touching sight is the הַבְדָּלָה, before our hands resume the labour which should be for God's service, as the rest is for his delight. Let us bless the Giver of the strength which nerves our hands, the skill which fires our brains, the energy which glows in our hearts. Let us bless the Giver for the power to work, for the happiness of work. Let us bless the Giver, with our young ones around us, for these dear precious gifts for whom we have to labour, for whose loved sake we pray our labour may be triumphant.

But it is vain to multiply instances. The poetry of the rite is, in truth, but the very shadow of its enduring influence. There is no home-ceremony that has not, apart from its grace and charm of beauty, an intrinsic solid good in the power it works in those who take part in it at the time; or in those who may remember it in the years to come.

And why do we now-a-days shirk their fulfilment? Is it apathy? is it idleness? is it a false shame lest we be, in our social practices, unlike our fellow country-men of other faiths? Do we fail to bless the Giver of food, to sanctify the feast, lest we be unlike other Englishmen? And yet, glorious as it is to be of this English nation, whose history glows with deeds of world-wide renown, whose position is magnificent in its dignity and splendour, how much more glorious is it to be of this Jewish race, whose origin and story are emphatically registered in the Book of books, the record which all civilization reveres? a race which received its guiding laws from the Divine voice? a nation which bears through the course of ages the inheritance of a Divine mission, the presence of a Divine priesthood, the recollection of a Divine deliverance, the assurance of a Divine destiny?

Let us be Jews above all things; Jews not only in the Synagogue, but in the home; not only in the presence of our brother Jews, but also in the presence of our brother Englishmen; not only before the Ark

H

which holds the Law, but also at the table round which our children cluster.

For the sake of those children, those dear young children, those soft, sweet faces, those loving, trustful eyes, those tender, innocent hearts, which the Father, whose cherished children we all are, has committed to our care; for the sake of our children let them see, day by day, the rites of our glorious faith! They may think of them in after days, far from home and its influences; far from the roof that sheltered, the breast that nurtured, the voice that counselled, their happy childhood.

In the feverish throb of the world's battle, in the crisis of fitful life, memory may picture some happy Sabbath eve, when the father sanctified the bread and wine, and the mother passed the cup from her loving lips to the lips she loved; memory may wake again the young voices of brothers and sisters clustering round the gay taper with the joyous chant of הַמַּבְדִּיל. Again may they feel on their weary brow the kindly pressure of the parent's hand and the breath of the hallowed blessing of boyhood. And, remembering these things, shall they never say in the throes of their re-awakened heart, "O God! I was once innocent, true, and happy. Let me be innocent, true, and happy once again!"

And the memories of a man's own childhood may follow him to his own home, when children of his own gather near him. Surely no modern fashion, no new refinement can ever compensate for the old, old fashion of our childhood's joyous observances. Shall he not yearn to hear from these fresh lips the sounds of days gone by—the uplifting of the Sabbath blessings, the tones of familiar hymns, the reproduction of his own hallowed boyhood?

Yet, not only for the sake of the old home, or the new home, or the home that we may hope to own on earth. Alas! to many, between them and the old home the prospect may be dimmed by a mist of tears; or the joys of a new home, and the homely loves, and the ring of children's voices may be all unknown, and never or never more to be.

But there is a home which is for all of us; a home which we only know as yet by name and by hope. Then, for the sake of that home in heaven, let us sanctify our homes on earth. Let us bless the hand that gives the bread and wine. Let us signalize the seasons of our deliverance from the Egyptian and the Greek; let us sanctify the Sabbath day, and thus prepare for a great deliverance from life's cares and sorrows; for a great Sabbath of rest from its struggles and its toils!

THE BENEDICTION OF THE COHANIM.

דַּבֵּר אֶל אַהֲרֹן וְאֶל בָּנָיו לֵאמֹר כֹּה תְבָרֲכוּ אֶת בְּנֵי
יִשְׂרָאֵל אָמוֹר לָהֶם : יְבָרֶכְךָ ה' וְיִשְׁמְרֶךָ יָאֵר ה' פָּנָיו
אֵלֶיךָ וִיחֻנֶּךָ : יִשָּׂא ה' פָּנָיו אֵלֶיךָ וְיָשֵׂם לְךָ שָׁלוֹם :

"Speak to Aaron, and to his sons, saying, On this wise ye
shall bless the children of Israel : The Lord bless thee and keep
thee ; the Lord make his face shine upon thee, and be gracious
unto thee ; the Lord lift up his countenance upon thee, and
give thee peace."—Numb. vi. 23.

On the festival days, when, in obedience to Divine
command, and in memorial of Divine mercies, we, the
children of Israel, assemble in our places of worship,
we signalise the rites by a ceremony of solemn import
and of sublime origin—a ceremony peculiar to these
joyful and hallowed times.   On these days, the descendants of Aaron, first of our long line of priests, stand
before the Law which is the silent witness of our faith,
and before the congregation which is its living witness,
and invoke the Benediction which has endured through
all the wanderings of our people in the wilderness of
the world.

As the Blessing is uttered in our midst, memory,
aided by tradition, may well revert to the past.   Time,
as it floats away from us, leaves its persistent murmur
with us, like the continuous murmur of a river as it

sweeps towards the sea. In the past, these words and
forms, this very chant, clothed the Benediction.
Shrouded in their טליתים, which now, perhaps, enwrap
their buried forms, our fathers spoke or listened to the
Blessing. Life's ardent tones may never more be
heard from their familiar lips, but they have left their
memories on earth, as the light leaves its track in the
sky, whence it has fled at evening. And, looking beyond these nearer years to a past more remote,
recollections embalmed in the grave dignity of history,
press on the mind. Centuries back, in the mediæval
synagogues, which have perhaps crumbled into dust,
like the hands that raised them, and the feet that trod
them, it may be that the steps on which the *Cohanim*
mounted to their station before the ark were stained
with their martyred brethren's blood, while the cries of
a frantic crowd and the clash of a furious soldiery
rang madly without the walls and mingled with the
chant! Still farther back, the brief day of a renewed
splendour flashes on the recollection. The princes and
sages of the captivity rise in majestic, melancholy
train, and take their stately places in the dream of
memory. We see their shadowy forms as they gather
on the holy dais in the dim old-world light, to utter
the threefold Benediction in tones, which, it is said,
have descended to us from the days of the Second
Captivity.* Thus history bears us back on its shadow-
laden wings, through varied years of glory and misery,
to the bright days in which the temple of our faith and
nationality lifted its imperial height; when a king on
whose brow gleamed the gems of the East, and a priest
on whose breast flashed the jewels of the Ephod, stood

* The late Rev. D. A. de Sola's Essay on Hebrew Music.

in its splendid courts, the one to receive, the other to
pronounce, the blessing which Aaron was enjoined to
utter three thousand years ago, and which, almost
yesterday, was trembling in our ears.

For the throng of the familiar and the unfamiliar
dead, those gone from life long since, and those gone
from us so lately; the faces which we picture to ourselves, though we have never seen them, and the faces
which we have so often seen, but may never see again;
the kings, the priests, the prophets, the historic heroes
of our race, and those nearer and dearer to us still, our
own homely dead; all these have passed away, but the
Blessing still endures! Living lips repeat the words
which those faded lips pronounced. Living ears
receive the sounds which their silent ears shall listen to
no more. The Benediction lives through time and
space, and all the turbulence of change; and though it
has passed through three thousand years of history, its
influence and intensity remain unimpaired—for the
light of His Countenance shines with unaltered power
and undimmed brightness, though it has flashed
through millions of leagues of space, on millions of
glowing orbs, through all the range of time lost in
Eternity.

More solemn than the influence of memory is the
sacred consideration that the words of the *Duchan* are
not of human conception, but were dictated by Him
who rules the world. And yet this Benediction, round
which so many dear and grave associations cluster,
and on which beams so radiant a glory, is not always
heard in these degenerate days, with all its due
solemnity. Do we all remember what it implies, and
does it reach our hearts? Do we strive to abandon

worldly thoughts beneath its sounds? Or, do we not, at times, disregard it, or listen to it with ridicule or apathy—failing to accept its meaning, or to appreciate its influence, as if, in truth, the benign light of His Countenance, for which we pray, had been withdrawn from us, and had left us in spiritual darkness, through which His Grace had ceased to shine?

For, if we thought profoundly and intelligently of what the Blessing implies; by whom it was framed; and what we should be, were its prayer rejected; should we then let it fall unheeded on pre-occupied ears, or despise it because at times its accents jar unmusically on the refined ear from untrained or unmelodious lips! Surely, its language was woven into the beauty of concord by a Divine Master, and its meaning appeals to a Nature which existed before the age of Art.

There is a shallow sophistry, which is to true logic what the mirage of the desert or the *fata morgana* of the Sicilian shores is to the substantial landscape beyond it—a semblance of reality, yet distorted, reversed or transmuted, striking the senses at first with plausibility, yet fading before the advance of tangible reasoning. This frothy argumentation, which being more blatant than quiet truth, shouts its inferences uproariously, and sometimes prevails for a time, is often applied to institutional religion. We have heard it directed to the particular instance of the *Duchan*. Men have urged that it is objectionable to hear and receive a blessing pronounced by unworthy lips; that as the *Cohanim* are not always individually better than their brethren, therefore it is unfitting that these shall pronounce a benediction, and that others shall accept it from them. We would deal earnestly with this objection—because it has had some practical effect. Yet we believe that its force will vanish under the cold scalpel of analysis. It is not the *Cohen* personally who blesses the congregation; he is merely an instrument, a means, a vehicle of transmission for carrying a spiritual purpose into material effect. It is a message from Heaven, embodied in the utterance of human lips. The *Cohen*, in pronouncing the blessing, is no more the giver of the blessing than the precentor who reads the Law is the giver of the Law. Heaven often condescends to work by human agency; and this is easy to be understood, now, since we have offended as a nation, and are no longer worthy of superhuman manifestation. The Presence has departed from the sanctuary; the cloud no longer fills the house; the awful voice is heard no more among the Syrian hills. Heaven has taken from us our Fatherland and our throne and our nationality, and our temple; but —tenderly compassionate—it has left us still its Blessing!

Now, the institution of *Cohanim* or hereditary priesthood, establishes an hereditary guardianship of the Benediction amongst the Jews, just as, by the institution of Judaism, an hereditary guardianship of the Law is established among the nations. The wisdom and advantage of a personal transmission of the duty of delivering the Blessing thus appear evident. Though a notoriously evil-doer may be debarred from fulfilling the sacred functions—because he is an unfit *instrument* —yet we simplify the question and give it an improving issue, if we consider that the matter concerns the *Cohen* because he has inherited the privilege of pronouncing the Blessing, not because he pronounces it. It is for him to ask his own breast whether he be worthy of his heritage—and, if not, to strive to render himself worthy of it. As a selected member of a selected people, as a priest in a kingdom of priests, as one especially privileged, among a nation especially privileged, he bears a high honour, a great trust, a solemn distinction — and, therefore commensurate responsibility. Because the *Cohen* has received this mission —to go up to the sacred place, to spread his hands before the congregation, and to bless them; it behoves him to sanctify and purify himself for the service. But what if, perchance, among the numbers of *Cohanim*, a person morally unworthy of transmitting God's blessing were found on the *Duchan?* Would this destroy the objects of his mission, and rob the blessed of God's promised mercies? We think not—if the blessing is received in a proper spirit, and with a heart truly raised in thankfulness to the Source of all blessings.

The duty, however, of the *Cohen* to purify himself for the sacred service still remains. And, indeed, this is true of all humanity. Every faculty which is given us to enable us to benefit and thus to bless our fellow men; every power delegated to us, by which we are permitted to be instrumental in the Divine scheme, is a privilege graciously bestowed on us by Heaven. In this sense all of us are privileged—all of us instruments of mercy, all transmitters of a heavenly blessing, from generation to generation. And, thus, we can all of us extend our hands and uplift our voices, impelled by pious hearts, in words, acts, and thoughts, which in themselves constitute a benediction. But we must all strive to sanctify and purify our souls to render them

worthy of this hallowed mission in the great temple of
the world—

וּמִי יָקוּם בִּמְקוֹם קָדְשׁוֹ : נְקִי כַפַּיִם וּבַר לֵבָב

"And who shall stand in His Holy Place? He that hath
clean hands and a pure heart."—Psalm xxiv. 4.

It is, indeed, wonderful that this one family of
Cohanim, these lineal descendants of Aaron, should
endure through thousands of years, as if it had been
expressly determined that the continuity of transmission should be perpetuated in one unbroken line.
Dynasties fall into oblivion, and pass away beyond human
recognition into the obscurity of ages. Great races
perish. The haughty oppressors of the Jews, the
proud houses of Pharaoh and Antiochus, nay, even
the imperial Cæsars, are swept away into those eddies
of forgetfulness which never return their dead. They
have faded away from the lists of living families, and,
save in the records of history and art, their "place
knows them no more." The same law which appears
to control the destinies of gentile dynasties has even,
to some extent, existed among the Jews. When the
"sceptre departed from Judah," the continuity even
of its heroic and its royal lines fell into the mists of
ages; and the dispersion in which our faith and our
customs were preserved, broke the chain of lineage.
The descendants of Gideon, Joshua, Isaiah, nay, even
of the royal David, are unknown. But it is not so
with the *Cohen* and the Levite. The priestly lineage
has been preserved, even to modern recognition,
through all the disintegrating influences of exile,
disunion, and indifference. If to-morrow, at length,

the long expected trumpet-call should awaken the world with the sound of our Salvation ; if to-morrow the Messiah should arise and uplift the banner of redemption and return ; if once more the Temple were upraised and the throne were restored, miraculous interposition could alone point out in whose veins coursed the royal blood of our ancient kings, and on whose brow their diadem should rest ; but for the *Cohen* and the Levite the abyss of ages is already bridged, and they could go up to the Sanctuary and take their places to minister as of yore, as if our history, our exile, our sorrows and our longings had been but a moment's troubled and terrible dream !

The *Duchan* is one of the few remnants of our ancient service.   The glories of the Temple have fled, its rites and observances have passed into the dim domains of tradition ; little is now left us save feeble emblems of historic splendours, and remembrances of departed ceremonials.   The *Duchan* yet remains : a glorious but a melancholy memorial.   It stands, a sad and solemn monument amid wrecks of fallen grandeur, as, in the ruins of the cities of the East, some rifted pillar lifts its lone height amid the recumbent columns, and broken battlements of shattered palaces.   Let us retain it.   Let these landmarks stand ; landmarks which resist the levelling waters of time as they rush over the plains of the world ; landmarks which tell of our lost land, our fallen greatness ; and which yet point hopefully forward to a future which we await, and steadfastly upward to the Heaven in which we trust !

These ordinances and practices, traditional in form, hallowed in origin, are connections of daily life with a higher world.   They are not mere types, nor fashions

variable by caprice. The *Duchan* is a fact ; an embodi-
ment of a command, a witnessing by modern living
men of the ancient living faith. By their endurance,
and by the belief manifested in their observance, they
bear evidence to the truth of Sinai with almost the
intensity of the faith which led men, in the days of
old, to answer the prophet, " We will obey, and we
will hear ! "

It is singular that, notwithstanding the gracious
privilege accorded to the *Cohanim*, there are some,
who, like holders of other high powers and faculties to
serve mankind, lay aside at once its burdens and its
blessings. At times they disavow and shun their
priestly duty. There are at times due motives for this
abnegation. The ordinance of the *Duchan* forbids or
releases him whose heart is newly charged with sorrow,
from taking part in the sacred rite. The mourner
must not mingle his tear-laden voice with the voices of
those who speak the Benediction. But it would be
well for those who can plead no excuse for omission or
absence, to claim, and to fit themselves for their part
in the holy service of the synagogue—their share in
the foremost inheritance of all the house of Israel.

We hear about the possible unworthiness of the
Cohen to *pronounce* the blessing, but we do not hear
whether men have greatly considered their own unworthiness to *receive* it. Have we ever applied this
touchstone of merit to ourselves ? For, indeed, with the
utterance of the Benediction, the power and the privilege of the *Cohen* cease. He speaks it, he cannot
bestow it. The gracious rain which falls from Heaven
fosters the fertile field, and blesses where it falls. Gay
harvest-sheaves bear golden witness to its life-awaken-

ing strength. The soil receives a blessing and yields its gracious growth. But the rainfall beats in vain upon the fallow ground, the rugged plain unploughed by the coulter, unenriched by seed. Thence no joyous growth springs up beneath its influence. Ah! when the threefold blessing falls on our hearts, may they be ready to receive it, to take it into their hidden depths, and send forth, evoked by Heaven, a hallowed produce! Pierced by the keen ploughshare of reflection, cleared from weeds of sin by the tearing harrow of repentance, may these hearts of ours be hardened never more, and never more repel the gracious gift.

We ask Him, our Father, to bless us and to preserve us. Without His aid, life would be impossible; without His blessing, it would be unendurable. The light of His Countenance pierces the deepest darkness with a living ray, and gilds the blackest cloud with a hopeful tinge. Without its gracious radiance shining on us, the world—the heart—would be lost in a terrible abyss. We are so apt to draw from the visible world our fancies of the invisible, that we may picture to our minds this fearful vacuity and gloom, as a vision of a physical globe whence all the glows and joys of light, and all the powers and energies of heat, and all the beauties of form, colour, and motion, had been withdrawn for ever. God's peace calms the storms of life, and He alone preserves its tempered beat in the breast. He alone can make life happy and give the peace which renders life sublime. Ah! may His face be turned to us and shine on us, and grant us peace, in all the shadows and struggles of death. Henceforth, when the *Cohanim* arise to bless us, may the Master's grace descend upon the hallowed words. For the *Cohanim*,

and for the congregation whom they bless, may the
Benediction render life holy, and sanctify the living;
and, when life be past, may the light of His countenance pierce the shadows of the grave, and glorify the
dead!

———————————

THE PSALMS OF DAVID.

It is singular that the superficial dabblers in literature and natural science, who imagine themselves to be profound scholars, and who—standing on the hollow and trembling basis of their slender acquisitions—try to analyse and assail the holy truths of Scripture, have never yet attempted to grapple with one point of Biblical difficulty quite as marvellous as the Mystery of Creation, or the Mystery of Historical Miracles. The point to which we refer is the Mystery of Inspiration.

Mystery though it be, it exists as a fact—a fact sustained by the inexorable logic of the ages. Centuries have passed, generations have lived and died, celebrities have left their "foot-prints on the sands of time;" yet the greatness of the works of the inspired men of the Bible remains practically unchallenged, because that greatness infuses, penetrates, and pervades all succeeding works and thoughts of non-inspired writers, workers, and thinkers; imparting to them a force, a beauty, and a spirit readily traceable to their sacred source—the inspired originals—the writings of the men on whom some mysterious influence, sent direct by Heaven, and called by us for want of a better name, Inspiration, was graciously bestowed, in order that the work of their hands might be more mighty, more permanent, more effective, and more saturating than the work of other hands, and—always for the highest of purposes.

Perhaps these inspired writers, these men on whom the gift of inspiration had been bestowed, were not in all cases better men than other men. There might have been in their days, as perhaps there are in these days, men more virtuous, more noble, more pious, than they. But what they did,—that is what they said or wrote,—far surpassed in its intrinsic substance, and in its resultant influence, all that other men have done, said, or written. They were mortal like other men, but their works are immortal. They lie in their cold graves, withered to dust like the ordinary dead ; but an undying light hovers above their graves, lighting all the world. The hand that wrote, the lip that spoke, have passed into the irrecoverable change of life quenched in death ; but the work of that decayed hand, the sound of that wasted lip exists, in themselves, in other works, in other sounds, infusing the works wrought and the sounds uttered age after age, in every clime of this revolving world, in every phase of our revolving time; living and active now as if they were like the wind that breathed on them, the inspired messengers when they were living men ; and breathes on us now —on us—from whom their earthly presence is divided by the chasm of centuries.

Such is the power of Inspiration that there have, as yet, been found but few, even among the noisy and arrogant throng of shallow critics of the present day, so bold as to dispute it. For who can deny its existence ? Among many salient instances, let us take but one, the inspiration of the minstrel king—David. Centuries have passed since he lived and wrote. Centuries have passed since the Psalms, which were for the most part written by him, were first sung in the now, alas! shattered courts of Zion. But he endowed the world with an immortal, an all-permeating literature. In how many a book, in how many a written page, in how many an uttered speech—aye, in every brain, in every heart, the spirit of the Psalmist lives! To him how many a thought of poet, romancist, essayist, preacher, may be traced; how many a word that flows from the ready writer's pen, the ready speaker's lips; how many a spoken, or unspoken, impulse of the suffering, the hopeful, the struggling, the broken, heart.

His was a strangely chequered life. It is one of the most marvellous and signal features of inspiration, that those in whom this Divine afflatus is infused are not of necessity perfect men. In other faiths, the imaginations of their framers have depicted the recipient of alleged inspiration in shining and perfect colours. A man without passion is taken, for instance, as the master prophet of one creed. Not so in the creed framed by Heaven. David, who as his name suggests, was beloved—David, the sweet singer of Israel—was by no means a blameless man. No; he was a man like ourselves, with passions like our own, guilty of sin, even as we all are; yet when he had sinned he was filled with poignant grief, burning remorse, and sincere penitence. Feeling, and yielding to, temptation, no doubt like us all; yet bitterly and tearfully lamenting his weakness and perversity, as perhaps we all lament them when too late, at least too late for aught save penitence. The shadows of deep sorrows hung heavily on his life, and many clouds dimmed the sheen of his diadem, and the lustre of his purple. We hear in the strains of his harp sad echoes of our own hearts. The

I

strings his fingers swept in plaintive or in impassioned
music, seem knitted to our own heart-strings. The
music of his Psalms throbs in unison with the music—
now wailing, now stormy, now harmonious, now dis-
cordant—of our own breasts.

With that restless disbelief that marks our age—the
exceptional longing for a disturbance of all recognized
landmarks and standpoints of ages—it has been for
some time the fashion to question the authorship of
the Psalms attributed formerly to the minstrel King.
Nay, as it is the fashion, especially of young persons,
to call every conclusion of variable Reason *certain*,
while every conclusion of unchangeable Faith is *uncertain*, he must be a venturesome if not an audacious
person, who dares offer an opinion contrary to that of
these sapient young logicians. Still we must venture
to express a belief that it is very likely that the
majority of the Psalms were written by David, even
if some few be due to different writers. It is true that
there is a difference in the style of some of them; but
what of that? Difference of style is noticeable in the
productions of many profane writers. For instance,
who could readily trace the light pencil of the author
of "Pickwick" in the grave pages of "Oliver Twist,"
or the "Mystery of Edwin Drood"? Who could
trace a similarity of style between "Measure for
Measure," and "Julius Cæsar"? or between "Mid-
summer Night's Dream," and "The Taming of the
Shrew"? Nay, who, not knowing it, would believe
that the hand that wrote the graceful and pathetic
story of "Evangeline," with its classic periods and
its soft touches of tenderness, could have scrawled
the platitudes and prose-jingle of "Miles Standish"?

Who would believe that the Bulwer who wrote "Ernest Maltravers," is the Lytton who wrote "The Caxtons"?

It does not seem strange to us, therefore, that we should attribute to the same hand Psalms so different in style and phase of feeling, as—for instance—the jubilant strains of the 150th Psalm, and the melancholy pathos of the 55th; the philosophical poetry of the 104th, and the homiletic vein of the 52nd. Yet there seems a general tone of sentiment that links them together; and when we consider the varied life-story of the minstrel King, the varied song seems at once explicable and natural.

The numerical arrangement of the Psalms cannot, however, be relied upon slavishly. They seem, whether classified according to style or subject, to be somewhat out of order. For instance, the 65th Psalm and the 104th, divided numerically from each other by nearly forty intervening Psalms, breathe the same spirit. So also Psalms lxvii., xcvi., and c., are tuned in accord with the spirit of Psalms cxlviii., cxlix., and cl., though many Psalms of widely divergent character are interposed.

Some of the Psalms are descriptive poems, even pastorals or idyls. Some are didactic—sermons or homilies in verse. Some are jubilant songs of national triumph. Others are melancholy elegies of personal grief, or bitter outcries of the passion of regret, repentance, or remorse. In one Psalm it is the preacher who speaks, in another the conqueror; in one the stately monarch, in another the weeping penitent.

Each Psalm presents its own scene. In one we see

the monarch standing in jewelled crown and purple robe, on the steps of his canopied throne, lifting his strain of royal dignity amidst his subjects. "Thy people shall be willing in the day of thy power, in the splendour of holiness."—Psalm cx.

In another Psalm it is the Royal preacher, the pious sovereign, who leads his people in their worship as well as in their battles. We can imagine him before the Tabernacle of the Ark on the Hill of Zion, while the votaries kneel around him, and the choral strains of sacred music float in the air. "Oh! come let us prostrate ourselves, let us kneel before our Maker."— Psalm xcv.

Or—"Enter into His gates with thanksgiving, into His courts with praise."—Psalm c.

In another Psalm we see him in the conqueror's military panoply, shining in his glinting armour, mounted on his caparisoned charger; while the legions of Israel, armed and arrayed, are gathered in review before him. "Who will bring me into the strong city? who will lead me into Edom? Wilt not thou, O God, who hadst cast us off? and thou, O God, who didst not go out with our armies?"—Psalm lx. 10.

When, at last, the glowing vision fades—the splendours of palace, sanctuary, or battle-field vanish—no courtiers press around, no priests or minstrels throng the hall, no soldiers in glittering lines wave their shining spears. The voice of singers is hushed; the clash of cymbals and the tender tones of the psaltery are heard no more. Alone in his silent chamber, away from pomp and pageant, the suffering, agonized, almost heart-broken man kneels in deepest misery, and uplifts his tremulous voice, stifled by tears:—"Turn thou unto me, for I am desolate and afflicted : the troubles of my heart have increased. Oh, bring me out of my distresses ; look on my affliction and my pain and forgive all my sins."—Psalm xxv.

Thus in the varied aspects of his life we see the royal poet ; thus each of the many phases of his career claims his poetic strain : the vicissitudes of that career are met by the variable powers of his lyre. *This* is true inspiration.

Delaney, who gave the world an "Essay on David," says of him that he was " in youth a hero ; in manhood a monarch ; in age a saint." We are not certain that the last part of the eloquent description is quite accurate ; but there can be no doubt that the heroism the majesty, and the sanctity of David's character pervade his whole life.

But what is most remarkable in him is his constant trust in his Maker. In his hour of triumph, he ascribes all glory to him :—"Not unto us, not unto us, but to Thy name be the glory given."

In the hour of his regal magnificence he bids his subjects give honour where honour is alone due. In his joy he thanks his Master. In his sorrow, in his troubles, even in his agony of remorse, he throws himself confidently on the compassion of Him who is the fount of forgiveness, the source of comfort and compassion, the " Rock of his strength, and the Shield of his salvation."

Neither time nor space would permit in these pages of a narrative of the life of David. Moreover, that life-story is well-known, and it is far better told in the pages of Sacred Writ itself, than it could be told by the comparatively feeble hand of even the most forcible

profane writer. It has been truly said that "perhaps
he is that monarch in the history of the world of whose
public and private character we have the most complete
and finished portrait."   His life-history becomes all
the more interesting when we trace it in the language
of his writings, just as one finds a special interest in
tracing a narrative in connection with the scenes in
which it is conducted. Writings are, perhaps, more
often autobiographical than the outer world is aware.
A man's heart often speaks through his pen, and his
experiences force themselves uppermost in his mind.*

We obviously have not space in this short paper for
a critical review of the Psalms ; but we would like to
point out that they seem capable of two distinct classi-
fications, viz., a classification according to *subject;* and
a classification according to *music.* The numerical
arrangement which obtains in our present revision,
seems not to follow either order ; nor does it probably
follow the chronological order. The Psalms seem
numerically arranged, as if according to the caprice or
convenience of transcribers.

It seems to us likely that the Psalms headed מזמור
were intended to be sung with musical accompaniment,
especially as the word מזמרות, which probably denotes
a musical instrument, is used in Kings,† and the primi-
tive meaning of the root, seems to favour this presump-

* We who in our days know how the great writer, whom we
have recently lost, tells his own story in "David Copperfield"
—perhaps the finest novel of the age—can in some dim way
comprehend how much the relation of events and thoughts that
were real in the writer's case, gives force and beauty to his
writings.

† 2 Kings xii. 14. .

tion, as if the singer's notes were marked or cut off by bars, or by the easily regulated notes of a musical instrument. The name of no musical instrument is, we think, derived from any of the other words applied to the titles of Psalms, viz., שיר, תהלה, and משכיל.

The supposition as to the meaning of the term מכתם is supported by the language of several נגינות, notably Psalms xii., xcviii., c.

The word משכיל used at the head of several Psalms, is ordinarily left untranslated. It is probable that it meant a didactic poem, a metrical reflection, or as it is sometimes rendered "a psalm of instruction," in fact, a sermon in song, as distinguished from hymns of prayer, penitence, thanksgiving, or triumph. An examination of the Psalms headed *Maschil* tends to confirm this interpretation (see Psalms xxxii., lxxviii., lxxxix.). מכתם probably meant a commemorative poem, a song written in remembrance of some great deliverance (such as Psalms lvi. to lx.). Several musical instruments are mentioned in the headings of the Psalms, probably as suited to the special symphony or accompaniment of the choir. Thus גתית, probably an instrument played by pressure (see analogous words, English *guitar*, German *zither*, &c.), perhaps an instrument of the character of an accordion, נגינות, a modulated musical instrument, from נגן.

The peculiar expression (יונת אלם רחקים) used in one of the Psalms, is either a musical instrument, as the Authorised Version has it, or it denotes the melody of an ancient song commencing—

"A silent dove flown far,"

according to which the Psalm was to be sung.

The " Songs of Degrees " are said to be either songs sung on the steps of the Altar by the priests, or sung by the pilgrims or travellers on their way to the Holy City to attend the Temple services. The language of Psalm cxxii. favours the latter supposition. Psalm cxxvii. favours the former supposition.

Psalm cxix. has the peculiarity of consisting of as many strophes as there are letters of the Hebrew alphabet, each line of each such strophe beginning with the respective letter of the alphabet. Each of the 176 verses of this Psalm is devoted to the so-called glorification of the Divine Law, to set forth the excellence and usefulness of Divine Revelation and recommend its earnest study and pious observance.

Psalm cxlv. consists of twenty-one verses, commencing with the letters of the alphabet in alphabetical order, א to ת excepting נ .

The psalms are written in strophes and antistrophes, and they should thus be sung, though it is not the constant practice.

Much of the beauty is lost by the neglect of this practice, which would even enhance the facility of comprehending, no less than of appreciating, the Psalms.

These glorious works have laid the foundation of the mass of more modern literature. We do not only refer to the quotations with which they have embellished literature ; but to the thoughts with which they have enriched it. These thoughts have lived immortally in books, in speeches, in the hearts of men. In one of the finest passages of a great orator, author and statesman of our age, Benjamin Disraeli, the debt due by humanity to the Psalms of David is well and brilliantly expressed. The Minstrel King has sown

a golden seed that has fertilized the world's broad field
—the broad field of immortal thought. What tears
have they not stanched, what minds have they not
refined? What noble passions have they evoked, what
vile passions have they checked! They have endowed
religion with archives of wisdom and knowledge.
They have purified society. They have blest humanity.
They begin with the doctrine of virtue clothed in poetic
imagery; they end with the praise of the Divine
Father. They teach the lessons of virtue; they
console the sufferer; they threaten the impenitent
sinner; they soothe the murmurer; they give hope
to the contrite. They open up in gorgeous lines the
brilliant scenes of earthly nature. The smile of hope,
the glance of immortality, beams through them and
lights the shadowy vale of death. In their earthly
music we hear heavenly music; and their strains as
they strike on the ear, on the mind, on the heart of
earthly man, prepare him for the strains which he
hopes to sing, to hear, to feel in heaven—in heaven,
when the earthly ear shall hear no more, the earthly
life be mute, the earthly heart be still; but when even
there כל הנשמה תהלל יה

All spirits shall praise the Lord. Hallelujah.

THE HUNDRED-AND-FOURTH PSALM.

THROUGHOUT the majestic range of ancient, mediæval, and modern literature, there is no collection of poetical writing capable of comparison with the Psalms of David, even when these are considered apart from the associations of the evidently Divine inspirations which imbue and permeate them.

If we consent even to regard them as a monument of literature, we cannot fail to be touched and moved by their solemn music, their profound philosophy, their imagery, their pathos and their passion. Above all, what may perhaps strike us most is their truth to nature. How many of us, in the varied drama of our own inner lives, may have felt a chord within our own hearts vibrate in unison with the strings of David's lyre! His music and his meaning strike—sometimes it may be suddenly—through the worldly garb which enwraps the spirit of us all, and reach the secret heart which feels full well the magic melody of the minstrel King.

It is evident that more than an ordinary mortal hand swept the Psalmist's harp: it is clear that the combination of characteristics that distinguish the Psalms proclaims a higher than human impulse. A human hand indeed may have penned them; a human voice may have sung them. But the immortality of their existence has been attained by the immortality of their origin.

With one Psalm alone it is now proposed to deal—
a Psalm which might be often read by us all; for it
seems that new beauties awake in it as we read it—
fresh charms rewarding the patience and intensity of
meditation.

It is a Psalm of no fewer than thirty-five verses, and
it is especially suitable for the portion of the service in
which it has been placed—the service of the Sabbath
afternoon during the winter months. For in what
mode can at least a part of the Holy Day of Heaven be
better spent than in considering and contemplating the
works of Creation, which reached its culminating point
on the Sabbath Eve, and received its seal on the
Seventh Day, "a memorial of the work of Creation?"
The day is Heaven's; hence thoughts should be
turned heavenward in this fashion on this day. We
should not, as some would have us, spend the Day of
Rest only in thinking of ourselves—our deeds and
misdeeds (and of our neighbours' deeds and misdeeds
still more often), nor set it apart for austere earnestness or cold formalism, over which no smile may
hover; but it is good on the Sabbath to think of the
marvellous surroundings amidst which we wend our
earthly pilgrimage, and which in their never-ceasing
wonders, their never-failing harmony, reveal the
Divine Hand as clearly and as forcibly as did the
burning of the bush, the parting of the waters, the
writing on the wall!

How easy it is to sympathise with the minstrel's
thought in the opening verse of this glorious Psalm!
It is his *soul* that breathes its blessing! It is not
here, as in many Psalms, a wearied heart, an anxious,
troubled heart, that speaks; it is not the jubilant lips

that are touched to psalmody by the evoked influence
of the varied senses, or the varied impressions of the
day.   It is his soul, the highest, mightiest, noblest,
most Divine part of him that speaks its blessing; it
feels in its own conception of the might of creation the
kinship of itself to the Highest, the kinship of a
feeble, trembling, ignorant child to an All-wise, All-
powerful, All-prevailing Father!   And what expressions could—were volumes to be filled with thickly-
studded pages—more amply express the bewildering
admiration of the awakened soul than the majestic
opening words of this great Psalm?

The figure that concludes the first verse—"Thou
art clothed with honour and majesty"—is carried
on to, and becomes amplified in, the second—"Who
coverest thyself with light as with a garment."   Light
is the greatest marvel, the first marvel, the first known
product of the work of creation.   Here, as in the
Biblical record, it may be said to open the solemn
narrative of creation.   And the light is "as a garment."   We believe the Creator to be incorporeal,
without form or similitude; in our vague, imperfect
conceptions, we imagine Him, as if robed in light.
Light is the only point of approach, between our ideas
of material things and our knowledge of His incor-
poreality.   We think of Him, as if a mantle of ethereal
light surrounded, not Him, but our indistinct notion of
Him, based on the finite nature of our ideas, which are
incapable of conceiving aught non-material.   But, as
if the brilliancy of that robe of light were too intense
for human eye,—as if when gazing upward, as man is
wont to do in the hour of prayer and praise, the burst
of light around His throne were so overwhelming that

no man could draw near it and live,—the Psalmist tells us that He "stretcheth out the heavens as a curtain!" As a curtain which hides from mortal eye some mysterious radiance too brilliant, too glittering to be borne. It is true that in fact His throne, His light, His glory are everywhere: not more beyond the sky than on earth below: but, as we are obliged to use words of human import, to render attributes of the Deity in some way comprehensible to us, so the eye in its gaze towards Him pictures His throne as if placed in the far heavens—the heavens extending as a curtain before His Robe of Light!

The heavens seem, in the vanishing line of the horizon, to spring from the seas, as if they rested on them,—as if the piers of the great arch were submerged in the ocean! How well the verse seems to render this idea—"Who layeth the beams of His chambers in the waters." Then, as the wild clouds drive over space, the poet sees in them the chariot of the Creator! He hears His footsteps in the awful gales! "He maketh the clouds His chariot; He walketh on the wings of the wind!"

In the next verse, the authorised version seems a little at fault. As it stands in that version it is feeble. But, what is evidently meant by the text is this: that he "maketh the winds His messengers, and the flaming fire (perhaps the lightning) His ministers!"

But, lest the mind should rest too forcibly on the evidences of Divine might and power,—the motive agencies, disturbing influences, and active forces of creation,—the next verse calms the imagination, and refers to the quiescent or passive strength which also dominates creation,—the *vis inertiæ*,—the power of stability—"He laid the foundations of the earth, so that it should not be removed for ever."

The Psalmist then seems to cite one instance in which it appeared as if the motive or disturbing power triumphed over the stable or organised natural order of the universe. He seems to allude to the great Deluge, which would, at a first inconsiderate glance, appear to controvert the idea of the previous verse—"Thou didst (*once* understood) cover it (the earth) with the deep, as with a garment: the waters stood above the mountains." But lest anyone should advance the record of this event as an instance of disturbance of the natural establishment of physical things, his mind is at once set at rest, and the proof of the triumphant power of a Deity vindicated, in such manner as to offer a fatal blow to materialism—

"At Thy rebuke they fled; at the voice of Thy thunder, they sped away."

Yes! the direct Hand of the Creator, after He had flung the waters of the deluge over the land—like a garment—proved its control over obedient nature, and drove the waters back, chaining the storm, and making the roaring flood of ocean—His instrument—His docile slave!

In the next verse, the natural arrangement of the waters is truly and beautifully told; the situation of rivers, lakes and seas, and of the rock-bound ocean, is perfectly described—"They flow on the mountains; they go down by the valleys unto the place which Thou hast hollowed (or established) for them: Thou hast set a bound that they may not pass over: that they turn not again to cover the earth." Here again is a climax to the argument of the joint powers of motion and rest,—

disturbance against the recognised order of nature, and quiescence within that order, present in the same hand.

And, now, the scene changes. The lyre assumes a gentler tone. The sweep of majestic music has passed over its vibrating chords with a loud and stirring sound: the golden strings now whisper a tender strain. When the waters subsided, and they streamed into their beds, not only did the angry torrents rush from the mountain crags, and the swift rivers pour their waters to the sea, and the lakes stretch their wide waters from shore to shore, and the frantic ocean beat its angry waves over fathomless depths far, far into hidden distances,—but, beside all these, soft limpid springs flowed softly amid the green grass of the smiling fields and—like shining crystal threads—murmured gently mid flowery brakes and dew-gemmed meads. "He sendeth the springs into the valleys: they run amidst the hills!" See in what charming verse the pastoral music melts. The tranquil country-side rises before the mind. One reads and hears not only the gurgle of the brook as it winds among the reeds, but the soft voice of the breeze as it scarcely stirs the flickering leaves in the dell; and the low bleat of the white-fleeced sheep that dot the meadow; and the call of the lark and the plover, as they wing their way to the skies; and the whistle of the ploughman on the lea; and the far off voices of the village school-boys as they speed along the hawthorn-lined lanes, and the paths of the tremulous woodland!

Our minds are floated, on the bosom of the springs, towards many pleasant scenes of field and flower, hill and dale, and grove! Hear the psalmist in his tender lines—

" He sendeth the springs into the valleys, which run among the hills ;

" They give drink to every beast of the field : the wild asses quench their thirst.

" Near them the birds of Heaven dwell—the birds which sing among the branches."

The *running*, flowing words of the 10th verse are remarkable—a sort of word-painting.

But this is not all. The bounteous Hand which sends the streams among the hills and vales, also sends from His skies the seasonable rain to fertilize the land —to cause the thirsty soil to yield its grass, its corn, its shrubs and fruit.

" He watereth the hills from His high domains. The earth is satisfied with the fruit of Thy works.

" He causeth grass to grow for cattle; and herb for the service of man; that he may obtain food from the earth.

" And wine that maketh glad the heart of man, and oil that maketh his face to shine; and bread which strengtheneth man's heart ! "

The 16th, 17th and 18th verses relate to familiar scenes of country life, depicted in terse, forcible, and poetical language.

In the 19th verse the changes of light and darkness, perhaps most noticeable by those who are brought face to face with nature in the field and the forest, are told in marvellously graceful words. The 20th and 21st verses, describing darkness, are wondrously fine. The picture of the shadow of the night " when all the beasts of the forest creep forth, and the young lions roar after their prey," is graphic and solemn. The touch of piety at the end of the 21st verse, reminding

man of the all-bounteous providence of the Creator
and Maintainer, is most forcible.   Then—morning
breaks; the beasts retire to their fastnesses in the
wood;—and

"Man goeth forth to his work; and to his labour
till the evening."

And here—at this culminating point—the minstrel
breaks off his narrative; and tuning his harp to a
higher chord, exclaims, as if in the over-charged fulness
of his heart,

"O Lord! how manifold are Thy works!   In
wisdom hast Thou made them all!   The earth is full
of Thy riches!"

The transition is natural from the marvels and wealth
of the land to the wonders and treasures of the sea.   The
25th and 26th verses refer to this mighty work, "made in
wisdom," in strong and telling words. One almost hears
the roll of the ocean, or feels its broad immensity, in the
verse זֶה הַיָּם גָּדוֹל וּרְחַב יָדָיִם

The description of Divine Providence, which occupies
the next few verses, is clear, true, and forcible.   The
utter and complete dependence of all created beings
and things on the care of the Creator is told briefly,
but wondrously well.   The heart droops with the verse
in the touching line—

"Thou hidest Thy face; they are troubled!   Thou
takest away their breath; they die, and return to their
native earth!"

The verse dies in a plaintive, wailing sound; but see
how in the next verse the trumpet-tone of poetry
rings in the triumph of renewed creation—nature re-
awakened and revived in spring—the symbolised
suggestion of the Resurrection!—"Thou sendest forth

K

Thy Spirit; they are created! and thou renewest the face of the earth ! "

And higher, and higher still, swells the jubilant note—

" The glory of the Lord shall be for ever : the Lord shall rejoice in His works."

The greatness and power of the Creator are told by the majestic figures of earthquakes and volcanoes contained in the next verse—

" He looketh on the earth, and it trembleth! He toucheth the hills, and they smoke ! "

*　　　*　　　*　　　*

And now there is a break in the continuity of the Psalm. The story of creation is told. The commentary on nature's marvels is ended. The pictures of the fair earth, and the rushing seas, and the changes of night and day painted by the music of the minstrel's lyre, have passed before the scene. And now the poet-king pauses and looks into the recesses of his heart—as men will look—to gather thence the impressions of these pictures, proceeding from his own strains. Influenced by the impulses he himself has evoked; overwhelmed by the marvels of creation and the might and wisdom of the Creator; he cries in the over-fulness of his heart—

" I will sing unto the Lord as long as I live; I will lift strains of praise to God while I exist ! "

And there seems to steal over his heart a very rapture of delight, born of his pious ecstasy ! a gladness of his soul, exultant in its praise—

" My meditation on Him shall be sweet! I will rejoice in the Lord ! "

And then it would appear as if it would be well to

banish from the scene of gladness, the heavenly sunshine of prayerful joy, all shadow, all cloud, all darkness—the heaviest gloom that darkens the world—the
darkness of sin. For, as we know, sorrow is not really
a dark cloud on the earth—it is but a mist which the
sun of faith pierces and dispels; but sin cannot exist
in the light of a jubilant divine world.

So the psalmist cries יִתַּמּוּ חַטָּאִים מִן הָאָרֶץ.

" Let sins pass away from the world! so that there
be no more wicked men (in it)."

And, then, reverting to the outburst of praise with
which the Psalm commenced, the initiatory thought
which woke his meditation becomes its climax—

" Bless the Lord, O my soul!—Hallelujah!"

And all hearts that read Nature and rejoice in it, and
see in the marvels of creation a revelation of a Divine
Master Hand, and in the varied scenes of earth, sea,
and sky, altars of worship;—all hearts like these swell
the chorus of the minstrel's song, and lift up their cry
of joyful praise—Hallelujah!

A MESSAGE OF LOVE.

וְאָהַבְתָּ לְרֵעֲךָ כָּמוֹךָ׃

"Thou shalt love thy neighbour as thyself."—LEV. xix. 18.

ALTHOUGH the words that constitute this text are widely known, it is well to append to them the name of the sacred book from which they are quoted. For some persons do not seem to be aware of their existence in the Pentateuch, but suppose them to have originated in the teachings of another faith; either because that faith claims, however unwarrantably, an exclusiveness in the doctrine of brotherly love, or because it has set up as a prominent maxim a portion or rather a single effect of this comprehensive and broad command.

That single effect is, "*Do* to others as you would that they did unto you,"—as if that were the whole import of the behest! If we would really love our neighbours as we love ourselves, it would be assuredly insufficient to *do* for them, as for ourselves. We must *think* and we must *feel* for them, as for ourselves. We must proffer no mere visible service, no cold mechanical performance of kindnesses, such as a paid servant would perform for hire; we must not be satisfied with action and behaviour, such as social laws exact and civil laws enforce. There is something more demanded of us; something which no money can purchase, no society can claim, no legislation can control; something which is neither to be wrought by the hand nor seen by the eye, but which is only felt by the heart—and its name is Love.

Self-interest or policy might be sufficient motives to prompt us merely to do as we would be done by; and, as before suggested, the laws of the land and of society, to a certain extent, oblige us so to do. For we might do to our neighbour as we would he did to us, and yet hate him in our hearts. Nor is kindly speech sufficient; since gentle language may be a smooth and false flattery for carrying out selfish views or for concealing cold indifference. It is not action nor language, not hand service nor lip service that is alone required of us; but it is the love which lies in the breast, the love which springs from an origin purer far than the shrine in which it dwells—this is the tribute which we must render to our neighbour—render freely, unreservedly. For this, what have we to do? We must think for him as for ourselves, wish for him as for ourselves, feel for him as for ourselves. Our innermost self laid bare, must have no thought, no hope, no prayer for the frame in which our own heart beats, or for the soul with which that frame is mysteriously linked, unless such thought, hope, and prayer, be combined with a like thought, a like hope, a like prayer, for our neighbour! Such is the import of the message which a loving Father has sent to all his children. Such is the command conveyed in Leviticus.

And how shall this command be obeyed? Surely, first, by learning to love our Father with all our heart, with all our soul, and with all our might. For if we love Him, shall we not love His children, the work of

His hands—the glorious work which was the last act
of the six days of His creation—the creature who treads
the earth with us; who has sympathies, hopes, fears,
aspirations, qualities, and desires in common with us;
who is nurtured by the same care, and nourished by
the same gifts; who is the object of God's love, and is
made in His image?

To love our neighbour, let us accustom ourselves to
think gently of him; to prize him highly, to bear with
his infirmities, to discover his merits, to accept his
peculiarities. We know how earnestly we do all these
things for ourselves ; how lightly we think of our own
weaknesses,—how highly we value our own miserable
merits !

Let us then carry into effect the Divine command.
Let us think charitably of our brother, and let us
think earnestly for him; let us take an active interest
in his welfare, consider the means of improving him
materially, intellectually, and spiritually ; talk kindly
of him—and, mean what we say ; strive to make him
happy, even at the cost of a little discomfort to ourselves ; speak mildly to him, respect his opinions and
tastes, and bear with his importunities and infirmities
as meekly and indulgently as we bear with our own.

And what if it be a sacrifice ? Will not the sacrifice
of a little pleasure, a little time, a little repose, a little
ease, a little thought, a little temper, serve as offerings
for us to bring to our Father's altar,—the altar that
must be approached with a willing tribute ? Not—
since the Temple has been cast down—with the sacrifice of bull or heifer, or the oblation of blood and
frankincense ; but the offering which each of us may
bring from his heart into the great temple of the

world, and lay on the invisible, but ever present, altar, round which all men are free to gather.

The poets, who are akin to the prophets, the priests, and the preachers, have sung the theme; and one among them, whose breast was keenly alive to affectionate sympathies has told us—

> " He prayeth best who loveth best
>   All things both great and small ;
> For the great God who dwells above,
>   He made and loveth all."[*]

Life presents various methods in which man may manifest his love for his neighbour,—methods contingent on individual character and on external conditions and circumstances. Sometimes it seems to take the form of public and sounding virtue. Abraham interceding for the inhabitants of Sodom and Gomorrah; Moses praying for the rebellious Israelites, Hillel scattering around him acts of goodness; John Howard visiting the fever-stricken dungeon; Vincent de Paul taking to his heart the innocent foundling;—all these, and many others whom we might name, no doubt, loved their "neighbour" as well, aye, better than themselves.

But others have neither the occasion nor the faculty to manifest their brotherly love by such acts of public heroism; and, happily for these, it may take the shape of a homely and gentle virtue. The humblest amongst us, in the most tranquil home, in the most secluded way of life, may love their neighbour like themselves. By a generous, a thoughtful, a well considered charity, given not with a lavish, careless hand, but with a

[*] Coleridge.

willing and kindly heart ; by the sacrifice of ease,
time, and personal comforts to the claims of those who
need our aid ; by that still more difficult sacrifice,
which, in any home that we would render happy, we
are so often called on to make, the sacrifice of temper.
By such charities, such sacrifices as these, we may shew
we love our neighbour.

Temper is often the main temptation of ordinary men
and women in every-day life ; trivial as the word may
seem, the indulgence of temper may mar the household
happiness, may exert effects of ultimate extreme importance on the career and character of human beings.
Our family circle may, for example, contain members
whose tastes, manners, and expressions—controlled by
influences other than those that govern ours, or
fraught with fashions and feelings of by-gone days,
or untaught by our experiences — may jar on our
susceptibilities and offend our sentiments or be dis-
sonant from our sympathies. The aged, the dull, the
eccentric, the young—how difficult it is at times to bear
with their ways and words !

But shall we deal hardly with them ? Shall we be
impatient because their opinions are not in harmony
with ours ? Shall we not rather think of the claims
on our forbearance which their very imperfections give
them ? The old, who have nothing to hope for save
the trifling pleasures of purposeless age, or the weary
longing for the repose of the tomb ; the dull, whose
life may have been overshadowed by the experience
of a great sorrow, or by having no creature very near
to them, to love them the most ; the eccentric, who
may carry into their intercourse with ordinary men a
mutilated heart, a blighted life ; the young, so weak

that a hasty word may bruise them, so loving that a kindly smile may charm them—ah! shall we not think of all these claims on our forbearance, and deal kindly with our neighbour? Shall we not think of the effect our temper may exert on the uncultivated, the neglected, the burdened mind? Or rather, shall we not be impelled by a higher motive than these relative conditions, and strive to recollect that by sacrificing temper and tastes to render others good and happy, we obey a Divine command; for He, who is so mighty that He gave His law on Mount Sinai amid awful thunders, and yet so tender that He brings the gentle tears from our touched hearts—*He* bade us love our neighbour as ourselves!

If the delicate and intricate systems of created organism impress our minds with the infinite Wisdom of our Maker; if the changing movements, the glorious beauties, the hidden forces, the stupendous sounds of Nature impress our senses with His awful Might, assuredly a consideration of the effect of this Divine behest may well impress our hearts with His merciful Love. For the injunction of love is addressed to me, to you, to all alike. Each individual is to have his feelings returned to him a thousandfold, reciprocated to him by all who come into contact with him.

And what a world would it be if all men obeyed, or sought to obey, the solemn and comprehensive command; if every man would strive so to subdue his passions, so to control his impulses, as to give to his brother man a love equal to the love which Nature has implanted in him for himself. War, dissension, fraud, tyranny, cruelty, coldness, would exist no more. No hand would be raised to strike; no word would be

breathed to wound; no deed would be done to harm.
Men would be knit together by a chain of tender affec-
tion—an emblem, though at an immeasurable distance
from the reality, of the Universal Love Divine. The
Poet's thought would be realised, "*Seyd umschlungen,
Millionen,*"—"Millions! be locked in one embrace."
Life would be as the "days of heaven upon earth."
Surely none but He, who is unspeakably, infinitely
loving, could have created the conception of such
glorious, world-embracing love.

But, since, in the presence of our failings, our
passions, our selfishness, our temptations, it is, alas!
so difficult to love our neighbour as ourselves—oh, let
us pray, let us entreat Him who is the Perfection of
Mercy, the Fountain of Ineffable Pity, to look down
on our weaknesses with His Divine compassion! May
we learn to love Him with all our heart and soul and
might; and through *that* love, may we learn to love
our brother as ourselves. And it may be, that the love
we bear His creatures may smooth the path of life and
calm the strife of death; and glisten in our fading
eyes, and glow in our fluttering hearts, when, in the
last supreme hour, we lift our eyes—we turn our hearts
—to Him!

PEACE.

—•—

בַּקֵּשׁ שָׁלוֹם וְרָדְפֵהוּ :

" Seek peace and pursue it."—Psalm xxxiv. 14.

WITH the exception of belief in the unity of God, there
is probably no sentiment which enters more thoroughly
and persistently into our Jewish national and devotional
life than the aspiration for peace. We sing of peace
in our Psalms; we pray for it, frequently and passionately, in our prayers. Peace is the last blessing in
the threefold Benediction of the priests. A petition
for peace concludes the prayer of the Eighteen
Blessings; peace is the last of David's tuneful words
that strike the ear as the Law is borne through our
congregation to its resting place. The familiar קַדִּישׁ
in which language almost exhausts itself in praise, and
which has so solemn an association with our mournful
hours, contains a supplication not only for peace, but
for "the abundant peace, the fulness of peace from
Heaven." Peace is the wish we proffer to each other
in our national salutation; and our sages, who are
lavish in their praises of peace and of peace-making,
tell us that the promotion of peace is the pursuit of
the wise, the duty of all men, and the highest of social
virtues. Peace is a sacred condition with which we
invest the mystery of death, and a supreme bliss which
we picture as one of the glories of the life to come.

It is easy to indicate a likely historical reason for the
recurrence of this sentiment. In the fighting days of
yore, when we were politically a nation, our country
was placed among hostile states and exposed to continual wars and incursions. Moreover civil dissension
was unhappily not unknown among us. To a people
so situated, and especially an agricultural people, with
fields to till and to protect, the advent of peace would
be a predominant desire. When we ceased to be a
polity, and were scattered among other nations, we
were long exposed to aggression and injury from
governments and governed. Our early history presents
a picture of almost continual disquiet. Well may the
hope of peace have been a prevailing sentiment in the
heart and on the lip of priest, prophet, poet, and people
in those troubled days. Anxiously must our fathers
have prayed for the blessing promised in Leviticus,
וְנָתַתִּי שָׁלוֹם בָּאָרֶץ "And I will give peace to the
land." *

But in these calmer times, when, save in exceptional
cases, we are protected from injury, even in countries
where Israel is despised; when we have mingled so
intimately with our fellow citizens that hostilities affect
us only as they affect them, and our hearts throb with
theirs in prayers for peace and enthusiasm in war; the
constantly recurring Jewish call for peace ceases to
have a distinctive political significance. But not on
that account has it lost its moral significance, or
diminished in its importance. For if war has ceased
from our border; if we may till our fields and pursue
our avocations in tranquillity, without fear of foreign
invader or civil tumult; there is yet war in our midst,

* Lev. xxvi. 6.

war in our hearts, an invader's step on the threshold, an enemy on the broad fields of humanity; and in the narrow inclosure of our conscience, which can only be met by an appeal to Divine Grace for peace, for "the fulness of peace from heaven."

Many may have observed in human nature the presence of two antagonistic principles, struggling for mastery, and contrasted as distinctly as light and darkness. Such antagonism Persian mythology dimly shadowed forth in the fantastic notions of Ormuzd and Ahriman, and a more spiritual teaching has presented in the good and evil genii of the baby's cradle. Such is the contrast of happiness and sorrow in human life, such the struggle for right and wrong in the human heart!

He who rules all breasts, and knows all secrets, can alone pronounce as to degrees of earthly happiness; but if the history of humanity, if reflection and worldly knowledge, if personal experience may guide us, we may infer that none can expect perfect happiness in this life; and those who seek it, seek a delusion and a snare.

On the other hand we need never be completely unhappy; there is no sorrow without a consolation, no shadow so dense as wholly to obscure the light; for divine mercy flecks the heaviest cloud with threads of gold, and in the darkest hour we may pray—we may hope for peace:

And he who prays for peace, prays a wise prayer. For him to whom the gates of peace are opened, prosperity cannot too much elate, nor adversity deject; his heart no passion can madden, no wild ambition torture with restless dreams, no broken hope nor disappointed

aim irritate with bitter regret. In the hour of its
keenest joy it will not be lost in delirium of rapture,
nor intoxicated in phantasies of impossible delights,
nor agitated by restless desire of change or shadowy
presages of evil. In the day of its affliction, though
blinding tears may for a while conceal the radiant
presence of peace, yet so surely as the sun pierces the
morning mist with its ruddy glow, so surely will the
peace that we pray for break through the veil of sorrow,
and lay her healing hand on the bleeding wound!

And now as to the struggle between good and evil.
To whom is that fight unknown? The campaign
begins in the bosom of the child, battling between the
attractions of appetite and the desire to obey. From
the nursery and the school-room to the after scenes of
life, wherever placed, the home, the counting-room, the
forum, the cottage, the palace, wherever temptation
rises in our way, like a gaunt ghost with fair face and
shrouded ugliness, or like the tormenting figure of the
old German story, with its alluring arms and its spiked
embraces, there the genius of good and the genius of
evil fight for mastery—there war is waged between
right and wrong, duty and passion, principle and
impulse.

We, who are growing weary with the struggle, may
well ask if to this war there be an ending, if there be
a day when the darkness of night will pass, and peace
be proclaimed, before at length the last silent peace of
the grave stills the throbbing breast? Yes, when we
pray for peace, may it not be peace in this life? Peace
that may be won, as other peace is won, by hard fighting, perseverance, and trust in a good cause; but never
without grace, favour, and mercy, and complete sub-

mission; never till we lay down our impulses as the
Romans of old laid down their arms, and pass humbled,
bowed, and broken, under the yoke of the law, as they
under the Caudine yoke of their victors.

If we disdain habitually the summons to do rightly,
and yield to temptation, there can be no peace for us:
"There is no peace for the wicked!" *אֵין שָׁלוֹם לָרְשָׁעִים׃

If the evil grow and strengthen from the hour of
its feeble and timid first assault till the day of its
maturity, we shall have a giant and not a dwarf to
fight. But there is a battle in which we need never
succumb. Divine help is for those who seek it by daily,
hourly sustained endeavour, unchecked by failure, un-
appalled by doubt or difficulty. If any effort, if many
an effort fail, let us not fear. If we find the enemy
beyond our strength to-day, let us take courage and
gather our forces to meet him on the morrow; if, as
we reach the wall's summit, we fall from the height,
even then let us remount, believing that at last the
thick front of the foe will be pierced, the rampart
gained, and triumph crown the fight with the fulness
of peace from heaven!

Having regarded peace in the abstract, in its spiritual
meaning, as a Divine boon for which to pray, let us
consider it in its relative, its applied, its human meaning, the peace which we may be the means of diffusing,
and which our Rabbins enjoin us to promote. For it
is a great privilege that we enjoy, we who are made in
the Divine likeness, that we may be the instruments of
transmitting the blessings which we ask as a hallowed
gift for ourselves. We can promote peace in the world
by example, and there is no human force more powerful

* Isaiah lvii. 21.

than the force of example : we can promote peace in the family circle by examples of forbearance, temper, and amiability. "Behold how good and how pleasant it is for brethren to dwell together in unity."* We can promote peace by precept, for we can teach the beauty of peace to children, pupils, servants, and all those over whom we have influence or authority; we can recommend peace by friendly counsel to our equals, and by respectful persuasion to our elders and superiors. And as the sphere of effort and duty enlarges, we can employ example, precept, and persuasion to promote peace in the circle in which we move, in the town in which we dwell, in the community in which we mingle, in the congregation in which we worship. We can promote peace between class and class, interest and interest, and thus work material service to the land in which we are born. We can promote peace in the earth by advocating the high doctrine of humanity, which sets its foot on wrong, and strives to a height far beyond the loftiest trophies of ambition, or the haughtiest majesty of imperial thrones.

Thus we can promote peace *outwardly* in the world, and by that effort promote peace *inwardly* in our hearts; we can spread around us a peace of earth, like a sun-picture of the spiritual peace we ask from Heaven for ourselves.

And then, how often soever the prayer for peace be repeated among us, it will be no idle repetition. If we promote peace in our families, and among Israel our brethren; if we advocate peace among mankind at home and abroad; if we desire peaceful lives, whether cheered by prosperity or chilled by sorrow; if we

* Psalm cxxxiii.

establish peace in our souls by suppressing the attempts and struggles of wrong against right; then hencefor-ward there will be a deep and solemn meaning for us in every greeting of peace, in every prayer for peace, in every blessing of peace, in every sound of peace, spoken to us or by us!

"May He who maketh peace in His high heavens, through His infinite mercy, grant peace to us, and all Israel. Amen."

HUMILITY.

לה׳ הָאָרֶץ וּמְלֹאָהּ תֵּבֵל וְיֹשְׁבֵי בָהּ :

"The earth is the Lord's and the fulness thereof,
The world and they that dwell therein."

PSALM xxiv.

THE heart which, in the flush of success in a noble aim, ascribes the victory to God, and brings to His altar the fire of its pride and the sheen of its triumph, is assuredly imbued with a spirit of true piety. Its humility, far from degrading it, elevates and glorifies it.

Humility has widely different natures. It may be a baseness; it may be a weakness; it may be an ennobling and dignifying virtue. It is a vice when it stoops to servility; when it springs from cowardice; when it masks' ambitious and selfish purposes; when it disguises pride, the "pride that apes humility." It is a weakness when it manifests itself in acts of objectless debasement; a dangerous weakness when it leads to undue self-depreciation, and thus destroys self-reliance, and checks the exercise of powers or capabilities which might be utilized for man's advantage. The humility of Sixtus, aspiring to the pinnacle of the papacy, was a vice; the humility of the Queen of Castille and Leon at the feet of mendicants, was a weakness; and a weakness, no less, the false humility of Diogenes, trampling with miry sandals on the purple draperies of Plato. "See," he said, "see how I trample on the pride of

Plato!" "With equal pride, thyself, Diogenes," replied the true philosopher.

But there is a humility of a different nature, a humility which springs not from cowardice, servility, misconception, self-seeking, or self-depreciation, but from a pure, a holy source : the humility which bows man's spirit, not before the spirit of his fellow man, but before the Mighty Power which made him ; the Power from whom spring, and to whom belong, himself, and his works, his genius, his strength, and his powers. This is the humility which does not stoop so low as to be incapable of great deeds, but which, when these are performed, ascribes their glory to their true origin ; the humility which impels the hero, in the hour of his triumph, to lift the laurel from his own brow, and to bring it, as an offering, to his Master's altar ; which teaches the man of genius not to be dazzled by the glitter of his success, but to track its rays to the everlasting Fount of light from which they flow ; the humility which acknowledges that great qualities are given, not for personal aggrandizement, but for the Giver's service ; because it admits the solemn truth that the earth and the fulness thereof, the world, and they who dwell therein, are all the Lord's !

And this should be the Jew's humility ; for humility is essentially a Jewish quality. Among the three points which our sages say should distinguish the disciples of Abraham are these two רוּחַ נְמוּכָה וְנֶפֶשׁ שְׁפֵלָה — "a lowly spirit and a humble soul." But assuredly this is not abject humility ; not the servile obsequiousness which exhibits itself in kissing hems of garments or whispering craven flatteries. The humility of the

slave is not for a race born to a heritage of freedom, a
race which God Himself once redeemed, and will again
redeem "with a strong hand, and an outstretched
arm!" Ours should be a proud humility, the pride
which will not bow its crest to man, but droops in the
dust, prostrate, subdued, before man's Maker.

David, our minstrel king, was deeply impressed with
this feeling. Though eminently successful in his career,
he seldom vaunted his own merits. Not only in his
adversity did he cast himself on the Divine compassion,
but in his prosperity he unreservedly acknowledged the
Divine control. His triumphant psalm—the twenty-
first—said to be a chant of victory, is no pæan exalting
his personal prowess, but an ascription of glory to
the Source whence all glory flows.

And near the close of his eventful life, he expressed
this feeling even more emphatically in his celebrated
act of thanksgiving, when he exclaimed, "All things
come of Thee, and of Thine own do we give Thee." *

So, also, king Solomon, when he had raised the
Temple with lavish pains and expenditure, did not
"mark the marble with his name," nor call for homage
as the author and architect of the magnificent structure;
but he sanctified his work by invoking a blessing on his
people, and by eloquent, thrilling, and majestic prayer.
Thus were the work and the worker hallowed.

And Holy Writ affords no more striking instance
of this sentiment than the example recorded in Exodus
—when Moses, having stretched his hand over the
seas, and beheld them part asunder, while Israel passed
through—and, having again extended his hand and
beheld the waters return and overwhelm the pursuer

* 1 Chron. xxix. 14.

—having thus been the instrument of a tremendous miracle—lifted his voice in exulting hymn, not to extol his own agency, nor the choice of himself as agent, but to sing to the Lord, for He had "triumphed gloriously."

Nor, need we draw examples solely from those early times, those hallowed days, when the Divine Voice spoke directly to the mortal ear, or sounded in the vision; when the Awful Presence, resting upon earth, cast a sublime halo on humanity; when man walked in the world amid visible manifestations; when the "bush burnt with fire," and the "cloud filled the house."* For, even in these cold, prosaic days, among ordinary men, engaged, like ourselves, in the every-day struggle of professional, commercial, or commonplace life, the pious sentiment has found a home in more than one breast, and is recorded in the history of more than one life. And, perhaps, it is wise to insist on such examples, because they afford evidence that right feeling is practically possible in all climes, and in all ages, for all classes of men, and all social conditions.

When Telford was on the eve of completing the Menai bridge, the master-work of his career, he paused before he struck home the last rivet which was to finish the achievement, and withdrawing to his chamber, no eye seeing him save the Eye which sees us all, knelt down to give thanks to his Maker! To Him he brought the work of his hands. Thus, also, when Reginald Heber had declaimed his prize poem in the hall of his university, amid the applause of an intellectual audience, he was missed from the assemblage, and—his ears

* 2 Chron. v. 13.

perhaps still ringing with the plaudits—his heart still
bounding with conscious pride—he was found on his
knees, lifting his thanks to heaven. Imbued with a
like feeling, a great man of a different order of greatness, the patriotic Nelson, after each battle had been
fought and each victory won, the heat of contest yet
glowing in his breast, and the flash of command
burning on his brow, was accustomed to dispatch home
the story of each exploit, not with a reference to his
own prowess, but with the acknowledgement that it
had pleased Heaven to " bless his majesty's arms with
victory."

Thus, these three great men, each in his own arena
—the one in arts, the struggle of mind with matter; the
next in literature, the combat of mind with mind; the
last in arms, the contest in which both mind and
matter are pitted against mind and matter; each
ascribed the glory to Him to whom they held it to be
due.

Nor is the expression of this thought confined to
individual instances. Public feeling distinctly recognizes
it. On the stately front of the commercial palace of
this metropolis are inscribed the words, " The earth is
the Lord's, and the fulness thereof." These words,
also, selected possibly by the gifted prince whom
England still laments, were displayed on the walls
within which the world's choice industrial and artistic
treasures were gathered. And they are placed appro-
priately on structures such as these, because they
remind men engaged in the pursuit, production, and
accumulation of wealth, that the treasures which they
produce and collect are not only not their own; that
not only the crude material torn from earth, tree, or

animal, is a gift of heaven; but that so also are the labour, the skill, the inventive faculty, the nervous energy and the muscular strength which fashion the material into shape by the subduing arts of manufacture, and utilize it for man's advantage by the pervading means of commerce.

Man's intelligence and strength proceed from God, the bestower of all things, and belong to Him as assuredly as does the crude matter on which that intelligence and strength are exerted. As he has enriched the earth with natural products, so also has he endowed the human hand with force to work; the brain with power to plan; the heart with courage to pursue. In the presence of this solemn truth, the highest genius may well droop its stately crest. Not only does the history of mankind forcibly remind us that "unless the Lord build the house, they labour in vain who build it," but we also know that the works of intellect and ingenuity long survive the hand that framed them, the brain that conceived them.

Long after the troubled heart, the weary brain, the striving hand, have withered into corruption or passed into unrecognizable transformation, the products of that heart, brain and hand still endure and flourish in the world—a tangible, a visible assurance that the product does not belong to the earthly producer; that he who has discovered, developed and cultivated a portion of the earth's fulness has appropriated nothing to himself.

All, all the world, and the abundance thereof; the treasures of light and heat and colour which sleep in its depths; the forces which reside in the gases that permeate it; the properties and capabilities which dwell in the fibres and juices of the plants that garnish it;—and not only these; but the treasures, the forces, the properties and capabilities of our human brain and heart and hand,—all these belong to God.

Rich are the lessons to be drawn from this solemn truth—gratitude to the Giver of these bounties which we enjoy, these wonders which we admire; the importance of employing His gifts for His service and His purposes; the vanity of human pride and human greatness. And, with this last lesson, let us next deal.

While great geniuses acknowledge gratefully the source of their inspiration and their success; while public feeling admits willingly the greatness of the Creator and the littleness of the created; it happens often that mediocre minds, giddy with their "little learning," plume themselves on their scanty attainments, and rear their obtrusive structures of vanity on miserably shifting foundations.

It is common to find unhesitating judgments laid down and positive opinions put forth by men whose profound ignorance is thinly covered by a superficial acquaintance with scientific, historical or literary knowledge. From this, in political history, fatal misfortunes, cruel, bitter feuds, murderous disturbances have arisen.

But it is in religious matters especially that the dangerous pride of a "little learning" exhibits itself with terrible effects. Few men would be so rash as to impugn the conclusions of science without a sufficient acquaintance with its first principles; yet it is certainly true that there are men who impugn the truth of a Book written in a language of which they are nearly ignorant; men who have dug just a little way into the upper crust of knowledge, who have disturbed the topmost film of the strata which conceal its treasures, throw up their tiny mole-hills of wisdom with noisy spades, smooth them with self-sufficient complacency, and lift their feeble selves on their puny heaps to storm the stalwart battlements of the frowning fortress built on the Rock of Ages.

For example, it has been truly said that the miracles recorded in the Bible are not more wonderful than the miracles registered in the book of present Nature, miracles whose effects are palpable, though the causes which produce them are undiscovered; whose effects are recorded by laws which can be learnt, collected and analyzed. while the laws of the causes are un-revealed.

Science spreads her branches far and wide like a majestic forest-tree, grand in its elevation, generous in its bounties, prominent as a land-mark to the passer by. Man may tend it, and trim it, and gather from it the treasures of its leaves, fibres, bark and sap ; man may transplant its branches, discover and study its properties and apply them, and learn the external laws which govern its growth and its decay; but the roots of the tree lie hidden in sods which no human hand has had—or may ever have—the cunning to penetrate: and even as time moves on, as wonders are daily developed before our astonished eyes, as Discovery, Study, and Invention draw the veil aside, fold by fold, the very laws we have framed as landmarks lose their fixity, tremble, and grow dim. The laws of induction are as a cluster bound together, but progress gnaws the binding thread, till the cluster, the law itself, gives way.

The poised needle starts from its polarity as the electric current passes near; the mute iron wakes to action as the unseen fluid winds around it; the glittering tints flow from the ugly coal; the burning metallic vapours proclaim their presence by bands of colour on the spectral disc; the subtle salt binds the fleeting light on the smooth plate, and retains the image long after the original has passed away; the lens discovers loveliness of device and ornamentation on bodies which the naked eye is unable to perceive; the inanimate metals resting in the briny bath evoke an influence capable of bridging leagues of land and ocean, defying distance, travelling swift as thought through realms of space. What is their secret? What is the secret held in the stagnant water which sleeps in the lazy pool, water which the soil absorbs, the frost enchains, the sun parches; and yet, which, when heat shall have transformed its particles into a less substantial shape, acquires a giant's force, plies ponderous weights with tremendous power, splits compact metal masses as children crush their feeblest toy, drags inert matter through wind, wave, and storm, on the rugged land and on the throbbing sea? What is the secret which resides in the cold, dead magnet, and bids it draw to its embraces the inanimate steel, as if one or both were endowed with sudden life, feeling, and passion?

Well, shall we witness these loud-resounding miracles whose trumpet-tongues speak to our bewildered ears— these miracles marvellous in what they reveal to our startled senses—still more marvellous in what they hold concealed? Shall we deem these to be facts, and yet doubt the power of their Creator's hand, to disturb or modify them at his will? Shall we stand dazed on the threshold of science, groping so blindly amid its mysteries, avowing our halting progress in its truths, finding, day by day, the laws we have established eluding our grasp and dissolving into new shapes as the clouds in a summer sky—shall we admit we know so little of science and of nature, and yet doubt or deny the miracles with which we fancy our miserable notions of science do not accord, our feeble knowledge of nature does not correspond? Shall we admit miracles of nature which to us seem to have no purpose, no object; and deny the miracles of the Bible, to each of which a marked, an evident, a recorded purpose is attached?

Human knowledge is, at best, but a fragile force in the presence of the mighty forces enshrined in nature: and since the fulness of earth, the world and they that dwell therein belong to nature's Maker; since matter and its laws; genius and its works; force and its effects; are all of His own creation and His own, even in this study of nature the aspiring human wisdom, which seeks to soar too high, and to fly where there is no passage, will break its wing against a rock, and fall drooping, sick and wounded, to parent earth.

Where then is the shifting sand on which we build our doubts? It is true that for countless ages the beating sea has swung and rolled on the face of a whirling globe,—now smiling in calm, now frantic with storm, for purposes that we cannot gather, or can only conjecture. Well, shall we doubt that once a limb of the mighty sea rose in its bed and stood apart, that the living witnesses of its Maker's word might pass through to tell His power and bear His truth to a benighted world—to untold generations?

Let humility, then, guide the Bible student, and teach him to learn a little more, before he flings his hasty decisions broadcast in the world. Sages who have pondered over the book of life, sentence by sentence, word by word, almost letter by letter—strengthened in their labours by concentrated study, accumulated and inherited wisdom, profound general knowledge, and brilliant abilities—have found those labours hallowed by the crowning blessing of belief. And those of you who have so little knowledge, such meagre wisdom, so weak an aspiration for study, shall you deny the truth because your lights burn so dimly that they fail to shew it on your mental disc ?

Then, let man, whose powers are given by God, and belong to Him, seek those powers and use them humbly, as he believes will be for God's pleasure and for His work. Let him yield to the Giver the wealth of his strength, his intellect, his skill, and his acquirements, and use them in the pursuit of great and good ends, never failing to sanctify his work and his thought by ready acknowledgment of the Source from which they rise. Perhaps, this it is, for those who have no other worldly wealth, to love God with all one's might. Let us listen to the voice of the prophet Micah, for in his words lies the gist of the whole matter, וְהַצְנֵעַ לֶכֶת עִם־אֱלֹהֶיךָ " Walk humbly with thy God."*

Not by the vanities of pride, nor the pomp of learn-ing, nor the presumption of opinion, is He to be served; but by hearts such as theirs, who, in the glow of their triumph, brought to His altar the laurels they had won, the work they had achieved ! Not by idle humi-lity that hides or checks the powers He gave, is His

* Micah vi. 8.

work to be done ; but by seeking out those powers by the lamp of faith, and employing them by the light of judgment. Not by undue reliance on our miserable wisdom, our flickering lights, our withering strength, our puny knowledge, is He to be approached ; but with the consciousness written in our hearts, imbuing our thoughts, inspiring our actions, and strengthening our wills, that the earth and its fulness, its gathering, its wealth, its inhabitants, their genius and their power, all are His own. His are the harvests of our labours, the triumphs of our toils. His no less the crop we reap than the seed which He gives us to sow. His no less the work wherewith we till the field, than the mystery in which He shrouds the secret of its growth. Let us then strive to do His work worthily, and raise a crop that shall be for His glory—a crop of which, though the seeds be deep in earth, the golden crests shall rise aloft and the perfume reach to heaven.

Be it ours, then, to uplift our minds to a sense of the high truth that the earth and its fulness are God's ; be it ours to remove the icy rigid bar of pride from our hearts, and to throw their portals widely open, that the " King of glory may enter " and fill them with a sense of *our* weakness and our duties, and of *His* majesty and might!

LOST AT SEA.*

הַנּוֹתֵן בַּיָּם דָּרֶךְ וּבְמַיִם עַזִּים נְתִיבָה :

"Who maketh a way in the sea, and a path in the mighty waters."—ISAIAH xliii. 16.

WHEN the intelligence of a great calamity—a calamity by which hundreds perish, and many households are plunged in mourning,—is borne to us on the wings of swiftly-circulating rumour, we should be less than human if we did not feel a pang of horror, or a throb of sympathy, even though none very near or dear to us may happen to be among those who have perished, or among those who are bereaved. But such is the charity of our earthly nature—a charity which of itself asserts that nature to have in it something of divine essence—that, when the news of a great trouble reaches us, though the trouble may not lie at our own thresholds, yet we take it home to our hearts in some fashion, —we turn aside for a time from our individual thoughts and hopes and fears, our personal cares and trials,—and at such an hour our faces grow grave, and our hearts chill, for those who have gone away, and for those who are weeping for their dead !

Only lately, such a calamity as we describe occurred near our own shores: a calamity which is of such character that it will be felt not only in this country, but

---

* Written on the occasion of the wreck of the " London," 1866.

will affect in like manner a distant region thousands
of miles away from us. In a dreadful hour of storm,
the frantic ocean beat to destruction a stalwart ship,
freighted with some hundreds of souls, and drove it,
all unresisting, into the trough of the terrible waves.
For long, long weary hours, the fated ship tossed at
the mercy of the foam and the gale. For long weary
hours, death, believed to be near, imminent and certain,
hovered like an angry welkin over these shipwrecked
human beings. Prayers, tears, and passionate supplications, sustained exertion, and calm courage could not
avert the threatening blow. No human help was near.
No human help could save! And the dread sea wrought
its work. Those brave hearts went down into the
"mighty waters," never, as we believe, to rise again,
till all the dead shall rise!

Among these, as we know, or may have known,
when we met on the succeeding Sabbath in our synagogues, were some of our own faith. Of course, such
is the all-embracing loving-kindness of our creed, that
the faith of those who perished matters not as to the
effect of this great sorrow on our hearts and minds.
We, Jews, are taught not alone to love our brother-
Jews, but to love all men on earth. Yet we advert to
the incident that, of these hundreds of sufferers, some
were of the brotherhood of Israel, in order to give
additional excuse, if such be needed, for our reference,
in our Sabbath Readings, to those who were "lost at
sea."

We have said that such a grief as this, whether it
be intimately our own or not, wakes an answering
chord in every heart. But shall this be its sole effect?
An hour's serious thought? a minute's sudden shock?

a moment's disinterested sympathy? No! for from this, as from many other acts of Heaven of which we are witnesses, though we do not always comprehend them in their profundity, there are higher, deeper, more enduring, more momentous inferences!

For these are the lessons of life! These blows that fall so unexpectedly—so swiftly—so heavily—so sharply —so resistlessly—these blows strike almost as if a bolt had fallen from Heaven in our midst, and had startled us from the dream of our internal life to a sense of the external life around us; these blows teach in a sudden, mighty, and awful manner, that, however great our powers, however strong our wills, however profound our plans, there is a Power, a Will, and a Plan, which we cannot control nor comprehend! a Power, a Will, a Plan, before which our brightest intelligence, our mightiest faculties, shatter, crumble, and are dissipated, as the bright strong light of summer "fades into nothingness" before the driving shadows of the storm-cloud.

Ah! those who were "lost at sea," are not lost to us, nor lost for ever. For, from the throbbing grave which yawned to gather them into its dread bosom, and then closed coldly over them, rise lessons that survive the dead! lessons of Life emerging from the heaving chasms of Death!

What, then, are the lessons which we may learn from this recent stroke of Heaven? First, let us learn from those who have perished, how

> "great a thing it is
> To suffer and be still."*

Let us learn a lesson of fortitude from men and women

* Longfellow.

who, suddenly called upon to yield up all bright hopes
of life, and to see their dearest ties of love torn
asunder, and believing almost inevitable death to be
at hand, could yet, in such a time, be calm and still
and resigned : could wait for the supreme hour as
gently and peacefully as the weary wait for the hour
of earthly slumber !

Let us learn too, how He, who is merciful, soothed
the last great struggle ; sent the " fulness of peace
from Heaven," and softened the anguish of impending
death with more—ah ! with how much more—than the
tenderest earthly love !

And yet let us learn another and a harder lesson.
It is for us who have still our dear ones round
us to learn the difficult lesson of due affection. On
the one hand, not to set our hearts too wildly, too
fondly, too madly on those we cherish, lest we raise
an idol in our breasts, and worship it—worship it till
the terrible hand—may-be in mercy to ourselves—
strikes it from the pedestal, and breaks it into dust
at our feet !

But yet, on the other hand, not to neglect the tender
kindnesses, nor yield to ungentle impulses, which, if
the former be neglected, or the latter yielded to, will
rise before us in a bitter hour, in the cruel light of
unavailing regret. To think that we have been unkind
—that we have spoken wounding words, or given a
hurtful pang to those whose stricken hearts will never
beat again ; that we have repulsed the loving glance
of eyes which shall look on us no more ; that we have
spurned the hands that shall never, never, press our hands
again in this our earthly life. Pray Heaven that none
of us may know at any time this hard, this keen regret.

N

For, regret for faults that can never be atoned, save
before the Throne of Him who is all love, will embitter
even the prayers we lift to Him for pardon.   Then,
may such thoughts as these draw us more nearly still
to those who are akin to us; calm our vain petulance;
soothe our childish jealousies; and wake our hearts to
all the joys of kind affection, and all the holy charms
of hallowed love!

Let us learn also the lesson that can never be too
often taught—the lesson of our miserable weakness in
the presence of the awful Power which rules the world.
We think; we scheme; we plan; we labour; we delve
into the recesses of the earth for the marvellous metal ;
we shape it to our uses, and work it and use it with
deft skill, and numerous devices.   We build our strong
ship without a chink in its seams, a flaw in its plates,
or an error in its design.   We launch it on the ocean,
and smile as we see it breast the parted waves, in all
its steady grace and its proud adaptability.   We note
its trim keel cleave the heavy pressure of the waters
as readily as our fingers cleave the elastic air.   We
equip it with the ingenious compass that shall never
fail from its true purpose, with its signals, and its
lights, and its life-boats, and its safety gear, and its
obsequious helm that answers to guidance almost as a
sentient being.   We set over it the well-skilled master-
mariner, who knows so well, with all his aids of science
and experience, "the way in the sea, and the path in
the mighty waters."   We throng its fair decks with
alert and vigilant sailors — and then, trusting our
nearest and our dearest to it, we bid it speed on its
outward road in all its strength and capability—when;
lo! there comes "a great wind into the sea, and a

mighty tempest,"* and the strong ship, with all its
power of freight—with all its hopes and promise—is
lost in the waves. "The wind passeth over it, and it
is not; and its place shall know it no more."†

And yet there is still another lesson to be learnt;
the lesson of the uncertainty of human life. Our
sages have bidden us repent the day before we die.
But when shall we die? This day—this hour—may
be our last. It is not only those who "go down to
the sea in ships," that are exposed to the peril of
immediate death. It is not only the hour of hurricane
and tempest in which the destroying angel wings his
way through the air! His pinions flutter near us in
every hour, in every place, in every phase of life. All
of us are launched in the frail ship of life that sails—
outwardly so strong, intrinsically so weak—on the
world's broad ocean. To us *all*, the storm that is
waiting to overwhelm us, may be near at hand! We
may look in vain to the bright sky that bends its
smiling arch above us, and may not see the faintest
shadow-birth of the cloud that is swelling into the
fatal fire-concealing nimbus, ready to burst over us,
and strike us to the tomb! We may not hear the
first low murmur of the gale that is rising to destroy
us—nor know its presence till its anger breaks above,
and drives us from our holdfast! In vain our hopes,
our plans, our fancied security. For, as with the hearty,
cheerful mariner on the seas—"Thou carriest them
away as with a flood!"‡

Then, let us try—oh, let us at least try—to be prepared; we who write, and you who read; for we who
write would be untrue to our mission if we did not take

* Jonah i. 13.   † Psalm ciii.   ‡ Psalm xc. 5

home to our own weak sinful heart the lessons we are
teaching—and learning too! We who write and you
who read, let us all strive to be prepared for the storm;
sooner or later, it must come.

> " For come it slow or come it fast,
> It is but death that comes at last."＊

Sooner or later we too shall know that our bark is
shattered and can never rise again to the waves; sooner
or later we shall see the billows ready to gather us into
their cold embrace; sooner or later to us, Conscience,
the captain of our ship, shall answer to our appeal, as
it was answered to these poor shipwrecked travellers,
"There is no earthly hope." Ah! but there is one
hope which never dies; no roaring gale can drown the
sound of the one dread minute gun, no sea can quench
the light of the one bright beacon-fire. A hope shines
through the storm and pierces the seething wave, for
though we may be " lost at sea " there is yet before us
a haven that we cannot fail to reach if we steer our
course aright. Then, may those who were lost at sea
in that terrible day have passed through the gate of
death to a rest and a bliss that shall be everlasting.
And may we take the lesson to our hearts, that when
the storm of death overwhelms us in the wave ; when
we are lost to life, far perhaps away from the earthly
port we have been seeking; may we travel through
the " way in the sea and the path in the mighty
waters " till we anchor fast in the tranquil Harbour,
where, as we believe, storms shall never reach us more,
tears no more be shed, and " death shall be destroyed
for ever."

＊ Scott.

HEAVEN UPON EARTH.

WE picture to ourselves a world of blessed beauty and deathless joy, which, when this world of ours, with all its cares, its hopes, its sorrows, and its tears, shall have passed away from us for ever, shall open in a flood of glowing light to our glorified awakening; a world which awaits us, as we humbly hope, when the dark grave shall have closed over us, and the sods of our last earthly home shall have parted us from all the pangs with which our hearts have throbbed. When life's cares weigh heavily upon our breasts; when our hopes grow very dim; and a stormy or a blighted Past chills our Present, and casts its shadow far into our Future, it is then that our souls are fain to see a light through the mist of tears, and rise exultant with the hope that the trial and the struggle will not last for ever; and that, one day, there will dawn for us a Festival of Joy, in which we shall never weep again—a Sabbath of Rest, in which we shall be weary never more.

But, since no revelation of the beauty of the world which we await has descended to the world in which we live; since the highest flight of intellect cannot escape the chains of association with the material world, we necessarily clothe our dreams of the life of future hope with the familiar attributes of the life of present being. Faith spiritualised, it is true, portrays

the fancied beauties of the world to be, in the lights
and colours of the world we know; though those
colours are heightened, those lights intensified.   And
no marvel is this; for, in the lavish mercy which
penetrates and illuminates Creation, this feeble world of
ours has been hallowed with the presence of a beauty
so sublime, that, even in itself, it seems to realise the
glories, joys, and charms, which, in our Master
Prophet's words, are " the days of heaven upon earth ! "

Not alone in the immeasurable loveliness of Nature ;
not alone in the treasures which glitter in the skies,
flutter in the breeze, rise on the crest of the waves, or
sleep in their depths, and cluster in a galaxy of glory on
the teeming breast of the generous earth. Not alone in
the intense, almost dream-like beauty of the physical
world, in all its triumphs of light and life; in all its
flow and flood of sound, colour, and perfume; in all its
grace of passive form and active motion.   There is a
greater beauty than in all these stores of loveliness ; a
beauty, more solemn and more bright, which dwells on
earth, and yet may serve to clothe our hopeful visions
of heaven.   It is said that there are gems which absorb
light from the skies and conceal it till evoked by the
burnisher, when it bursts from the polished surface in
a flood of rich radiation.   So, also, the rays drawn
from heaven lie deep-buried in our hearts, ready for us
to bring them forth, and send their glow throughout
the earth, to hallow it, and to bring upon it the " days
of heaven."

Yes, rays of light lie in our hearts. We carry with
us a fount of blessing, and have only to unlock its
source to bid it freely flow.   Formed, as we are, in the
"image of our Maker," we, although at the immeasur-

able distance which separates the feeble creature from the Omnipotent Creator, bear within us, and can give forth from us, the glory of a delegated power, by which we ourselves and others may be rendered good and happy. He is all love, all mercy, all compassion, all forbearance. And we, dust as we are, may be loving, merciful, compassionate, and forbearing. From Him all bounties flow; yet we are hallowed with a reflected light, which streams from Him, and, like angels, who of old bore messages to man, and the words of heaven to earth, we may bear His bounties to our fellow beings, and bring to earth the days of heaven.

And this is a lesson we have to learn from Him who, through the "faithful of His house," told us all that was needful for the mission of our lives, and its due accomplishment. When, in the later days of the wanderings of our ancestors, the first taint of their former bondage had passed away, and their emancipated minds were prepared to receive a spiritual creed; He who had before proclaimed Himself to them by His awful power, His signal deeds, at length declared Himself by an appeal, not to their thrilled senses, but to their aroused hearts. He asserted the majestic attribute of His unity, and then announced the method and measure in which He would be served. *Love* me, He said, with all your heart, with all your soul, and all your might! This was the sacrifice, this the service, this the worship which He demanded. Human intellect can devise no purer, holier, more transcendant creed. It is the creed of love, the creed of Heaven upon earth!

In all our ways, then, we must be led by the gracious guidance borne to us on the wings of these words.

We must not merely serve Him for the awe induced in us by His power to save and slay; nor for the worldly blessings which His bounty has provided for us, and promised to us.   No, not even for the reward which we await, and the promise which we infer.   Virtue must be no incident, no compromise, no barter.   Not from fear; not for worldly advantage; not even for hope of heavenly recompense alone; but, as has before been truly said, *for love* of Him!   Love, complete, absolute; untarnished by selfish motives, unalloyed by outward influence!   And loving Him thus, and therefore, serving Him, we may safely trust to Him for an accomplishment, according to His wisdom, of the worldly recompense declared in words, and the heavenly recompense deduced by thought.

Now it is this creed of love which is so rich in meaning, so ample in its development, from which the lesson we would convey is derivable.   It is by a love of God, properly understood, and rightly felt, that we, in our fulfilment of it, can learn how to carry out the mission of conveying to mankind the bounties of our Father.   It is in this mode that we can be the messengers of His mercy, and His love.   Thus each of us, in his humble way, can be a reflex, however pale, not the less certain, of that Divine " Sun of Righteousness " which illuminates mankind.   Thus, then, can we kindle in our hearts a glow of holiness, and bring on earth days like the days we hope to meet in heaven.

Yes, we can render earth an almost heavenly home, and earthly life a state of blessing.   The way lies before us, ready to be trodden ; a way which is no wild chimera of a fantastic philosophy, no empty phantom of a poet's dream, no impracticable dogma of a visionary faith. We, the children of Israel, are not bidden to perform impossible feats, to sacrifice our manhood and our affections, our human tendencies and natural feelings on the altar of our Faith. We are not enjoined to yield to the claims of a fanciful virtue the tender home-charities by which life is rendered happy and complete. We are not told to strive against the very nature of our being. We may be good men and yet our hearts may beat with manly courage, our checks flush with honest passion, our minds be filled with human aspirations. We need not turn the left cheek when stricken on the right, nor impoverish ourselves to enrich the poor, nor let the guilty go free because we are not righteous enough to punish, nor leave the holy charms of family delights to follow the standard of fanatical self-denial. But what we have to do is this. True to the teachings of our faith, we have to take our nature as it is; with all its aims, its passions, its impulses; and, beating the evil from it as the thresher strikes the chaff from the grain, or the smelter frees the dross from the gold, we must shape and trim the pure material into its best form, and work it to its best purpose; drawing from it all that it has of good; giving to all its strength an upward tendency. For our thoughts and our powers, even those of our earthly nature, if cultivated in the pure atmosphere which flows from heaven, will, like the growth which springs from seeds and roots buried in the sod—like corn, flowers, and trees—rise from earth and point through the air upward, from earth to heaven, flinging around the graceful presence of their use and beauty, yet ever tending to the lofty skies!

And we shall better understand that it is within our

nature to render earth a blessed home, if we—however unwilling we may be to recognise it—reflect how many of our sorrows and our cares proceed from our own mis- deeds, our faults of omission or commission ; how much of struggle, grief, and despondency are due to errors, many of which we might have avoided. The mariner cannot drive the storm from the air, nor the lightning from the cloud, nor the chafing billows from the tempest-tossed sea ; but the ship can be built to breast the wave with a stalwart strength, and to cleave the mighty water with a deft and lithe prow ; and it can be steered in the right track, and away from the hidden rock and the fatal surf. And its sails can be trimmed to the wind, and every heart can be set to the work, and thus the better will it make its course, and meet the winds as they blow, and even the gale if it rises ; and, at last, it shall come to harbour, either safely sheltered from the storms at sea, or still more safely sheltered where life's storms shall never rage again.

Yes, many of life's sorrows are in our own control. Not all ; for death and sickness fall on us, and around us ; and our hearts grow sad beside a sufferer's bed,— before a new-made grave. But even as to these, had the Divine laws of temperance and health been duly followed, it may be we should have less sickness to assuage, fewer untimely losses to deplore. Not for our- selves only, lest men should barter, for a few so-called happy years, a life's moderate exercise ; but for others, on whom the excesses of intemperance, and the dis- obedience of physical laws strenuously tell their tale, should we seek to adhere to a code sanctified by the ordinance of heaven, and spoken, even in words, to our forefathers, round the base of Sinai ; and, by another sort of revelation, spoken to every mind in every age. It is not, however, to this part of the subject that we call attention now. It is to another, and almost a higher, injunction that we appeal.

If we would bring on earth the days of heaven, there is a lesson, among others, taught us from on high, and by many a holy example—the lesson of Forbearance. It is difficult to acquire; but it brings close in its wake the blessings of its reward. In how many ways, at how many times, its exercise is required of us, let every man declare from the story of his own life, and the struggle of his own heart!

It is a hard lesson to learn, so great are our temptations, so signal is our weakness; yet not an impracticable one, so great are our examples, so strong is the power of the soul! In the history which has been miraculously revealed to us, and by an equal miracle has been retained to us through all the vicissitudes of ages, are recorded bright and enduring examples; and a heavenly power beats triumphantly in our hearts, capable of combating and overcoming our earthly feebleness.

When Aaron the priest, and Miriam his sister, spoke evil of their brother Moses, and assailed him with invective, Moses, who had been, under Providence, their deliverer from bondage, and their redeemer from captivity; he who had been the founder of their exalted fortunes, and was the leading spirit of the nation—how did he meet their insults! He, the beloved and chosen of his Master; he, who notwithstanding all his sublime honours and peculiar exaltation, was "the meekest of all men who were on earth," bore the unmerited reproach, the poignant blow, with calm and gentle forbearance. He did not resent it; he manifested no mean spirit of retaliation. Scripture tells how he returned good for evil; for, when Miriam was visited by grave punishment, a punishment which took shape in the form of a loathsome disease, the meekest of men avenged his wrongs by a prayer— "Heal her," he cried, " I beseech Thee!"*

When Joseph, who, in his youth, had been the victim of vindictive jealousy; for his hard and malicious brethren had torn him from the joys and comforts of home, and the tender love of his father, and had sold him, a miserable slave, into the hands of strangers, thus inflicting on him the most cruel of wrongs, for they robbed him of his freedom, and

> " The love of liberty with life is given,
>   Life is itself the inferior gift of heaven!"†

yet, in after days, far from resenting the injury which, but for a higher interposition, would have blighted the promise of his manhood as it blighted the bloom of his youth, he *forbore;* he forgave his brethren willingly and graciously. Vengeance, anger, and resentment had no place in his noble heart. He gave to all succeeding ages an example of a generous and high-minded forbearance, which, considered apart from the touching poetry of expression which is the vehicle of its narration, appeals to our intellect and our spirit as heroism to be admired and imitated.

The conduct of Gideon,‡ when kingly rule was offered to him, is an instance of forbearance of another character, yet not less difficult to practise, for there is perhaps no struggle more severe than to turn a deaf

---

* Num. xii. 13.   † Dryden.   ‡ Judges viii. 22, 23.

car to the voice of ambition and the joys of power and position, when the cold hand of duty intervenes between the tempting purple and the heart that in its glow of triumph pants for glory. In after ages we know how this example was followed. Cincinnatus, Cromwell, and Washington met the temptation and overcame it; but the glorious instance of Gideon is probably the first record of a man, with little, if any experience of the career of heroes, raised to power by a people, rejecting an offer of empire, when that offer had been deserved by a triumph so brilliant and a result so important.

The instance of Samuel is a remarkable one. The people had grievously offended him, as it would appear, by refusing to be governed by his sons; and urged him to appoint a king to rule over them in their stead. When evil days came, when the king who had been raised by their own desire oppressed and misgoverned them, they, in their distress, turned to Samuel for relief. He did not reproach them. "Moreover, as for him," he said, "he would not sin by ceasing to pray for them!"*

But there is a higher, mightier, holier example of forbearance, which man may seek humbly and hopefully. By one of the mysteries of Creation, there is an example far beyond humanity for comparison, yet near to it for imitation. In an awful moment, when the divine attributes of mercy were proclaimed to Moses, mankind learnt the lesson of Divine Love.† And if we would truly be God's children, and gather to ourselves a ray of the light of His countenance; would we, when that light falls deeply into our hearts,

° 1 Sam. xii. 23.　　　† Exodus xxiv. 6.

diffuse its beauty through His holy world ;—ah! we too, then, must learn, in our own poor feeble way, to call forth the love He has implanted in us ; we must learn the difficult lesson of forbearance.

Almost every day of our social domestic business, or public life, our life in the home circle or in the wider world abroad, forbearance is sorely tested. The failings of our surrounding fellow-men are serious, and the occasions of our having to cope with them numerous. We do not speak of forbearance in its absolute sense—forbearance from all sin or fault—for that might in truth be a chimera, since "there is no man who sinneth not."* Nor do we speak of forbearance manifested by an active suppression of all natural impulse, or a passive abnegation of self; since our own nature, far from been impure, bears with it a fount of goodness ready to flow forth freely in the sight of men and under the sunlight of heaven, unless we clog and fret the fair stream with our iniquities. But, let us forbear with our fellow-men ; forbear with their frailties, their faults, their resistance to our wills, guidance, and opinions. There is no condition of existence or society which can claim immunity from the necessity of such forbearance ; rich or poor, high or low, young or old. The poor seem importunate to the rich ; the rich seem hard to the poor. Yet, if the rich forbore generously, and considered the trials and temptations of the poor ; if the poor forbore willingly, and considered the claims and anxieties of the rich, charity would indeed be the two-fold blessing it is said to be. It would be no question of giving or taking of alms, but an inter-

* 1 Kings ix. 46.

change of heart. The rich, thinking kindly of the poor, would give as joyously as a father gives to a child; the poor, thinking gently of the rich, would receive as proudly as a child receives from a father.

And thus, too, let the old and the young mutually forbear with each other. The sunshine of life would never pass away from home; the cold shadow would not gloom the familiar gathering of kindred. Let it not be supposed that religion, in its world-embracing tendency, takes too broad a grasp, or soars to too high a point, to regard matters such as these. The story of Moses and his sister, which we have just cited, reminds us that the wondrous book, in which the bases of civilisation, society, and general legislation are laid down, and the awful revelation of Heavenly Will is majestically interpreted, contains also the simple narrative of a family episode, and thus teaches a lesson of home forbearance. Hence we may well suppose that family government and home trials are not matters of indifference to Divine consideration, which rules highest and lowest, powerful and feeble, helpful and helpless; and that the great scheme of Religion includes, not alone public performance, outward observance, and inward devotion, but the milder charities, whose scene is the home, and whose actors are those whose careers lie in the narrow circumference of our family experiences.

The spirit of our prayers confirms the impression that, if we would be truly religious men and women, we must think gently of each other. We pray, not singly, but in concert. According to the chaste language of our liturgy, we pray in the name of a congregation, or rather, perhaps, of all Israel, more

than as individuals. It is to *our* Father we address
our supplications. We ask Him to lead *us* not into
temptation, to deliver *us* from sin, transgression, and
contempt. We bless Him in the joint name of Israel.
We praise Him, not singly, but in our conjoint names.
We, calling on Him as *our* Father and our King, ask
Him to forgive *our* sins, declaring that *we* all have
transgressed, including many forms of words in which
the unhappily too numerous shades of sin may be
comprehended, lest anyone amongst us, guilty of his
own special iniquity, stand confessed and shamefaced
before the rest. If, thus, in the presence of the Maker
of us all, we link ourselves together in our prayer, our
praise, and our repentance; surely when we go from
His house, in which we worship in words, into His
world, in which we must worship by act and thought,
we must not break the tender chain. If our voices
mingle, let our hearts mingle also. Nor will this
seem so difficult, if we only forbear with one another.
Kindness grows apace in the fruitful soil of humanity.
The more we learn to love, the more hard it seems to
hate. The habit of gentleness and affection soon takes
firm root, for it is more akin to the intrinsic beauty of
our human nature than is the artificial habit of harsh-
ness and unkindness. And the world, instead of con-
tracting before our eyes, in the winter of indifference
or bitterness, will expand under the warmth of the
heart's own sunshine, and become a world of beauty,
triumph and glory.

Even in the troubles which, it may seem, we have
in no wise occasioned, in adversity, in sickness, in the
deeper and more solemn sorrow, when those we love
pass through the gates of death into the house of life;

ah! even then, and then, perhaps, more than ever, the tear is sweetened, the gall is dashed from the cup, the very bitterness of death is half removed if we can call forward in the mirror of our conscience the angel-presence of Forbearance; if that mirror is undimmed and untarnished by lack of love and gentleness to those who have suffered; to those who have for ever left us!

In ourselves then, with divine grace, it mainly rests to make of earth almost a heaven. Not indeed to be always happy, but to be always at peace. Our hearts, attuned to a divine concord, will be ready for the home they await. The days of heaven upon earth will prepare us for the days of heaven, when earth shall be a dream. If, when the last scene of our life's history draws to its close, and our story is about to end; if, then, our hearts, soon to be still, shall yet beat with exultation, because in the days of strength and action they had sent forth and around, in world-wide radiation, their light of love to humanity; those glows shall enwrap the parting soul and bear it upward, as in the chariot of fire in which the prophet was lifted to the skies! To the skies, from that earth on which he himself had brought days almost as blessed and holy as the days of the heaven into which he ascended!

N

THE SOUL'S RECONCILIATION.

כָּל תְּפִלָּה כָל תְּחִנָּה אֲשֶׁר תִּהְיֶה לְכָל־הָאָדָם לְכֹל
עַמְּךָ יִשְׂרָאֵל אֲשֶׁר יֵדְעוּן אִישׁ נֶגַע לְבָבוֹ וּפָרַשׂ כַּפָּיו אֶל־
הַבַּיִת הַזֶּה : וְאַתָּה תִּשְׁמַע הַשָּׁמַיִם מְכוֹן שִׁבְתֶּךָ וְסָלַחְתָּ :

"What prayer and supplication soever be made by any man,
or by all thy people Israel, which shall know every man the
plague of his own heart, and spread forth his hands towards
this house : then hear thou in heaven thy dwelling place, and
forgive."—1 KINGS viii. 38, 39.

As the revolving year pursues its circling march, it
treads with the steady step of Time, but its way lies
through many varied experiences of human life, and
many varied scenes of Nature—and, there is one season
of the year more solemn than the rest. It is the season
in which the first dull shadow of autumn falls on the
bright face of smiling Nature, and its first chill breath
whispers in the gay summer air ; the season in which
the fulness of the golden beauty of summer seems, as
if, from its very exuberance, to pall into the sullen
sickness of decay. A faintness steals over its fairest
flush ; a dimness clouds and mellows its gayest glow.
The rich reds and purples of the orchard and garden
merge almost imperceptibly into the sober russet of de-

cline. The fatal speck mars the hectic bloom of the fruit; the tender flower droops at the lip, parts with its smile for ever, and crumbles in the rough breeze. The leaves on the forest trees grow tawny, crisp, and frail; and, as a blighted life resigns its vigour, its action, and its place in the world's ranks, so these yield up their proud strength and their glowing colours, and fall from their stately height on the lowly ground; writhing, as if in the mute agony of death, till scattered far abroad into forgetfulness. Chill winds rise from the secret distance and sweep across the sea, stirring amidst the woodland and the cloudland, and bearing the breath of winter on their wings from the icy regions whence they float, as heralds of the coming desolation. Men look grave in the country-side, and gather in the yellow sheaves and garner the stacked hay; and men look graver still around the coasts, and hoist the storm-drum, and make the life-boat ready—as, from time to time, the broken flotsam and the shrieking gull bear to the shore tidings of tempests far out at sea, and tales of shipwreck and disaster. And, thus, the face of Nature, even ere it has lost its golden summer smile, bears the autumn shadow on its brow, and there is a voice of Death in the air.

But, meanwhile, at this very period of the year, while on one side of the globe nature is drooping into winter, on the other side it is blushing with the opening beauty of the spring! While, here, the fields grow thin, and the flowers fade, and the winds are shrill with a sad murmur—there the meadows, the hill sides, and the glades are awakening to the mantling flush and cheery call of the coming summer. Here, decay broods like a falling shadow on the swelling uplands and the silent vales ;—there

> " To mute and to material things,
> New life, revolving summer brings,
> Its genial call, dead Nature hears,
> And, in her glory, reappears."—SCOTT.

There, the limpid rivers sparkle in the growing heat—the new-born blossoms wake to life and joy ; the gay trees wave in the gentle breeze and fleck the laughing sunlight as it shimmers on the grass. The world is in a glow : or, as the sacred Psalmist sings in joyous numbers—

וְגִיל גְּבָעוֹת תַּחְגֹּרְנָה
לָבְשׁוּ כָרִים הַצֹּאן
וַעֲמָקִים יַעַטְפוּ בָר
יִתְרוֹעֲעוּ אַף יָשִׁירוּ

The hills rejoice on every side,
The pastures are clothed with flocks ;
And the valleys are covered over with corn ;
They shout for joy, they also sing.—PSALM lxv. 13, 14.

Thus Nature, the great primeval Revelation, which descended from heaven to earth, when the charmed eyes of man first opened on the marvellous beauty of Eden—Nature, which is the revelation of heavenly greatness, as the Law given on Sinai is a revelation of the heavenly will—teaches us by these signs and wonders—these varying phases—these striking interchanges of Life and Death—of renewal and decay—a mighty and pervading lesson, which appeals to us in a voice not loud but deep ; a voice borne by the senses to the soul ; a voice laden with the wealth of great truths and types and the records of the " constantly renewed work of the creation."

On the one hand, life and youth, hope and promise ; on the other, decay, death, and desolation. Here, a world fading sadly into wintry gloom ; there a world bursting triumphantly into strength and gladness ; emblems of the history of nations and of individual man, in which hopes and fears, joys and sorrows exist contemporaneously, side by side, and weave the continuous band of life ; types of the gladness of a spirit striving upward to the victory of triumphant virtue ; of the misery of a soul sinking beneath the crushing burden of its sin ; reminders of the scheme of life, in which the summer glory droops beneath the blight of age ; and, as we believe and hope, a brighter summer glory awaits our re-awakening from the winter of the tomb ; images of the truth that, as summer sunshine does not for ever glitter, so joy and prosperity shall not be for ever ours ; but, as wintry frosts do not endure for ever but melt at the step of spring, so even care and sorrow pass away at last. Yet all these are but types and emblems on this outspread page of Nature's revelation. That page, open to us all, bears a still mightier, a deeper import.

Tradition has on good grounds taught us that this wondrous season of the chequered year, rich with such portentous changes, is the world-long recurring anniversary of creation ;—the epoch at which the human soul, whatever it may have been before, whatever it may be hereafter, whatever the inferences of science, or the inspirations of faith, first received the impress in which all that we know of human being is enshrined ;—the period in which the history of wedded body and soul first was unfolded to the world ; the era at which, launched on its mysterious voyage—starting we know not whence, steering we know not whither —the soul first rushed forth on its marvellous career ; tossed on the ocean of life between the shores of time ; making for the unseen port of Immortality through the narrows of death, and under the all-extending arch of Heaven!

To the Jew, this season of the year is not alone the most solemn and suggestive of nature ; it is also the most solemn and suggestive season of his life. It is at this epoch that he is called upon to regard the question of Creation, as far as it affects himself. At this anniversary of the first blending of spirit and matter, within the scope of his intellectual vision, he is summoned by the trumpet of Faith solemnly to consider how spirit and matter, blended in himself, have worked and lived! He need not, at such an hour as this, call in the aid of abstruse science nor of profound philology, to gauge the meaning of the word Atonement, nor the powers of Expiation ; nor need he even base his mental exercises on, nor direct them towards, a consideration of the nature of a future state, nor proofs of an immortality beyond the grave. There is a louder, nearer call! Some things he knows full well, without the aid of science or research. He knows and feels that he is not all material, but that he has an inner life which lies deeper than in mere outward seeming ; he knows that he is not alone responsible for powers, duties, and trusts confined within the narrow bounds of worldly limits ; but that he has other powers, duties, and trusts for which he is responsible ; he knows that there are in

him, and of him, senses and hopes (whether instinctive
or whether instilled perceptibly or imperceptibly, it
matters not); senses and hopes not restricted by the
aspirations, pursuits, dealings, and language of the
world; he is conscious of a portion of himself, or of
an influence within himself, not tangible, visible nor
audible; not imaginable by the senses, nor producible
by human means nor of earthly matter. He is aware
that not only the earth on which, and its marvels
among which, he dwells, are beyond his mightiest
control; not alone that events occur around him which
he is all incompetent to guide, and all incapable to
understand; but that he lives in a torrent of wonders,
as a man struggling in a rush of an ocean; and that
high above all is a God, all-seeing, all-knowing, all-
mighty, in whom he believes, whose will he must
obey, and whom he has been solemnly adjured to serve,
to fear, and to love!

And oh! merciful Heaven! what have we done
with these trusts? what have we done with these
duties? There are powers within us so gracious
and sublime, that they would, if carried into effect,
permit us to take part in the glorious scheme of Mercy
which pervades Creation, and to confer on the world,
which is around us, a happiness which is almost Divine!
We know that our Master—He who rules and controls
us all; who rules and controls nature and humanity—
life animate and life inanimate— he who is all Mercy,
Goodness, and Wisdom—has given *us*, His creatures,
some faculty of being merciful, good, and wise; and
thus He has infused within our nature, and imbued our
being with some of the fire of His divinity. In us,
with us, of us, we carry from the cradle to the grave a

portion of ourselves far, far beyond our base humanity, but partaking of the glorified state of holy heaven. It is as if, in the hour of our birth, an angel, brilliant with a heavenly light, came down and passed into our frame, to dwell with it for life, to dwell with us for ever. And if this be so, let us ask ourselves, what have we done with this angelic visitant, this Divinity within us? How have we polluted it! How have we defaced its beauty, and dimmed its hallowed light!

For these powers which we have are surely trusts, and unlike other trusts, or trusts of earthly origin, they carry their reward with their fulfilment. הַכֹּל נָתוּן בְּעֵרָבוֹן say the Sages. Everything is given to us on trust; powers, virtues, faculties, senses, and lights, not of our own producing, not of own fashioning, not of our earthly nature; surely these are trusts for which we are accountable to the hand which gave them. What have we done with them? What account shall we give of them? What shall we say, if the hour should come, when a Voice, mighty as the Power which fashioned these virtues, these faculties, these intelligences should ask us to render, in the story of our lives, a reckoning of the fulfilment of these awful trusts of existence?

Miserably we err, if in our presumption we imagine that because we have never been guilty of what the world calls a heinous sin, therefore we are wholly innocent. For let us here bring logic to our aid, if faith suffice not. Persons, doubtlessly, become habituated to interpret sin as signifying the commission of some notorious crime, or the practice of vice. Conscious that they are free from these flagrant transgressions, these iniquities of a public and striking order, they grow to consider themselves unstained by sin, preserved from the very necessity of repentance. Ah! alas for these, the measure of iniquity is not result, but temptation. Temptation which we children of earth cannot gauge, but which is, if reason fail not, the standard test of a higher estimation. And when some of us reflect on our few temptations, we, perhaps, may well dread to reflect on the character of our lives. Born under the influence of a virtuous home; reared beneath the sacred shelter of a father's roof, within the tender refuge of a mother's arms, the gentle teaching of a hallowed childhood may have kept temptation from the threshold of our lives; as if an angel stood on guard with flaming sword before the threshold of our homes. Yet we dare to pride ourselves in our not having succumbed to sins, sins of which, though our ears may have heard the names, our hearts could have never known the nature. Senseless pride! Mercy kept the sin far away from us. Mercy descended on our lives and fenced them from the stroke of iniquity, and we thank *ourselves, our* strength, *our* forbearance! when every power of thankfulness within us should be spent, as if in a torrent of our powers, to gratefully render to the Strength and Forbearance which saved us, and made us what we are, our feeble meed of thanks; thanks which should never end while life wakes the throbs of our heart.

Measured by the gauge of temptations, what have our lives been? Surrounded by virtuous associations, guided by right teachings, impelled by sacred influences, the vulgar crimes of more unhappy men may have been kept far from us. But yet, what have our own lives been? It is not possible that every act of

our lives shall have been a right act, or a wholly
virtuous one. Nor, in the exigencies and hurry of our
existence, could it have been possible for us to shape
our every deed with a perfect impress, nor bend it to a
perfect end. But what we might have done is this :—
We might have shaped our manhood in a right mould,
we might have directed the aim of our lives to a right
end ; once on the true road, the little breaks on the
way would not have turned us from the main path.
It is the manner of our manhood which is at fault.
We sin because we fail to form our lives as we should
form them, and we do not turn their direction to a
true purpose ; because we do not fulfil our trusts, nor
lift ourselves to the glory of the Nature which is
mingled with our own, a nature so sublime that, if we
were but true to its holy inspirations, we should walk
through the valley of the shadow with a halo on our
care-worn brows, and hope to rise, transfigured into
angels, from the darkness of the grave !

Let us, then, take small credit to ourselves for our
avoidance of the snares which have been removed from
our path ; and recollect that because our temptation to
wrong-doing is so small, therefore the greater becomes
whatever little wrong we do. It may be, indeed,
measured by such a test, that he, whose sin would be
characterised in worldly language as a venial fault, a
weakness, nay, perhaps, in the gentle jargon of the
day, an amiable eccentricity ; he may be a greater
criminal before the high tribunal of Heaven than
many an outcast, many an untaught, unbefriended
wretch, who has expiated his discovered crime by public
ignominy, or by the most terrible of public chastisements.

Indeed, in the so-called better classes of society, the small vices assume alarming magnitude, for two reasons—first, from their effect on the sinner himself; because a man whose career, moral or material, is assured to him, or made easy to him, and whose surroundings are of a nature to improve him either by example or by precept, is just the man who, as we have before urged, is thoroughly guilty in the commission of sins called small by a worldly standard; just because his excuse is so small; and, secondly, his sins become the greater by reason of their effects on society and humanity, which are most liable to impressions from the acts of those to whom moral power and influence are given. Whether it be true, as some philosophers have told us, that every act of our lives travels with the travel of light from star to star, through all the realms of space and all the ways of time, till time be lost in eternity, never hidden from vision nor blotted from existence; whether this be true or not, surely it is true that the effect of every action of our lives never perishes; that the past is in this way irretrievable; that it lives on, and that its result once stamped on the face of events or on the mind of humanity, is indelible; and that, though divine compassion may pardon the offender, his offence, as far as our feeble intellects permit us to comprehend the Divine scheme, endures in its effects to the utmost verge of time, and perhaps far beyond—for ever, and for ever!

We know that no human intelligence, however powerful, no human perspicuity, however profound, no human experience, however vast and varied, can probe every human heart, and bring the light of conscience to bear on every soul's particular iniquity. For each

sincere breast knows not alone its own sorrow, but its
own sin. *Here* the preacher and the homilist can be
of small avail; the occasion is too solemn for other than
general admonition; too sublime for the narrow sphere
of human instruction. *Here* the free heart, and not
the trammelled mind, must speak. Yet the homilist
has, at least, this deep strong sympathy with those
whom he ventures to address. In the painful consciousness, each of his own transgressions, he, and
those for whom he writes, can comfort each other in
the sorrow of sin, and with the solace of its acknowledgment. For it might be vain to appeal at this time
to any one heart against any one especial sin; or to
warn it against any one vice or weakness. We repeat,
every candid heart knows—and knows alone on earth
—its own sin, its own temptation, its own struggle.
Perhaps, in the silence of the night, when the world is
shut out by the darkness, and the Father, ever present,
seems more near to us in the loneliness and the gloom;
and perhaps (pray Heaven that it be so!) in the faintness and weariness of the Day of Reconciliation, the
heart speaks aloud, and breaking through the trammels
of materialism, stands, like an accusing angel, before
our awakened eyes! It is, surely, the day, not the
formalized word, which touches the secret spring, and
lays open the hidden wound. Heaven will see it, will
hear it, though the world may know it not, may never
know it. When, in the great public confession of sins,
that brotherly avowal in which, impressed with the
love which is the holy key of Judaism, as taught by
our leader—the children of Israel passionately pray
for pardon for their joint sins, careful not to lay
on any one man a public self-confession—in that

combined avowal, it may be that the lip may tremble, and the tear stand in the eye, and the heart beat faster, when the voice pronounces the name of the one fault, for which any one soul may need to cry for a pardon for itself!

We will not dare, therefore, to speak of individual iniquities, nor imagine vainly that any words of ours, however deftly aimed, could fly straight to every bosom. Each life has its own story. Each life is lighted by its own lights and shadowed by its own clouds. But there are faults, nay, vices, appertaining to us as a nation; and even to us when considered in a division of classes—vices, of which we burn to write. Dare we speak out at such a moment as this? Dare we say to the rich, how often they forget that the poor are their brothers, to be loved as themselves—not an alien class to whom charity must be doled sparingly, with cold, cautious and sharp reprehension; and idle pursuit of old, vain aims, in the old worn-out grooves, which, though they may strike forward for better ends—for triumph over the results of poverty—always wind back in a circle to the old origin, the tangle of causes of misery and indigence? Dare we say to the poor that they blindly, madly, neglect the powers which are in them—the powers to work; the powers to think; the powers to *feel;* that they do not strive to be self-helpful, but rest carelessly on the minds, hands, and hearts of others, forgetful that there are no moral, mental, or spiritual faculties of the rich which they have not themselves? Dare we say to all, rich and poor alike—upper class, middle class, lower class—that they are untrue to the spirit of their faith; unfaithful to the practices and precepts of their religion ; alarmed lest by pursuing its ordinances publicly they might move counter to fashions, tastes and susceptibilities; careless of its high moralities which breathe a spirit of immortal love; or perhaps content to shelter themselves beneath ceremonial observances, whose sole animation would be, if practised in the inspiration of faith, as evidenced in virtuous lives, and which are mere dead, soulless practices when unlit by the star of holy feeling ? Dare we say that they, though they inherit from the days of Sinai the duty of setting before mankind by example, and teaching by precept, the sublime truths of virtue, morality, humanity and love, have shamefully abandoned and neglected their solemn, inherited, inspired and hallowed duty, and who are almost only known by the neglect of their own religious ordinances, their abject suppression of the salient peculiarities of their code, their unhallowed levity in their assemblies of prayer ? Dare we speak truths such as these ? Ah ! may Heaven have mercy on a people who stand so far from that Redemption which can alone be expected when holy lives and purified hearts shall mark their scattered thousands—whose dispersion shall be one day gathered together, and in whose midst the standard of Freedom shall be raised.

Not perhaps that we, considered as a race or people, are worse than any other race or people; but, if we may venture to tell this truth—a truth not told for the first time—we *ought to be better*. We have the strongest inducements to be better. In the first place, we have a pure, rational faith, in which a man may believe without sacrificing his reason, judgment, or knowledge. Ours is no fantastical creed ; no jumble of notions half monastic, half pagan. Ours is a creed which men may follow without abandoning the natural impulses of their human nature, or surrendering their intellect and their senses. With us, a man may be a devoted adherent of his religion, and yet avoid nothing save the attractions of evident sin, and the vile appetites which injure health, destroy peace, and affect happiness so clearly, so prominently, that educated reason, nay, uneducated reason, almost the instincts of intelligence, come in aid of faith, and set a seal on the mandates traced by faith itself! But more than this; we have been kept together as a nation—miraculously, we may say—because it is contrary to the precedents of history, and the disorganising influences which have marked our career; and we thus present an evidence of the truth which was first transmitted to ourselves, and intended to be transmitted through us to the world. "He shall not fail, nor be discouraged, till he have set judgment in the earth, and the isles shall wait for his law."* And, surely, it is not enough that we should hand down the law intact by the fairly written scrolls of the synagogue; we must hand down the spirit of the law, by the example of the virtues which its tenets enforce, the moralities which its precepts so persistently, so sedulously, so majestically enjoin. If we be untrue to this mission, we are untrue to a duty incumbent on us as a nation, but possible of fulfilment if the individuals of that nation undertook, *each*, to bring his element of the tribute to the altar of humanity.

The season of self-examination is at hand. Two days for the summons to repent, yet seven more for penitence, and one for the culminating Reconciliation.

* Isaiah xlii. 4.

Brethren of the house of Israel, what will it be for us
if the summons sound, and our hearts fail to hear?
What if the days of penitence pass by, and our
contrition be incomplete? What if the hour of Reconciliation strike, and our souls be still unshriven?
For who shall say whether for *us* in this life—for any
one of us—that hour may strike again! The seasons
come and go; the year pursues its round; the leaves
grow thick on the tree; they wither, and they fall!
but, ah! before another autumn shall have mellowed
into winter; before another summer shall have waned
into autumn; it may be that some ears shall be for
ever closed to the summons to repent: some hearts, as
yet untouched, shall throb no more: some souls that
now are all unreconciled may have passed from the
bonds of that mortality to rest until the dead shall rise
again.

There was a man, no romantic, sentimental youth,
but a man in the stubborn prime of life, who, in the
silence of his chamber and the darkness of the lone
night, set his mind to consider his position and his
hopes. The night's gloom was not darker than his
thoughts; the night's chill struck not so keenly home
as the cold whisper of his miserable retrospect. For
he was a lone and sad man. The tender charities of
wife and child did not cheer his heart, nor beautify his
life. His ambition was crushed, his aims unsuccessful,
his health impaired, his vigour abated: he was not
rich, nor happy, nor beloved. For him no dawn shone
through the shadow of the night, but a murmur of
despair stole on its silence. When, *suddenly*, as by an
impulse which we cannot fathom nor analyse, the
thought woke within him, that he had yet a friend, a

comfort, a hope, a mine of wealth, a rock of strength. He thought of the tender Love which never fails— the mighty Power which never yields—the glowing Promise whose light no darkness can obscure. He discovered that he had one Hope left; and, clinging to that Hope with all the strength of faith, in the stormy ocean of his vexed life, and amid the fury of the tempest, he saw through the welkin "the sun of righteousness arise, with healing on its wings;" and he understood, even as if an angel had borne the message to him, that life, before so dark, need never more be unhappy, never more shadowed by despair, but beautified, sanctified, glorified for ever! He then earnestly sought the ways of Reconciliation.

The secret life-story of many a man has perhaps had in it a like chapter; for this man felt, as a child feels, when suddenly awakened to the true meaning of a parent's love. The analogy may be a trivial one, and wholly insufficient to express the fulness of the fact; but we must borrow from material life, which we all know well, instances which render us capable to consider spiritual things of which we know so little. True, there is this difference. A knowledge of a parent's love may come too late—may come when the love we failed to seek is now for ever lost in the stillness of the grave. But the love of Heaven fails never; it is immortal; the grave does not hide it; death does not part it from us. No, let us hope, not even death. We may all of us have felt the misery of awakening from a night's sleep to the recollection of a sin or regret of the previous day. Ah! what would be the misery of awakening from the sleep of death to the recollection of past sins never more to be atoned! but

what the glory of awakening from the still grave
to the triumph of a heavenly home attained, and a
heavenly love won to us—for ever!

But not for the life beyond the grave; not for the
reward which is promised to us, whether on the familiar
fields of earth, or in the mystic plains of heaven; not
for the fear of death, though death may hover near at
hand; but for life—actual, present, earthly life—and for
love, without reward—let us strive, at this hour, to be
reconciled to the Father of us all. He knows best the
secret struggle and the silent sin; he sees the tear that
mortals cannot see, the pang we hardly own to our
own consciousness. Let us not impiously shroud our
spirits in the presumption of a supposed innocence, and
weave out of our vanity a mantle of obduracy to veil
the impurity of our hearts. We cannot hide in the
glades of a fancied Eden, an Eden bright to the eye,
but blighted in the root of every fairy tree. We
cannot hide from the Voice which will call us in the
cool evening of our days. May every heart plead for
itself. Its own agony, its own passion of regret will
be its best advocate. The thought of the powers
intrusted to us, and of the miserable use we have
made of them; the thought of the love given to us to
lavish freely on mankind—love which we have with
such base selfishness garnered in our breasts for *ourselves* alone; the recollection that, with so much power
to confer happiness, we have conferred so little; the
reflection of our dull insensibility to bounteous favours,
our cold ingratitude for lavish mercies; these, alone,
are bitter, cruel thorns, however fair the garland of our
twined years may be. But, far more bitter still, far,
far more terrible, is the anguish of a heart which

wakes to a consciousness of having offended Him, whose pity guards us, whose mercy spares us, whose might preserves us, whose love accords us every joy that stirs our pulses.

Not because His might controls the universe, unchains the storm, and holds death and terror in His mystic leash; not from a craven fear of a power too awful for expression, but manifest in ways which thrill us beyond the ordinary feelings of our nature; not from a dread of the death which may await us near at hand, to-morrow, to-day, this hour, this actual fleeting minute! Nay, not even for the anticipation of the unknown waking from the grave—from the sleep of which we know so little to the hereafter of which we know nothing, save its promise and its instinctive hope —but for a holier, a better impulse of our nature. Let us rather weep for His offended love than tremble at His offended majesty. For the Hand which rent the earth asunder, and bade the fire pour forth to wreak its wrath on Korah and his sons, gave the gladdening stream to the fainting child in the wilderness, and sent His angel to save the little lad whose mother moved far from him lest she should see him die! The Power which smote the house of Eli, yet preserved the gentle Joash from the tyranny of Athaliah. The awful Might which flings the lightnings from the skies is shewn in love and pity near the feeble, the sufferer, and the young. His ruling strength thralls the streams in the ice of winter, sends forth the roaring winds on the bleak steeps and the furious seas; casts aloft the fatal fires of the volcano, and pursues the fated ship with the terrifying storm,—yet, in the fulness of time He bids the tender flowers spring from the earth with all

the charms of their colour, their fragrance, and their
grace; permits the feeble birds to build their soft nests
in the waving boughs, and throws the laughing
sparkles of the sun amid the ripples of the brook.
For the seasons come and go.   Now summer laughs
in the breeze, now winter shrieks amid the woods;
now the blossoms gaily garnish the glades, now the
branches wave in the blinding gale.   So at one time
joy gladdens the heart with its merry glow, at another
sorrow girds the brow with its cold bands of steel;
now the mirth of new-born life and the glee of marriage
sports wake the resilient air; now the chill sadness of
a life passed from the dull shadow of grief, sickness, or
death steals on the face of the home.   Joy and sorrow,
spring and winter, sin and virtue, fall and triumph;
all take their hasty round.   But high above all, far
beyond all, with a glow that summer sunshine cannot
equal, with a warmth that winter frosts can never
blight, with a beauty that the glitter of joy cannot
outshine, nor the shadow of sorrow destroy—nay, with
a sheen that even sin cannot for ever tarnish—burns
the towering fire of faith!   Faith given by the unseen
hand, poured into our souls, glorifying our lives, rendering us angelic even in the lowliness of our humanity.
Ah! may gracious Heaven in this dread hour of our
appeal, the hour of our contrition and our passionate
prayer, the hour of the awakening of our conscience,
in which our spirits wait for the rising in the sky of
those three stars of hope which seem like heavenly
acceptance of our prayer, our penitence, our charity—
in this solemn hour appointed for our reconciliation,
may Heaven have pity on our tears!

For, guilty of polluting our Divine element of being,

guilty of treason to the sacred trusts reposed in us; guilty of want of love to our brothers on earth, and want of love to our Father in heaven; guilty of rejection of His tenderness, His compassion, and His care—we throw ourselves wholly, passionately, heartily, on His enduring pity, and we ask Him for a Father's pardon. Pardon now in our lives, pardon beyond the grave, so that this day, in the hour of our tribulation, and in the inevitable day which will be the day of our death, our souls, hopeless of their own merits, may blend their tears, their terrors, their struggles, and their prayers in all the torrent of their love for Him from whom all life proceeds, from whom all mercy flows.

THE EVERLASTING LIGHT.

לְהָאִיר לָהֶם אֶת הַדֶּרֶךְ אֲשֶׁר יֵלְכוּ בָהּ׃

"To give them light on the way wherein they should go."

Nehemiah ix. 12.

ONE Sabbath morning, when a congregation of our
brethren had assembled for public worship in one of
our metropolitan synagogues, a dense mist such as
occasionally broods over London (as we Londoners
know to our cost) had penetrated into the sacred
building, and rendered its interior dim and obscure.
A young boy, calling the attention of a man beside
whom he stood in the Synagogue, said to him some
such words as these; "Look at the נֵר תָּמִיד (the
Perpetual Lamp)—how beautiful it is!"

And he was right: truly it was beautiful. Shining
in the mist, as it hung above the steps of the ark, it
was the chief bright point in all the gloomy building.
Possibly its light had acquired especial beauty from
its contrast with the surrounding gloom. All near it
and about it was shrouded in the dull mist. Men's
faces were indistinctly seen; indeed, at a short distance
they were scarcely perceptible; certainly undistinguishable. The words of the open prayer-book were
scarcely visible. The pale darkness which pervaded
the solemn hall rendered the whole scene coldly
obscure. But through the clouded air, one point of

light shone brightly, distinctly, and beautifully : it shone as a glowing beacon in the mist ; a lamp in the shadowy darkness ; a signal in the uncertainty. It was the Perpetual Lamp which shone before the ark, as if to guide the steps of the doubtful and the blind— groping through the mist—to the Law before which the Lamp was suspended.

Oh! symbol of that other, that higher, brighter, everlasting lamp—the light of faith—that hangs before the Law, and shines in the mist of Life : perpetual light which gleams in steady, constant beauty through all the shadows and the clouds—through the darkness and doubt that surround us! We, who stand enwrapt in the life-long mist, in which we know so little of our nearest comrade, and so imperfectly understand even the most familiar things ; we who grope blindly, doubtfully, and need a guiding ray—oh, happy are we that we can ever lift our dim and shadowed eyes to the Perpetual Lamp of Faith which hangs in its enduring beauty—an everlasting light to lead us to yonder ark!

For all the world is veiled in the cold pale shroud, and its mists will never lift, it may be, till we pass from its darkness to the greater darkness or the greater light of death. The world is dim, not so much with the heavy shadows of sorrow as with the gloom of doubt. We know so little ; we understand so little. Life seems so strange to us. Our feeble judgments fail ; our frail hearts tremble in the presence of events in which we take a part, or which pass before us, beneath our eyes. Yet they pass as the visions that float through the night, and we take part in them as the phantom figures of a dream.

Have not all of us, or at least many of us, known
and seen in our own experiences so much that renders
life difficult of solution ? If we charge our recollection
with the story of our own lives, or of the lives of
those whom we know, or of whom we have heard, will
not our amazement, our doubts and difficulties raise
around us a mist, a shadow, a cloud, through which
we wander in vain, wander as without full perception
or intelligence, until we lift our eyes at last to the
one enduring light, the נֵר תָּמִיד ?

Let us cite the one most striking example of these
great problems which can only thus be solved. See
how death—which, whether it bring joy or sorrow to
those who die, assuredly brings great grief to those
who are to live on, parted from their dead whom they
loved, ah, so dearly in their lives—see how death falls
in our midst in a manner and with incidents that we
cannot understand. The shadows of its cold pinions,
which fling a pall of gloom on our sad hearts, cast a
mist of doubt on our troubled minds. They die—those
whom we might well imagine would be most likely to
live on: the young, the hearty, the helpful. They
die—those whom we might well suppose would be
most desirous to remain on earth: the happy, the
hopeful, the ambitious. They die—those whom, as we
conceive, can be spared the least—the useful, the
generous, the wise : fathers of families, mothers of
young children, friends of the poor, workers in the
world, helps to society.

Oh ! look through the record blotted by our tears !
Who, gazing into the veiled future, or resting on his
own weak pedestal of judgment, would have dreamt
that the lightning darts of death would have fallen

where, alas! they have struck so fatally? Sad and sorrowful are the tales of human experiences. No fiction writer ever drew more melancholy pictures from his free fancy than some of us know are imprinted by the stern hand of fact upon the tablet of our hearts and memories. The earnest worker, treading his noble path of usefulness and charity; caring for the poor, teaching the young, preaching the truth, founding good works, directing the eyes of men from earth to heaven, and filling on this material world what we deem to be an angel's mission—suddenly is checked in the midst of his ardent career, his burning energy! He dies—dies, while the idle, the useless, the thoughtless, and the vain live on, and mouth their silly platitudes above his grave, and lounge with useless strut about the world which he adorned. Again; the young husband—the young wife—gay and blest in their new-born happiness, treading lightly on the threshold of their first home, as if they floated through the golden clouds of the fragrant dawn; with life's young love circling their hearts, and nothing save its silent depth checking the glad outburst of joy almost too great to bear! with the seal of all this love and happiness, the cry of the first-born trembling on the ear; with a vista of a long, long future, a visionary future, belted by rosy garlands and leading to sunshine; —they die—die in the midst of all their love and joy. Alas! the vista led but to the grave. The hope of so many lives breaks, crumbles, and is scattered to the winds. They float from the fairy present into the unknown future—away from the grasp of hand and heart, and all the household ties. They die, while the broken-hearted, the blighted, and grieving still live on ; still trail, through the melancholy years, the ravelled thread of a weary, withered life. One other picture, and no more. The fair young child, the pride of the household, the dear joy of the mother, her golden curls glistening in the sun of love—falls asleep in death—dies in her angel youth ere life has bloomed into fruition ;—while the evil-hearted, the hateful, and the mischievous, whose presence is a cloud in the home, and a blight on the household joys, lives on—lives, and scatters sorrow as he passes by, in his career.

And bitter pain, the great grief of incurable malady, falls at times on the gentle, the happy, and the good—while the wicked and the rough seem to revel in their impunity. The true-hearted and the loving, whose hand is ever open to the poor, and whose foot is ever on their threshold, struggle almost in vain for daily bread, or fail in the schemes and plans of their lives—while the cold, the harsh, and the hard, who never sympathise with sorrow and suffering, luxuriate in golden prosperity, and gather in the stores of lavish wealth. These things seem strange to us, and amidst our mourning and our wonder, the old cry, " Why does this happen ? why is this so ?" rises in our heart, and hurries to our lips. A great mist of doubt and dis-couraging amazement hangs over the scene of the event and the mind that contemplates it. We cannot penetrate it with the dim lamp of experience and reasoning. The darkness resists our gaze so long as " men see not the bright light which is in the heavens." *

But high shines the everlasting light—the Lamp of

* Job xxxvii. 21.

Faith. By its bright rays, calm and strong, the shadows are pierced, and the doubt grows clear. Let us have Faith! let us look through the mist to the perpetual light, and trust to its guiding beam! Then, oh brother, oh sister! "The light shall shine on thy ways,"* and we shall read the enigma of life's strange story, the answer that Faith discovers, "all, all for Love!"

At first it may not seem so; the certainty may not lie on the surface, but rest in the depths. Not the less is it there. Shall we, with our puny loves, our feeble ·affections, so frail that they scarcely survive absence, so fickle that they hardly endure a life-time, or scarcely brook a moment's petulance, or admit a moment's sacrifice of temper; shall we pretend to gauge or reason with a love of which our own is the merest shadow? With what measure of ours shall we mete a love so great, that when judged beside it our fondest, firmest love is scarcely love at all? And yet so gently by analogy are divine things familiarized with our earthly natures, that we can even from our poor worldly affections form some weak estimate of the strength of heavenly love. Oh! fathers and mothers, to whom your little ones are so dear! oh, you friends of young children, to whom the blessing of offspring has been denied: you can understand in some fashion the love that at times must needs afflict. To some hearts it is a penalty to force the lip to speak a chiding word; it is a punishment to turn the cheek away from a proffered caress, be the present chiding or the pretended coldness ever so needful for the future advantage. It does seem so hard to punish a child one

* Job xxii. 28.

loves; to inflict pain of any sort seems a pain so
acute. And yet have not tender mothers held their
darling little ones in their arms with averted eye and
compressed lip, while they have stretched the cherished
shrinking limb to the lancet of the surgeon—and—
all for love ?

Thus may we form some frail notion, very weak but
very clear, of the nature of that great love which—all-
potent, all-wise, and all-enduring—subjects at times
our shrinking breasts to the keen and scathing knife
of pain and grief. We human creatures, when we
make others suffer, even as we believe for the best, do
so always in a sort of ignorant blindness. It is a
necessity of our ignorant and blind nature. But the
blow that strikes from heaven is dealt in wisdom.
Knowing this so well, and understanding it a little
even from our earthly experiences, we feel that the
pain is none the less keen, the blow none the less
severe ; yet the mist of doubt is somewhat brightened,
and at least the way through its pale shadows seems
more clear, when our eyes, upturned to the everlasting
light, read by its rays, the rays of Faith, the true solution—all for love.

But let us understand it well, and not read it too
lightly. It is not enough to say these things. Let us
feel them. Let them enter into our hearts. We must
be guided by them, and led by them. They must pass
into the spirit's deep recesses, and into the channels of
life's action. And it is needless for us to grope vainly
into mysteries which Faith itself is insufficient to
unravel—the mysteries of the special reason for each
manifestation of this supreme love, the special application, in any special instance, of the truth we propound.

Let us remember that the Perpetual Lamp which lights our steps to the ark, does not penetrate the curtain that conceals it. Thus we need never ask *how* heavenly love is evinced in any special instance, nor battle for some motive which we cannot unravel; enough for us to know, by the Faith which should never fail us, that it is all for love; enough for us to have been so assured by those extraordinary men who were privileged to penetrate the curtain—the inspired seers of Israel—who solemnly declared, " Whom the Lord loveth He correcteth."* " Happy is the man whom God correcteth; therefore despise not thou the chastening of the Almighty."§

And if this lesson be well taught, better taught than by these humble words of ours, if the heart be well saturated with this conviction; the densest clouds will roll swiftly away, and leave the blue expanse in its serene solemnity. He who made *our* love, which we believe so strong, and placed it in our hearts, which we believe so loving; how strong must His love be! He who sustains *our* love, which we think so enduring; how lasting must His love be!

Have faith, and it all seems easy. Lift up your eyes from the bed where the dear one lies so sadly—lift up your eyes from the cold lone grave where the dear one sleeps so calmly; nay, uplift your eyes from the inmost recess of your own torn heart which holds the dust of shattered hopes, and the ashes of blighted passions; uplift your soul from the mist which surrounds these dead visions, to yonder everlasting lamp—the light of Faith! Its beams will pierce the darkness, and the

---

° Prov. iii. 12.   § Job v. 17.

visions of the past will no more be bedded in the cold
shades of troubled cloudland, but will float in the holy
peace and warmth of a sunny sky.

When we fail to see that this must be so; or when,
being willing to believe this to be so, we grope blindly
for reasons, as if to justify Providence to our hearts and
understandings, we are miserably weak in Faith. We
trust to the dull torches of our own intellect and
inferences, which we carry with us as we grope through
the mist; but these fail to illuminate the shadow in
which we struggle. How can we rely on such feeble
lights as these? We know, in sober truth, nothing of
each other. It is a common saying, "The good are
taken, the wicked remain; the happy die, the wretched
live on." But we do not know who is good, nor who
is wicked. We do not know who is happy, and who
is unhappy. We, who are absolutely ignorant of the
workings of the secret heart, nay, who scarcely understand our own, can only judge from outward evidences.
We cannot penetrate the veil which shrouds every
·bosom. We judge of men's virtues by what they
choose to shew us of themselves, or by what we happen
to infer. And, indeed, it may be that while we are
forming our idle estimate, we know nothing of the
hidden sins, the real temptations, the master-virtue of
a man's true life. For perhaps that master-virtue
may not be his outward acts of good works, his
efforts for the poor, the helpless or the sick, which
may be easy to him; but the daily, hourly, constant, mighty struggle with some great temptation
of his life!

Still less do we know who is happy, and who unhappy. We cannot penetrate into the hidden chamber

of which each heart keeps the key. Human beings live together perhaps for years, sleeping beneath the same roof, breaking bread at the same table, having ties of kindred and close interests in common, constantly interchanging the ebb and flow of conversation, and yet they may pass each to his grave without any knowledge of the secret thought, the hidden hope, the ruling joy and grief of each other.

For not our nearest and dearest know the breast's own mystery. None on earth; none save the Father in Heaven, as the wise king cried in his glorious prayer, "For thou, even thou only knowest the secrets of the hearts of all the children of men."* And let us learn from Faith to understand this thoroughly, and to forbear recording inferences drawn from our feeble experiences, our unenlightened intelligence, and our restricted means of knowledge.

But lifting our eyes through the mist of life to the Perpetual Light of Faith, we see very clearly that we are all, not one more than another, creatures and subjects of an overruling Power, all equally objects of divine care and solicitude. The work of which each human soul is in some way permitted to be an instrument is not confined within the scope of each man's career. Man is but a link in the universal cha Nay, each man's work is not even restricted to his o household, his own family. Perhaps not even to his own community nor country. Perhaps, if science aid the eye of faith in its upward tending glance through the realms of space; if wisdom turn the beams of its everlasting light towards the unnumbered orbs which glitter in the ethereal dome, the sphere of each im-

* 1 Kings viii. 39.

mortal soul may even not be limited to this one planet which we call our own. The soul may be called from the orbit in which it fluttered for a while, as a forest bird in a golden cage, and bidden to stretch its impatient pinions for other higher flights, to make for other spheres! The task of the undying spirit may not be bound by the range of our material world; but the soul, like the light which streams from the central sun to star on star, in countless order, may strike from its source through the realms of unknown ether, from orb to orb, from world to world, spreading blessings where it goes, glorifying its Maker in its passage, like the blessed glorious light itself; until it is merged in the awful and mysterious Fount of Light, Glory, and Blessing!

And Faith, the perpetual lamp, shews us also, and shows us clearly, that death, and pain, and grief may be a very blessing to us, and a "joy for ever."* If in some supreme hour the secrets of all hearts shall be made known; if the histories of human spirits be spread before us as a written scroll; it may be that we then may learn how many souls have been saved by the influence of a great grief, or by the power of a great awakening, brought about by the advent of death! Its fearful presence, its surroundings, its inferences, warnings, and results may rouse the apathetic, and inspire the thoughtless. The key that opens the charnel-chamber to admit the dead, may open a secret chamber of the heart, and let some holy *living* thought pass out; some thought that may fructify for everlasting good. Death may sometimes check not only the useful career on earth of him who dies,

* Keats.

but the evil or useless career of him who lives on. How many hearts may be uplifted to the sacred skies by the flight of one heart thither! How many angels may be newly born on earth the day on which one angel is newly born in heaven!

Still, steadily lifting our earnest eyes to the perpetual light, the נֵר תָּמִיד of Faith, we may see through the mist other things, and learn other lessons. We shall understand that because that light is everlasting, it cannot, it must not perish with our perished joys, nor die with our dead hopes, nor be buried in the graves of those we dearly love. Oh! no! Faith is immortal! Let us not cast away with our lost happiness the duties we have still to do, the work we have still to accomplish. These duties may seem cold, and the work cheerless, when the long cherished inspiration, the long fostered ambition, the warm sweet smile of those we once dearly loved, shine on us no more. But the undying light still lends some pleasant, some tenderly cheerful beam even then: and beneath its rays they cease to be utterly darksome.

Oh! brothers and sisters, you who have loved and lost, you who have struggled and have lived to mourn over many shattered hopes and withered ties, do not bury your hearts and energies in the tombs of your dead! Give to your dead, to your dead hopes and ambitions, give to your dead dear ones the sad tribute of your tears, your sobs and sighs, but not the sacrifice of all your life's best strength, all your life's energy, work, and duty. For the Perpetual Lamp shines in its enduring radiance, not to make things clear while we rest, while we only "stand and wait." It beams through the mist to guide our steps, so that we may pass firmly, hopefully, reliantly, to the ark before which it hangs. Then may the lamp which never perishes, even when the lamp of earthly love has quenched its ray; may love eternal light us, cheer us, guide us on our sad way, may it light us through our tears on the earthly paths which we have yet to tread through life's cold mists to the Ark of Rest. May we truly exclaim with the Psalmist, "Thy word is a lamp to my feet, and a light to my path."*

We may not hope, it is true, that in this our earthly sphere, all things will be made wholly clear to us. The mist may never wholly lift, some things be never known; but at last, at the supreme time, we may say as Schiller said, "Now is life so clear,"§ and we may look back like Job to the hours "when by His light I walked through darkness."||

But, while life lasts, and its mists endure, let us learn our lesson. Let us lift up our eyes faithfully, trustfully, persistently, to yonder everlasting lamp! the lamp which time does not affect, which no "rain of tears" shall quench, no storm of struggle shatter, no hurricane of passion overthrow. It gleams in its solemn beauty, a beacon in the gloom. Oh! brothers and sisters, who have loved and lost—whose sun of earthly joy may never rise again; oh! brothers and sisters, to whom life seems so dark, so doubtful, and so cold! Be comforted! Take courage! May the undying ray, the perpetual light of Faith guide us on our way through the throngs of our fellow men, and lead us through all the mists of life, and through the

* Ps. cxix. 106.
§ "Nun ist das Leben so klar."—*Last words of Schiller.*
|| Job xxix. 3.

curtain of Death and the gates of the Grave, to the Ark of the Future, in which we hope that at last, the " light will break forth as the morning,"* when in the divine "light we shall see light,"§ and all our troubles and doubts being ended, the Father of Love will be to us an "everlasting light."‖ .

° Isaiah. § Ps. xxxvi. 9. ‖ Isa. lx. 19.

A GOSSIP WITH BOYS.

שְׁמַע אַתָּה בְנִי וַחֲכָם וְאַשֵּׁר בַּדֶּרֶךְ לִבֶּךְ :

"Hear thou, my son; and be wise; and guide thine heart on the way.—Prov. xxiii. 19.

Boys! you are the hope of the world! You are the heirs of the future, if time shall endure. When we, who are now writing for you, who think of you, and work for you, shall have passed away from this busy life, and shall be cold in our silent graves, you, if you are spared, will inherit our labours and our cares, and the world which we shall have left. You will be sailing smoothly—or tossing roughly—on the ocean of life, when we shall have drifted far away into the hidden distance beyond the low lying line of the horizon. Pray heaven that the rudder of Wisdom and the beacon of Faith may guide you, and may then have guided us into the harbour of immortality!

Boys! we who are now addressing you, understand you, like you, and sympathize with you. We will not flatter you in a false fashion, nor will we weary you with lectures or censure. We will not imitate the style of certain tracts for boys which are simply absurd, because written as if you were angels or fools; and usually you are neither. However good some of you may be, and however foolish others, there are in your aggregate, ordinary virtues and good sense.

Some tracts we wot of are severe punishments—stories of impossibly good boys who talk like saints! render themselves remarkably unhappy (and their friends also) and die, "talking good," at an early age. Now, boys, we, your Jewish brethren, do not wish you to talk like saints, but had rather you talked like boys; we do not wish you to be unhappy, because our faith is intended to make boys and men very happy; we hope you will not die at an early age, nay, not even if you spouted a Bible-full of virtuous sayings, like a collection of copy-slips, on your death-bed. We would rather—ah! far rather—that you should live an honoured, holy life, to a green old age. For we belong to a religion that every-day people can understand, believe, and practise; and for that reason, if for no other, you should be grateful that you were born and bred as Jews.

Boys, we once said in a previous paper,* something, which, in effect, we will repeat to you, as it leads to what we wish to say: we said that men often treat boys inconsistently; they talk to them as if they were sages, but treat them as if they were babes. They talk to boys as if their judgments and experiences were equal to theirs, but treat them as if they had no sensibilities or affections. But *we* would talk to you in quite another fashion. Your experiences are, perhaps happily for you, not equal to ours; but your affections are as vivid, your hearts as stout, your sensibilities far more fresh. Hence, when we, with our minds, appeal to your hearts, we think you will understand us, and we shall get on well together.

Jewish boys! we say that in you rests the hope of the future—the hope of the world. You are not

* Barmitzvah (page 84).

ignorant of what is passing around you. Do you not
see that men's minds are disturbed in their old ideas
and creeds? Do you not notice, you boys, who read
newspapers and magazines (instead of silly sensational
stories), and who listen to the conversations of men,
that your fellow-countrymen of other creeds, are
abandoning long upheld notions, and veering round, or
rather "tacking" to the old, yet always fresh, principles
of right, laid down in the Mosaic law, and its proper
interpretations, familiar to you by hear-say and
practice?

Now, some examples will bear us out. Some years
ago, when we who write were boys, people were hanged
with as little compunction as they are now imprisoned.
Yes, readily hanged on circumstantial evidence, which
leads too often to frightful mistakes. Well, at present,
as you may be aware, public feeling revolts against
capital punishment; and reverts, in theory, if not in
practice, to the merciful doctrine of the old Jewish
criminal law. Those who say that such law was
sanguinary really know nothing of the subject, though
when you reach our age you will find it common—alas!
too common—for persons to talk very much and
boisterously on subjects of which they know little or
nothing. Again, when we were boys, our fellow-
countrymen were accustomed to bury their dead in the
midst of the living—a most unseemly and unhealthy
practice; but now they pursue our old Jewish custom,
and lay them far away—where the dear ones who were
so good to them in life cannot harm them in death;
and where they may be at rest, distant from rude
business haunts, and under the calm skies, with the
fresh country breeze playing on the grass beneath

which they sleep. Again, gradually, in every day life, as if circumstance — a strong lever in the world's machinery—were assisting to a result—our fellow-countrymen are approaching a sort of Sabbath observance of Saturday, treating it as a day of rest and sensible enjoyment, in good Jewish fashion, and not as a gloomy, silent, uncomfortable day like the English Sunday. We will not touch upon the proofs offered by the modifications of religious opinions noticeable in these days, for it would neither be delicate, nor gracious, nor politic, to refer to our neighbours' religion, which we are bound to hold in respect. But leaving this last topic to your reflections, we believe you will agree with us when we say, that public feeling and intelligent opinion are turning towards Jewish laws and institutions as positively as the magnetic needle of the compass-card points to the north.

Now, is it not likely that one day the world may look to us—or perhaps not to us, who may be gone, but to you who may be here—to be the witnesses of the beauty of the Law, as we are now the witnesses of its Truth; to raise its banner, and show all men that it makes men and men's lives good, true and happy ? We cannot help being the witnesses of its truth, you understand. That does not depend on us. For our very existence as Jews bears witness of its truth to the world. But what does depend on us, under Heavenly will and aided by Divine help and grace, is to show by our lives the use and beauty of our religion. Just think, boys—especially those among you old enough to understand us—what a glory it would be for your manhood and your race to be the leaders of the world ! to be its teachers and its examples, by your interpretation of the Heavenly will, and by the goodness of your earthly lives—no longer to be the despised and rejected of nations, but to prove their blessing and their light!

Of course, we do not mean that you are called on to teach all men to be Jews, to adhere strictly to observances not intended for all the world. That may never be, nor be meant to be at any time. Conversion is not our business, nor yours; and if our neighbours were as rational in that respect as we are, and were to leave attempts at conversion aside, they would be more wise and useful, and have more money to spare for their poor, and fewer persons in their prisons. We have no reason to suppose the gate of Heaven to be only open to the Jew, nor that a man is better than his neighbour only just because he is a Jew. That would be a silly doctrine, foreign to the generous creed of Moses our Master. But assuredly we might try, by *precept* and *practice*, to teach all men to be good, and to do right; to love each other; to take care of their own health and the health of other people; to avoid injuring others; to be truthful, honest and charitable; to be kind to the poor, to all men, nay, even to the meanest creature of the field, the air, and the sea; to be just in dealing; to honour their parents and their aged; to keep the Sabbath in holy joy; to renounce cruelty, envy, cant, and hypocrisy; to judge justly; and above all, things to lift up their minds to two of the solemn and precious truths taught by our Father—that He is One, and that He must be served in love.

For, boys, all these things are among the plain doctrines of our Religion. If you question this, read your Bible, which we fear you do not read too often;—

we have been at the pains of setting down "chapter and verse" of some of these ordinances.*

But, independently of the grand future, which may be more or less remote, there is a definite future, which, if you live, will be your lot—the future lives which you will have to lead. Now one of the many beauties of our sacred law—when properly interpreted and understood—is its adaptability to modern life, and to every man's life. It is not an impossible religion, which only angels can believe and only saints pursue. But it is a faith which, though one may not exactly perceive its presence, may be present and make itself felt in every waking hour and every pursuit of one's life, and may beautify and illuminate those hours and those pursuits, just as the light is present in the air, makes its presence known in it, and beautifies it.

Indeed, boys, it is by following our religion in all your life, as boys and as men, that you will be happy ; whether as the children of your parents, or as—we suppose you expect to be one day—the parents of your children. When we speak here of happiness, we do not mean that sort of temporary enjoyment or pleasurable intoxication, which lasts for a short time, so long as its immediate producing cause endures ; and which "fades into nothingness," or changes into misery when such immediate cause is withdrawn ; a sort of pleasure like that which greedy boys experience when eating a quantity of indigestible cakes, which, when eaten, have the disagreeable effect of making the eaters violently ill. Ah! boys—if you

* Exodus xxiii. 12; Lev. xi., xiii., xiv., xix. 9 to 18, and 32 to 36, all inclusive; Deut. x. 19; xv. 7, 8, 11; xvii. 6 ; xxv. 4, etc.

only knew how many indigestible cakes we do eat in
after life! How nice they are during the repast! How
horribly wretched we are when the banquet is con-
cluded! Before we taste we envy the full-grown boy,
rich enough to buy as many as he likes! But
when we have eaten to repletion, we envy the sensible
boy who leaves them alone, or even the poor boy who
has not money enough to buy them! But the happiness to which we refer, the happiness which religion
affords, is a description of happiness which you, in
your boyhood, can comprehend as thoroughly as we in
our manhood—the happiness of *conscience satisfied!* the
happiness which endures continually; in which the
moment's joy is sacrificed for everlasting joy; a happiness so powerful that it shines through the deepest disappointment, the most gloomy sorrow, and most bitter
pain; the happiness of pleasing those we value and
those we love; the happiness of pleasing our own
hearts, when "not led astray;"—the sublime happiness of believing that we are pleasing Him who,
though we cannot see Him—is near to us in every hour
of life!

We are addressing—we hope—many readers of
various ages, various dispositions, classes, and modes of
training. Some of you are rich, others of that middle
class, which, in happy boyhood, hardly knows its own
position; others are poor—a class which, alas! always
does know its own position. Some of you are sensible,
others foolish. Some grave, others gay. Some well
brought up, others badly. Some have certain virtues
and faults, others other virtues and faults. We cannot
hope—unless we wrote at a length beyond our time,
space and strength, and beyond your patience and

temper—to say words likely to tell home to every one of you; you know far better than we or any around you what faults you have, and you best can mend your way by curing yourself of these. The Greek sage, Socrates, taught "Know thyself"—the English poet tells us—

"The fittest study of mankind is man."*

But all this was far better told, ages ago, by our own royal bard;—"Stand in awe, and sin not; commune with your own heart upon your bed, and be still."§

רִגְזוּ וְאַל־תֶּחֱטָאוּ אִמְרוּ בִלְבַבְכֶם עַל־מִשְׁכַּבְכֶם וְדֹמּוּ

Here, in a few words, lies a mass of wisdom; take a little time, each boy, and commune with your own heart! Take ten minutes each night—as some one we know is in the habit of doing—before you read your קְרִיאַת שְׁמַע or each morning after the morning prayer —and, instead of wasting the minutes in idle nonsense as some of you do, or instead of taxing them with too much study, as others of you do, sit tranquilly by yourselves, and "commune with your own heart, and be still." Think of the day's events. Try to recall your deeds and thoughts; ask yourselves how you have thought and acted, and whether you have thought and acted wisely, and well. Have you done your duty? Might you have acted more bravely? spoken more truthfully? pursued a better course? Have you controlled your temper, recollected your religion, done all the good you could, avoided all the wrong? If your heart's reply be Yes,—praise Him

* Pope.   § Ps. iv. 4.

who guided you. If it be No,—well, have courage;
He is near to help you; near in the loneliness of your
chamber; near in the silence of the night; tenderer
far than any earthly father or master. He understands
all that your heart would say to Him. He is ready to
guide, teach and forgive you. Oh ! boys, young as
you are, seek Him; to pray to Him, or to praise Him !
and then " ye shall not be afraid of the terror of the
night," for you may well hope " He will give His
angels charge concerning thee, to keep thee in all thy
ways."* Then " be still," for you may say with earnest
lip and sincere heart, בְּיָדְךָ אַפְקִיד רוּחִי "To thine
hand I entrust my soul."

But, boys, though each of you must alone be the de-
tective of his own secret sins, though each alone must
test his own conscience according to his own weaknesses, sins and cravings; yet there are some faults
common to you all, as Jews; at least we mean common to so many of you as to be a fault which leavens
the mass. We do not know whether certain qualities
are inherent in races, but certain qualities do *belong*
to races, possibly as the results of their education or
mode of living. Jews, either because they are Jews,
or because, owing to their being Jews, they are taught
certain things in a certain way, or brought up in a
certain manner, have peculiar faults and failings.

And they have certain virtues also. And of one
of these we would speak; for it leads—like a pleasant
road to an ugly village—to the special fault of which
we would speak. Boys, we have noticed one particular
qualification in which you contrast favourably with
other classes of Englishmen. *You are not bullies.* You

* Psalm xc.

do not oppress those weaker than yourselves, or dependent on you. This is true of you in all classes of
life, and we wish it were true of your young fellow-
countrymen of other creeds. We are not afraid to say
this, because perhaps, if they or their friends should
read these pages, our words may be of service to them,
—for, as you probably are aware, in the great public
schools this cowardly bullying is embodied in the dis-
gusting form of fagging—a vile practice which clergymen approve, and ignorant public opinion tolerates.
If Eton and Winchester were filled with Jewish boys,
fagging would be unknown ; big boys would not make
little boys nearly die of fear in the river, nor keep
them in the hot cricket ground till they sickened and
died utterly. It is too common to see in the London
streets big boys insult and assault little boys, with
cowardly injuries, until some one interferes. We never
see Jewish boys bullies in the higher, middle, or
poorest classes. We never see them otherwise than
kind to their younger brethren.

Perhaps this may arise from the innate or inherited
courage of our race, combined with the instilled mercy
of our faith ; courage combined with mercy is the
master colour of the hero's character. And there has
been from days of yore a stout spirit of heroism in our
people, when aroused by emergencies. You boys of
the upper and middle classes, who read of the exploits
of Greek and Roman heroes ; you boys of the middle and
lower classes, who read of the deeds of English worthies
who did exist, and of various sensational characters
who never did exist ; do not imagine that heroism and
daring were confined to the banks of the Tiber, the
Scamander, and the Thames. The leap of Marcus

Curtius into the gulf of the forum was not more glorious than the exploit of Eleazer, the Maccabee, who perished beneath the elephant. The martyrdom of Regulus in the nail-studded cask for the sake of Rome was not more heroic than the martyrdom of Rabbi Akiba, for the sake of Heaven. There is no incident in the lives of English soldier or sailor, or in the mock heroics of the penny literature of brigands, banditti, or buccaneers, more romantic than the self-devotion of the Jews of York, or of the two youths of Worms, who died to save their brethren. Pray spare time from a perusal of the doings of Leonidas, Cæsar, and Nelson ; or the thrilling deeds of heroes of the Dick Turpin, Red Rover, and Jack Sheppard class—to read of Hyrcanus, Almeida, and Don Solomon ; of Simon ben Gioras, of John of Giscala, and Judas the Maccabee !

Yet, boys of Israel, there is one description of courage in which you fail lamentably—and especially in your passage from boyhood to manhood—the moral courage of adherence to your faith. Boys ! you do not stand to your colours ! You quit the flag on which are written the precepts and practices imprinted by the instructions and recollections of your childhood. You think it " fine " to cease to act as a Jew ; you do not desire to be " taken for a Jew." You neglect, gradually, one by one, the customs of your people ; one omission leads to a second ; you break away the wall, fragment by fragment, until you undermine the rock itself ; until the towering height, reared with so much care—that height of which it may be said—

" Eternal summer settles on its head,"[o]

—crumbles at last into the abyss of infidelity.

[o] Goldsmith.

Yes, you abandon customs one by one. You neglect the blessing on the food placed before you, or the food of which you have partaken, until you eat carelessly of that forbidden food on which you dare not ask a blessing. You neglect the binding of the *Tephillin*, until at last the *Tephila* itself is forgotten. You throw aside the *Tsitsith*, and at length you throw aside the precepts of which they are to remind you. You cease to be Jews in practice, until you cease to be Jews in theory. Of what are you afraid? You break down the fences which hallowed wisdom has reared around your heart's sanctuary, until the day comes, on which you find your own unaided moral force insufficient to defend it from the invasion of irreligion.

Pray bear in mind that you may be very good Jews, and none the worse for it in any way of life; very good Jews and yet very happy ones. We would not have you angels before your time. We do not expect you to develop the false wings of Icarus. Virtue and enjoyment are not incompatible. It is not unmanly to be good. Your right arm will fling a cricket-ball none the less deftly because your left arm had worn the *Tephillin* an hour before you went into the play-ground. Your heart will beat none the less bravely, because it throbs against the four cornered band of the *Tsitsith*. We welcome muscular Judaism as a new glad feature of the day; but we welcome brave intelligent Judaism more gladly. We would have every Jewish boy lift a proud calm brow to his comrades and to the world; not only because he has the privilege of being born a Jew; but also because he is conscious of the glory of obedience to the precepts of his religion, and of the endeavour to become an example of all manly virtues to all the world.

When a non-Jewish Lord Mayor gave an entertainment to the pupils of a great public school which comprised many Jewish scholars, he offered as portion of the amusement—and a very pleasant portion, no doubt—a sumptuous repast. But ignorant, possibly, of the dietary observances of our people, or judging from observation that they did not all regard those observances too rigorously, he crowded his board with food which Jews must not eat, either because not *kosher* in itself, or not *kosher* by the mode of its preparation. Nevertheless some Jewish boys partook vigorously of the forbidden dainties; others, though equally hungry, rigorously abstained. Well, who were the manlier boys? Those who conquered appetite for their faith, or those who bartered its teachings for the leg of a roast fowl?

There was once a dinner party of merry young men —very young men; during the repast some forbidden food was handed round; it was probably the horridly unwholesome monsters called oysters, which feed on the drowned. All partook except one young man, who, utterly regardless of sneers, jibes and jokes, refused the dainty nastiness. Well, was he not manlier and happier? He might have found it never very difficult in after life to resist—not only forbidden food, but the other things forbidden by Heaven—life's many temptations. Some days after the dinner, one of the guests said to him, "I wish I had had your courage; I wish I had acted as you did." Perhaps finding it was not so difficult to be brave, this second guest—and it may be others of the guests—may have been more manly on other occasions. For great is the force of example. Every good, wise action drops around it seeds of promise, whence other good, wise actions may spring and flourish. These tales are trifles, but trifles make the sum of life. Boys, learn from trifles, and be wise!

Yet, this want of moral courage is not your sole fault of *race*. Another fault characterizes every class of you. Monstrous pride. The rich are insufferable in their pride of wealth; the middle class in their pride of caste; the poor in their pride of race. It is the sole cant of our people. How the children of a people taught to love their neighbours as themselves; a people who were "bondsmen in the land of Egypt;" a people whose greatest teacher was a foundling and the meekest of men, and the founder of whose royal race was a shepherd boy; how such a people can thus build supposed excellence on social rank and position, or on a heap of wealth which their fathers amassed for them, is surprisingly inconsistent. The pride of the wealthy, it is true, has only one trifling disadvantage; it simply renders them disagreeable in society and to themselves. But the pride of the poor results in a greater disadvantage; for it prevents them from engaging in certain humble but very honest pursuits, and encourages them to a style and expenditure beyond their position, and thus they more readily become, and remain, paupers, unable to earn a living and incapable of independence.

And now a word as to learning. We are not going to fatigue you with the hackneyed conventional sentence that *now* is your special time to learn. *Your time to learn will last as long as your time to live.* But

Q

that is no reason for your not learning as much as
you can at the present more favourable season of your
life. Not only in your grammars and arithmetic, your
Livy and Virgil, your Euclid and Keightley, but in
another and far older book, the Book of Books—the
Bible ; and in that yet older Book, the Book of Nature,
which speaks aloud of Heavenly might and wisdom ;
and in that younger book—the pages of your own
heart—which speak softly of Heavenly help and love.
You live for some great purpose; then cease to be so
frivolous as you sometimes are ; do not be so fashionably
supercilious and punctilious, thinking, as many of you
seem to do, about your visitings and your smart clothes
and your *Barmitzvah* watch-chains, when you had far
better be thinking a little more of your *Barmitzvah*
duties. Do not be so fashionably uncharitable and
censorious—after the fashion, we mean, of your elders ;
but try to set a new fashion, on an old type—the
fashion of loving one's neighbour and never hating
one's brother. And, since you are not always happy—
for if extremely silly persons tell you in books that
boyhood is a season of unmitigated enjoyment, they
know nothing about you, and you and we don't believe them—since you are not always happy, you can
well understand how sorrow loses its sting, and how
happiness doubles its charm, when the mind tells the
heart that the soul—even the young boy's soul—has
done its duty !

We have spoken to you of the future duties you
may have to fulfil, and the future life you may have
to lead. But the voice of religion, the belief of wise
and pious men, the arguments of reason, and, it may
be, the instincts of your own young hearts, point to

another and a brighter future hidden in the secret world beyond the barred portals of the grave. But to you, who are so young and full of vigour and energy; you whose blood flows so gaily in your veins, and whose spirits are so elastic that the rebound of your sorrow is in itself a joy, it would be useless to speak of a future in heaven from which you are separated by the hopes of a long life on earth. And thus, indeed, the rewards of an immortal hereafter were not distinctly indicated to our fathers in the boyhood of our race. Young inexperienced spirits do not grasp the idea readily or availably. Perhaps only those who know life's cares and trials, its sins and sorrows, and who have grown very weary and very penitent, can see through their tears the vision of the Golden Hope.

But there is one recompence we all can understand, receive and welcome. Yes, the young and the old, the happy and the sorrowful, the merry and the weary— we can, all alike, lift our eyes from earth, and hope to win the love of the Father in Heaven. May that light of love shine on you, boys, in the spring of your youth and the summer of your manhood, in the autumn of declining strength and the winter of old age. Come, boys of our hopes and affections, strive to be brave, wise and good, so that you may become better men than we are; so that your own boys, in far days to come, may profit by your example, and become better than you; and thus from generation to generation, improving and yet improving, while time and the world endure. It may be that we shall have the joy of believing we are links in a chain of generations, rising from the ranks of impure humanity to the spiritual beauty of the angelic world. And, it may be, too, that the sun of heavenly love and blessing, shining on an age of grace, in a far distant future, may even shed in our times a forecast of its glory, to brighten our clouded lives, and penetrate the dark shadows of our graves.

HOW WE SPOILT OUR HOLIDAY;

OR,

ALL IS *NOT* WELL THAT ENDS WELL.

A Story for Jewish Schoolboys.

FIVE and twenty years ago I was a schoolboy—a pupil of a great London School. I had some three hundred comrades of various creeds, countries, classes, and capabilities. We had broken up for the summer vacation after a hard struggle in my class for an important scholarship. I had fought for it and had been beaten; not ignominiously but decidedly. However, I did not complain, because it was won from some twenty competitors by a Jewish boy named Percy Arnold—a lad of great talent, industry, and good nature. He was a hard worker, full of genius and assiduity, and peculiarly modest and gentle—a great favourite of the masters, and of a few of the boys—though not generally of the school, for some of his school-fellows used to have an occasional fling at him. He was rather a friend of mine, however, and I was glad he gained the scholarship, not so much for himself, but because his success reflected honour on all the Jewish pupils. And in those days, boys, we had a little trouble to " hold our own " at school.

Arnold was not intimate with any of the boys, and
neither gave invitations to them nor accepted any from
them. He was what you boys might call "close."
All we knew about his domestic matters was that he
lived in a small house at Islington ; for it is needless to
remark that his reserve naturally urged us to conspire
together, and to fee a small but trustworthy junior boy
to follow him home and ascertain where he *did* live.

Percy was awfully shy and sensitive. He would
blush like a girl under the slightest provocation ; and
he once burst into tears when taken down in class ; a
sort of thing, you know, boys, we forgive in the lower
forms ; but really we cannot pass it over in the fifth
or sixth upper ; where we are all stoics and philosophers, and do all our lessons at school, and all our
crying and other expressions of feeling at home.

It was clear that Arnold was very poor, for his
clothes though neat, bore evidences of cheapness and
coarseness ; and—dreadful to relate—they were ready-
made clothes ! The lunch he brought with him to
school was beyond a joke. There was a tradition,
almost too dismal to record, that it never went beyond
thick bread and butter. And, indeed, there was a
current legend that his *Barmitzvah* was passed over
without any festivity or increase to his personal adorn-
ment. Boys, fancy a *Barmitzvah* boy without a breakfast or a watch ! Let us hasten to draw a veil over
the melancholy picture.

The term was over; the scholarship gained; the
vacation in full force. Most of my schoolfellows had
gone to the sea-side or the country, while I was
wasting the holidays in town, idling three parts of the
day, and persuading myself that I was studying during

the fourth part. When lo! one morning, joy of joys! I received an invitation. And such an invitation! Not to the monotony of Margate nor the beatitude of Brighton; not to revel in any one boy's exile, where opportunities for quarrelling would be varied and numerous; but actually an invitation to spend a month with Ben Barnett! the richest, proudest, and most stupid boy in all the school. To spend it, too, at his father's lovely country seat, Hillside house, Hertfordshire, where fifteen schoolfellows were already assembled or expected as guests! There would be boating, bathing, and boys! Cricket, football, and fives! Driving, riding, walking, running, and wrestling—such a programme as I can best describe by calling it intensely jolly.

I obtained parental consent, accepted the invitation, and packed my portmanteau, with, of course, a quantity of articles I could not possibly require, while I naturally omitted such trifling essentials as shirts, shoes, and tooth-brush, and had to undergo the humiliation of re-packing, under maternal supervision. You will quite understand that I was ready to start three mortal hours before the coach which was to convey me could possibly put in an appearance, and that I arrived at Hillside house in a wild flutter of expectation—a pure and pleasurable excitement, which I pray Heaven might be awakened in me again in these hard years of after life!

But in the days of youth, even our hopes are sometimes realized. The weather was glorious, the house and grounds magnificent; there were boats enough for us all, though we all wanted to row; and ponies enough for us all, though we all wanted to ride; a number which sensibly diminished after the first day's experience, when the large majority of us came rapidly to grief and violently off the saddle.

Among the guests were some Christian schoolfellows, and, moreover, a middle-aged gentleman, named Hyde, a friend of our host. Mr. Hyde was the head of a mercantile house of great wealth and high standing.

Among the Jewish guests was the very Percy Arnold of whom I have spoken.

Mr. Hyde took little notice of us boys, with one exception. He showed great interest in Percy Arnold, and frequently would he saunter with him through the shrubberies; his hand on his shoulder, each evidently deriving pleasure from the conversation of the other. And sometimes, when they were walking together, Mr. and Mrs. Barnett would exchange approving and significant glances.

Percy's favourite resort was a romantic and thickly tangled wood, which extended over some miles of country, about an hour's walk from the house. Hither he would frequently wander, either alone or with any companion he could capture; and his great delight was to lie down at the foot of some shady tree. He haunted the wood, and we used to banter him, by styling him "Pan," "Dryad," "Jacques," or such other designation as our readings and imaginations suggested.

I think that jealousy of Percy's abilities and success was at the root of the disfavour with which he was regarded by some of his schoolmates.

Now, one evening, we boys were sitting late round the supper table, talking of school feats in study and playground; and some were dealing unmercifully with the characters and scholastic reputations of our absent schoolfellows. In this talk Arnold did not join, but sat apart, and abstracted. Presently, he rose and left the room. He had scarcely closed the door when Ben Barnett, who, to do him justice, rarely spoke scandal, because he rarely spoke at all, said, " Well, I suppose, Arnold is too fine to join our talk about school. He thinks himself a touch above us *now*."

" Oh, as to that," observed a boy, named Phillips, " Arnold is as great a humbug as ever breathed!"

At this remark, spoken very loudly, Mr. Hyde, who had been talking with Mr. Barnett, and had not hitherto paid attention to our gossip, turned his head and glanced at us. I noticed that after this first mention of Arnold's full name he seemed to listen attentively to all we said.

"I do not agree with you," observed a mild boy, called Millington. " I think Arnold a jolly good fellow and not a bit of a humbug."

"Ah! " said a boy named Frank Marks, "you don't know as much of him as we do. I tell you Arnold is a sneak."

" Yes," added Barnett, " he never joins in any of our fun. He is always getting made monitor, and getting other fellows in a row."

" He told of poor Watson, and nearly had him ex- pelled for copying at the written examination. He said it was his duty, you know. Fine duty ! When *he* came in second, in consequence ! " Here broke out a storm of invective.

" Cost him nothing, his duty. He never lets any- thing cost him anything," said one boy. " He would not subscribe to the Head Master's testimonial."

" He only gave a shilling to the fund we raised

for poor Partridge, the porter, when he broke his leg."

"He's an awfully sulky fellow, and dreadfully mean."

"But," said mild Millington, "he won the scholarship, you know; so he must be clever."

"Clever!" answered Phillips, "not *he*. He won it, in my opinion, by cribs. I know he has access to the City library."

"Yes, and worms himself round old Grosvenor, the Greek Master, and gets lots out of him somehow."

"He never comes to see any of us, nor asks any of us. I am sure I wonder he came to you, Barnett; but then your father's rich ; and Arnold is no end of a snob."

"He isn't a gentleman, though ; " said Phillips, in a slow sententious manner; "in fact, how *can* he be?"

"Why not?" asked a chorus of voices.

"It is not possible," said Phillips, mysteriously, "don't you know all about him ? "

"No ; what is it ? Do tell us ! "

"It's a secret," said Phillips, in a pompous voice ; and immediately, boy-like, he proceeded to reveal it. "I heard it as a fact from a servant of ours who, in their better days, was a servant of theirs. His name is no more Arnold than yours. His real name is Abrahams ! He changed it, because his father—well, perhaps I ought'nt to tell—"

"Oh ! do tell—do—."

"Well, as you are all confidential friends,"—(there were twelve confidential friends present)—"I don't mind mentioning it. His father forged, and was transported for life to Australia; and died there a convict! There's a fine fellow for you ! "

I observed that, at this juncture, Mr. Hyde rose from his seat, and paced the apartment twice or thrice contemplatively; and then, suddenly, as if actuated by a sudden impulse growing out of his meditation, he quitted the room.

When he had gone, Mr. Barnett said gravely—

"I wish, boys, you had not spoken so sharply against Percy Arnold; I do not think he ever did you any harm; but I fear you may have done him a great harm. The fact is, he was strongly recommended to Mr. Hyde by your head master—(though he could not afford to contribute to his testimonial). Yes, recommended to fill a position of high trust in Mr. Hyde's office—a sort of secretaryship, which he requires, as he has many public duties to fulfil in addition to his ordinary business. He asked the head master if he knew of a clever well educated youth, of respectability and *unimpeachable* character, and pleasant temper, to whom a salary, a home, and a promise of advancement would be inducements. He offered a very handsome salary. Dr. Parker at once named Arnold. And, to tell you the full truth, I invited Arnold in order that Mr. Hyde might have an opportunity of seeing and knowing him."

We all glanced at each other.

"Now," continued Mr. Barnett, "Mr. Hyde was delighted with Arnold, and offered him his situation; he nearly closed with him, and told him that if he was as pleased with him as he anticipated, he would— to use his own expression—be the 'making of him.' And this is no trifle, boys, for Arnold is very poor, and dependent on a widowed mother, who ekes out a scanty living by her arduous labour as an embroiderer for a London warehouse."

We looked rather uncomfortable. Alas! our unruly tongues—I fear I must say our unruly hearts—had run off with our discretion. We felt it was but too possible that we had done a little mischief, and we were sorry. I then thought of Scott's words—

> " Full many a shaft at random sent,
> Finds aim the archer little meant ;
> Full many a word at random spoken,
> May heal or wound a heart half broken."

I don't think Hood had written his Lady's Dream in those days, so, of course, I could not quote—

> " Evil is wrought by want of thought
> As much as by want of heart."

We gradually filed off to our bedrooms in a sheepish style: but we soon forgot the incident. For long before our usual bedroom conference—prolonged school-boy fashion far into the night—had subsided into slumber, we had allowed all thoughts of Arnold, and of his—or our— shortcomings, to pass away from our minds.

Morning dawned : and before the sun had dried the dew on the flowers, we were all, as usual, up and about. We assembled for prayers, but missed Arnold. He was usually one of the earliest amongst us ; but he did not appear either at prayers, or even at breakfast. We fancied he had overslept himself; and as he occupied a small chamber in the upper part of the big house, we could only obtain information by sending a special embassy. Breakfast being over, we sent up a servant to look after him, and our emissary brought us the astounding intelligence that he was not in the room, nor anywhere in the house; and that his bed had evidently not been slept in; for it remained in its last night's "made" condition.

We then surmised that Arnold, who, as that disagreeable boy Marks growled, "always was eccentric," had started for a morning's walk and had lost his way; and we imagined that he would soon return. But the morning wore on. Morning was crowned by noon. Noon waned. And still he did not come.

Where was he? Where could he be? What could have happened? We questioned the servants, but no one could give any information. No servant and no boy had seen him since he left the room at supper time on the previous evening.

At length, Mr. Hyde, who had appeared indifferent hitherto to the general excitement, said that *he* had seen him after supper, because having had a private communication to make to him, he had followed him to his bedroom, and finding him there up and dressed, and hard at study, he had spoken to him a little.

Mr. Barnett, anxious about his young guest, asked Mr. Hyde if he might enquire the nature of this communication.

Mr. Hyde hesitated: but, after a pause, he said, "Well, it need not be a mystery. I did not care to mention it: but it may as well be told. I had thought of offering an appointment to your young friend, Arnold. But when I heard all that was said of him last night—all that was said of his character and connections, by those who must have known most of him, and by young boys who could have no possible motive for aspersing him, I distinctly and decidedly withdrew my offer. I told him that I could not possibly engage him to fill a position of trust and responsibility, requiring tact, temper and talent."

We boys were aghast! What had we done? Our discomfort of last night was a trifle compared with our horror now! The uneasy feeling of the evening gave place to a sickening remorse. For myself, I was terror-stricken. I could not divest my mind of an apprehension of evil. And while I was in this confused condition of mingled regret and alarm, a man-servant entered with a letter which a maid, in arranging my room for the night, had found on my bed. Its position accounted for my not having seen it when I went to dress for dinner. The letter was addressed to me. I tore it open. It was from Arnold! Eagerly, impatiently, I read it aloud. I have kept it ever since on my person, as a reminder. Here it is :—

"Dear Bernard,—You have always cared for me more than the other boys. I cannot go without a farewell word to you. I am too wretched and confused to write to my kind host and thank him as I ought. For I am heart-broken. I am utterly miserable. The main hope of my life is shattered. My terrible home secret, my father's condition, is known! known to all the school! known to Mr. Hyde, the best friend I had ever gained. What will my mother say when she hears it? I yearn to lay my weary head on her dear bosom to comfort her—or to die! But my limbs ache; and my head aches; and my heart aches; oh, how my heart aches! So I cannot meet her. I can never go back to school. I can never face the world. I will wander in the wood till it is all over. Say good-bye to my mother for me. Oh! what will my mother say when she hears it?"

In one moment the truth flashed on me. Young as I was, I thoroughly understood how terrible, how fatal to a boy of Arnold's sensitive disposition, must have been the knowledge that the dreadful secret of this father's disgrace was known to the school. The world's opinion assumed gigantic proportions in the boy's mind. Its black shadow fell on his heart, blotting out the sunshine of happiness. And it was no imaginary sorrow. For his hopes were blighted. The bright position, the promising career opened to him by Mr. Hyde's brilliant offer were lost to him—lost to him all through our idle, senseless, heartless talk; nay, let me say the true word—our wicked calumny!

I was a boy of positive character, and I at once resolved to set out in search of Arnold. I felt a cold fear at my heart. The dread of the terrible possibility urged me forth to seek my schoolmate. Mr. Barnett condemned, nay, ridiculed, my project. He said that night was coming on, and that a search for a boy in the wood, in the darkness, was a wild, mad scheme. I was firm. The boys, eager for adventure, were anxious to join me in my expedition. Mr. Barnett forbade his own son and some of the younger children to go out. But, to my surprise, Mr. Hyde decided that I was right, and declared that he would accompany me in my quest.

In a quarter of an hour from the reading of the letter, we had set out,—Mr. Hyde, a few of the elder boys, two men-servants, and myself, in all eight. We walked to the wood, where Mr. Hyde marshalled us in four parties of two each, and each party had a lantern, for the thick trees of the wood, full of July foliage, made our way very dark indeed. We agreed to search in different directions and to meet at ten o'clock (we started at seven) in the centre of the wood, where a woodman's cottage stood.

At a quarter past ten, we had all met at the woodman's cottage—our search utterly in vain! wearied and discouraged; and, to be candid, some of us very hungry, for we were but boys. Three of the boys and both the men-servants resolved to return; one of the latter, a coarse country hind, angrily declared that "it was a wild goose chase for a fellow who had never tipped them a sixpence." But, with one accord, Phillips, the ringleader of last night's mischief, but now heartily repentant, and Mr. Hyde and myself, determined to resume our search; for I felt convinced that Arnold had not left the wood!

We three, abandoned by the others, and keeping close together, set out again, exploring the least frequented and most tangled brakes of the wood. Eleven o'clock struck. Oh! that weary, terrible night. Oh! the grief and remorse that tore our hearts. Oh! the fear that almost paralyzed them. Never shall I forget our misery and alarm. The hours dragged on, and still we found no clue to Arnold. Our anguish and anxiety grew almost too great to bear. Twelve—one—struck through the still air from the village clock, and we heard the dull sounds in the dark lone wood. But we found no trace of Arnold. But at last we said to each other—at least I do not know who said it first—we said in a whisper what we had thought for hours in our hearts, " The *river !* oh, the river ! "

For a narrow but deep river edged the wood on its farther side, and the trees reached to its brink as they clustered in fantastic shapes on its steep bank. And thither, though we knew it was vain, we bent our weary way.

What was THIS lying on the shelving grass, where the trees were thin? What was *this*, lying stiff and still—stark, cold, and damp? A pale face turned upward to the chill moonlight, a face so motionless that it looked—ah! and felt—like stone! Oh! Arnold—oh! our dear injured schoolmate! Dear boy! dearest boy! had we found him at last? And was he dead? Had his poor stricken heart ceased to beat for ever? Oh! what would his mother say when she heard it?

* * * *

No! boys, no. He was not dead. We felt faintly, but assuredly, the slow throb in his breast as we laid our hands on him. But his eyes did not open, nor his lips move. Mr. Hyde knelt on the damp sward, and raised his head on his knees. And oh! boys—I am not ashamed to tell it, though Mr. Hyde and Phillips were looking on, and though I was a sixth class boy, I knelt down with a great passion of tears and pressed my trembling lips to the cold pale cheek of my schoolmate.

Perhaps the hot rain of my tears, or the touch of my kiss revived him. For he opened his eyes slowly, and his lips parted—and though he closed eyes and lips again almost instantly—we just caught the words, "Oh! what will my mother say when she hears it!"

Need I tell you, boys, how we raised him, carefully and tenderly, and bore him to the woodman's cottage, and laid him on a bed? how we sought medical aid

and used every wise expedient to revive him? The
night wore on—the dawn broke—and, ere noon, he
had woken from his stupor, but was in the first
throes of brain fever!

But at noon his mother, whom we had sought out,
was by his side; and in all his delirium, though he
did not know her, he spoke but one sentence—
again and again—"Oh! what will my mother say
when she hears it!"

*   *   *   *

No, boys. He did not die. My story ends well, or
I would not have told it on this Sabbath day, the day
of Heavenly Joy and Earthly Peace. He recovered—
far more rapidly than we had dared to expect. He
recovered to forgive us all, as we gathered round his
bed, with tearful eyes and quivering lips.

We tried to expiate our fault by boldly seeking Mr.
Hyde, who had returned to his London duties, and
telling him that we had exaggerated every weakness,
and distorted every characteristic of our schoolfellow
—that we had ruthlessly, cruelly, heartlessly vilified
him.

He was a good man, though hasty. He believed us,
I think; but it was clear that he could not quite divest
himself of the impression against Arnold left by our
calumnies. He never took kindly to him again. No,
all is not well that ends well. He did not renew his
offer of a situation. But he treated Percy charitably,
and gave him money to start him in life.

Percy Arnold is now a happy, prosperous man;
married; the father of many children. His mother,
too, is living. And the story of his father's shame is
unknown to the new generation. You may be sure

that I have substituted a fictitious name, therefore, for the real one.

And, though Arnold is prospering, yet the impression of that miserable night has remained on my mind through all the years of my life. It stamped my heart from the hour in which I knelt on the grass beside the prostrate form of my schoolfellow. But I do not regret the hours of misery I passed in the wood, for I believe they made me a better man than I might have been otherwise; and perhaps you, who have listened to me, "may profit by my tale."

For, be assured, our religion is really a religion of love. And we pray wisely when we pray that our tongues may be kept from speaking evil, and our lips from uttering deceit.

THE SCHOOLBOY AND THE ANGEL;

OR,

"THINK AND THANK."

Another Tale for Jewish Schoolboys.

"I'M the most unfortunate fellow on the face of the earth," cried Vivian Davis, passionately,—his hand clenched, his eyes flashing, "the most unhappy wretched fellow that ever breathed," he continued, violently striking the playground gate with his left hand;—his right was in a sling.

Let us see what, in respect of the speaker, the scene, or the circumstances, justified these strong observations.

The speaker was a lad of fifteen; strongly built, graceful, good-looking, well-dressed. Nothing in all these personal qualities to render Vivian "the most unfortunate fellow on the face of the earth."

The scene was as pleasant a playground as you can imagine—the playground of the Rev. Mr. Morris's boarding-school down at Seaford. Gravelled in one part, grass-covered in another; with a few tall trees and no brick walls. Sloping upward to the picturesque red-tiled school-house at one side, sloping downward on the other side to a bright flower garden which belonged to the boys and was cultivated by them; and beyond which was an acre or two, divided into patches, where corn and vegetables grew, and to which the boys had free access.

For Mr. Morris was a sensible man in one respect. Not sensible, inasmuch that he did not look upon a boy as a coupon representing a dividend payable in half-yearly instalments, when presented at home at the end of the term; but he actually thought boys were rational beings, with minds to cultivate, bodies to strengthen, hearts to draw to his own heart, and souls to render pure. He really went so far as to imagine that because parents entrusted their children to him he had undertaken a solemn parental responsibility and was called on morally to fulfil it. And one way in which he accomplished his task was this; he taught his pupils the great lessons to be learnt by the marvels of the garden, the meadow, and the field; he told them of the seeds which, when carefully planted, grew by mysterious influence into flower and shrub; the sheaves which, when carefully tended, yielded the bursting ear to the reaper; the tree which woke to life in spring and grew rich with leafy shade in summer and withered in the winter, preparing for its new awakening. Ah, well! some schoolmasters fancy all lessons may be taught by one single vegetable production only, vulgarly called the cane; but Mr. Morris took a broader and truer view of nature, and enlisted other offspring of the soil in his service.

Over the fair playground on the day that Vivian spoke the words which head my story, there arched a blue and beaming August sky, flecked here and there with a few feathery clouds. And beyond the

playing-fields stretched the broad bright country in
its green summer beauty. And the soft cool breeze,
laden with the breath of the salt sea, near at hand,
stirred the gay leaves of the playground trees. Surely
there was nothing in this pleasant scene to render
Vivian miserable.

Now as to the circumstances. Well, to tell the plain
truth, they *were* annoying. At least, I think you will
say so. Vivian Davis was the head boy of the school;
that, of course, was only an annoying circumstance
to the boys who were not the head boys. But he
wanted, naturally enough, to retain his position, and
hold the ground against all comers.

Caleb Ellis was close on his heels—always trying to
trip him up, but never yet quite succeeding. It so
befel that a rich gentleman named Barnett, the father
of that very Ben Barnett of whom you have read in
a certain history narrated in these pages, called
"How we spoilt our Holidays," desiring to render
himself eminently agreeable, commemorated his
sojourn that summer at Seaford by offering a really
handsome prize for competition to the first class
of Mr. Morris's school. You know that what we
public-school boys call the *sixth* form in *our* schools
the boarding-school boys are so obsolete as to call the
first class in theirs. Well, the prize was—of all things
in the world—a pony! It was suggested by young
Ben Barnett; and those who knew him best declared
it was the only sensible suggestion he had ever made
in his life.

It was agreed that the test should be a set of printed
questions which had just been used by a great public
school to which Ben Barnett went, and where, though

he was taught a great deal, he had not learnt anything.

Vivian thought he should win easily. He glanced
at the questions (which he had, of course, to answer in
writing), and when told that he had three hours in
which to answer them, he laughed rather contemptu-
ously, and said he could do them in half the time.

Ellis said nothing; did not laugh at all; set to
work, and—won!

Not quite fairly, *I* think. The fact was, the questions of one subject were printed on both sides of one
sheet. Vivian, in his superb disdain, forgot to turn
a page, never saw the question on the reverse side,
did not answer it, and lost just marks enough to lose
the day!

Such an easy question, too; that was the worst of it.
You know, boys, that famous arithmetical question,
which is not at all likely to be put to anybody in any
walk of real life, and which therefore is considered a
highly necessary portion of a sound practical education : "If A could do a piece of work in 24 hours,
and B in 12 hours . . . ." I will spare you the re-
mainder of the hideous fiction, worthy only of a
Colenso.

Well, Vivian protested; Mr. Morris would not listen
to his protests ! Vivian became angry, a state of mind
with which he often inflicted his schoolfellows, especially his dearest friends amongst them ; Mr. Morris
persisted in his decision. The marks were read aloud
in the schoolroom: Maximum 100—Ellis 90, Davis 87;
all the rest nowhere. Pony duly adjudged to Caleb
Ellis. *Hinc illæ lachrymæ !*

And that was not quite all.

An hour before the declaration of marks Davis went with two or three intimates to examine the cricket apparatus; for a tremendous match was to be fought on the morrow. Not at Seaford; not in the school only. Oh, dear no! The annual match between Mr. Morris's Jewish boys at Seaford, and a Mr. Smith's Christian boys at the rival town of Cliffsend (a match with the fame of which the world ought to have rung, for it woke wild frenzied enthusiasm in twenty-two boys for three months beforehand!)

Davis was intensely fond of cricket. He batted well, he bowled better. They had a first rate bat at Smith's school; but as to a bowler! There was not a boy in all Cliffsend who could have held a candle to Vivian (even if such an operation had been customary at cricket, which for the benefit of you boys who do not play cricket, I must mention is not the case).

Well, now comes the climax of poor Vivian's misfortunes. While passing through the outhouse in which the cricket apparatus was kept, he trod on a fallen ball, which rolled from under him and brought him down heavily, his arm somehow beneath his body. He sprained his wrist fearfully; and though— for he was a manly, resolute fellow—he determined to make light of it, he suffered great pain, and sustained a serious injury. No cricket for poor Vivian to-morrow!

To say the least of it, it was aggravating. But even these troubles did not justify Vivian's annoyance. Assuredly they did not justify his violence and discontent.

The truth is, Vivian Davis was a thoroughly discontented boy. He had what persons call an unhappy disposition; he was always fancying himself illused, injured, and sinned against. This self-tormenting quality made him appear far more ill-tempered and selfish than he was by nature. He rendered himself thoroughly wretched, and, what was far worse, he rendered persons around him thoroughly wretched also.

Vivian had not even the cause of complaint that some boarding-school boys have. He had left no happy home, no loving parents, no dear young sisters and brothers to live away from those tender ties, under a stranger roof. He had no sisters and brothers, no home—nay, worse still—and this was his greatest misfortune, though he did not in any way recognize it—he had no father or mother!

This deprivation is a sad blight to a young life; it makes boyhood so imperfect. For the strong love of the father and the tender love of the mother bless and beautify the life that clings to theirs. They are the angels of the home, the angels who guide our hearts forward in the way of earth—upward in the way to heaven.

I have a great compassion for fatherless and motherless boys; I think each of us should try in his way to be very gentle with them, and very forbearing, knowing what they lack, knowing the love that they have lost.

If amongst us there are some who have no little ones of our own, let us give some of our spare unapplied care and affection to these children who need them, ah! so much. Blessed are they who shelter and befriend the orphan! What if they have no boys of their *very* own? The life story of the fatherless whom they have guarded and led aright will chaunt a hallowed קָדִישׁ over their silent graves!

No, Vivian had no father and mother. Perhaps if he had had, his character might have been moulded by parental influence into a better shape. But so it was. He had in other ways very much to make him contented. He was strikingly clever, he was healthy and strong, he had an affectionate, sensitive heart, and an imaginative mind, and he was rich. He had succeeded to a large inheritance, which had accumulated since he lost his parents in the third year of his life.

   *   *   *   *

"I am the most miserable wretch that ever lived," said Vivian again, " everything has gone wrong."

" Well," answered Harry Bennett, a sympathising young schoolfellow, "you *have* been unlucky. Nothing short of an angel would set the matter right."

"Bah!" cried Vivian impatiently, "don't talk bosh about angels. I don't believe in such nonsense."

" Don't believe in angels!" exclaimed Harry, aghast, his big eyes opening to their widest expression of surprise, "why Mr. Morris was only telling us about them last Saturday, and that's what made me think of them."

" Ah well! angels don't come now-a-days," rejoined Vivian, " it was all very well in former times, little stupid, when there were all sorts of things that people don't understand; but angels don't come down from the clouds in these times and set all our troubles right."

" Don't be too sure of that, Davis," said, in his usually slow dreamy tone, a boy named Franco, an imaginative young fellow, who (like some twelve years old boys I knew,) wrote poetry, or rhyme, when he ought to have been doing his exercises, or playing prisoners bars, "Don't be too sure of that: I often fancy angels come to us now-a-days, though we do not see them, at least all of us don't see them, but I am sure that——"

What he was sure of never will be known, because Vivian with a fresh gesture of impatience, strode angrily away, frowning, muttering and giving vent to various outward manifestations of savage discontent.

Strode away and came bolt up against his rival Ellis.

Now Ellis was not the most amiable of boys, though he differed in character from Vivian. He was not violent, nor discontented, not sensitive nor affectionate. His main annoyance was that though he was anxious to enter professional life (he wanted to be a physician or surgeon,) his father considered him intellectually incompetent, and intended him for a foreign counting-house, a subject on which he was especially sore.

How it happened I do not quite know, but Ellis, very foolishly and unkindly, taunted Vivian on the result of the examination. High words ensued and Vivian worked himself into a towering passion.

The passion, the heat of the day, the annoyance of his defeat, the disappointment regarding the cricket match, the pain of the fall, acting on Vivian's sensitive temperament, or, it may be, some physical indisposition, seemed to affect the boy very remarkably. He felt languid, complained of severe headache and giddiness and before evening he was really very ill. The illness increased as the day waned, and when Vivian went to bed he was distressingly feverish.

As "head boy" he slept in a small chamber by himself, a pleasant room looking over the fields towards the sea, but the soothing murmur of the waves failed to lull the boy to sleep, and when the stars woke in the sky and glittered through the pane, the lad was still awake, tossing feverishly in his bed.

Mr. Morris was alarmed. Nothing could have happened worse. Mrs. Morris had been the previous day summoned to the sick bed of a relative thirty miles away. The house servants did their best, but the anxious schoolmaster, deprived temporarily of the calm aid and tender advice of the dear partner of his cares, missed her more then ever at this critical moment. You understand; his pupils were his children, not mere coining dies with which he stamped money.

Backward and forward during the hours of midnight, poor Mr. Morris flitted to and from the boy's chamber, of course disturbing the lad very much every time he came in; trying to walk on tiptoe in a hushed manner, and consequently making a most absurd noise; and being, like many learned men, just a little clumsy and awkward, he woke the boy from his brief dozes, first by the crash of a cup which his dressing-gown swept to the ground, and next by the fall of his candlestick on the top of the stairs, whence without apparent provocation or mechanical justification, according to known principles of gravitation, it rolled step by step to the stone pavement below, rousing half the sleeping boys, and rendering poor Vivian more feverish then ever.

But the last exploit proved fortunate to Vivian, for Mr. Morris visited the boy no more that night, and

Vivian manfully endeavoured to compose himself to sleep. Woke up once arguing with little Franco, woke up twice imagining that an angel was going to attend the cricket match on his behalf on the morrow, woke up thrice with a confused notion of an angel bearing off the coveted pony from Ellis' grasp and presenting it to himself, woke up a fourth time in a blended confusion of cricket, angels, boys and examinations, and finally fell fast asleep.

*　　　*　　　*　　　*

Was he awake or was he dreaming? Was he in the possession of his faculties, or was his brain distempered with delirious fancy? Was he alive? What was it that the boy, drowsily opening his heavy eyes, saw at the foot of his bed?

Surely he was not dreaming! surely he had his usual intelligence. For, there was the bed, there the window, with the moonlight gleaming through! there the familiar furniture; there, carelessly thrown on a chair, the clothes he had worn during the day; there lay his bandaged arm on the pillow. He felt his temples ache as they had ached when he went to bed; he felt the keen smart of his arm as it had smarted since his fall; he even heard the distant murmur of the sea; yes, he heard the town clock chime the hour! Surely he was not asleep.

Not asleep, not dreaming, not delirious, not dead; and yet, at the foot of his bed, between the parted curtains, there stood—an angel!

An angel, if ever boy saw one; an angel if the fancy of the painter, the dream of the poet, the tradition of all men, be true!

In the soft light of the moon, which formed a broad

silvery shimmering track sloping upward behind her, as if she had glided down the shining path from her native sky, the angel stood. Yes, surely an angelic apparition. Her face, fair, smiling, gentle, and oh! how beautiful! Her bright, tender, loving woman's face, such as we see in pictures and dreams, with rich golden hair, shining like opaque light, and wreathed with a heavenly garland of azure flowers, on which it seemed the dew-drops sparkled; while other flowers, oh! how lustrous in their varied colours! were clustered at her breast; she was robed, it seemed, in a cloud of blue, a feathery mist that appeared in the soft moonlight, like a vapour fading from the hills at dawn; and just on each fair shoulder was a glimpse of a white glistening ridge, like the folded edge of an angel's wings.

Some sparkling crystals, beaming coloured fires, girded the upraised arm—upraised to hold aside the parted curtain. A perfume sweet, like the breath of violets or hawthorn, floated all around her, and her face—ah! it was lovely, like a dream!

He looked, he looked again, drank in her presence with his eyes—"Ah!" he murmured, "an angel! an angel has come to me, to set it right."

She smiled a radiant smile, and then she sang. It seemed to him she sang in notes of an unearthly melody, a sort of gentle lullaby, so softly, that her voice scarcely rose above a murmur; so sweetly, that it soothed him inexpressibly; so harmoniously, that it woke some feeling of sleeping poetry in the boy's young breast, and led it upward like the voice of a sacred song, heard for the first time.

He opened his eyes more widely. Oh! no, he was

not dreaming. There she stood, the angel of the night, the angel who came to the schoolboy, parting his curtain with her jewelled hand, and singing him to sleep.

And again murmuring "Angel," he sank to slumber once more, lulled by the smile of her brow, the grace of her presence, the music of her voice.

He slept, yet not so soundly but that he felt (or perhaps then he was really dreaming) that a tender hand turned and smoothed his hot pillow, and bathed his aching head with cooling, soothing, sweet-smelling waters, which lessened its heavy pain ; and that the same tender hand relaxed the bandages of his suffering arm, dressed it with some kindly balm which checked the smart, and laid it in an easy fashion, on a softer and cooler cushion.

He slept ; but it seemed to him (though perhaps then he was really dreaming) that as he closed his eyes, calm loving eyes were looking into his ; that a tender kiss was pressed on his heated brow ; that the song was checked for a moment, while a voice, as lovely in its music as the song, breathed gently these fond words, " Poor motherless boy ! "

*   *   *   *

With the pressure of such a kiss he woke. Woke as some pleasant drink was held to his parched lips, and he saw that it was broad day-light, and that near him stood the angel of the night.

"Are you," said he, half closing his weary eyes, " an angel come to set it right ? "

" I hope so," said the angel. " I hope I have come to set you right ; but I fear I am no angel."

" Who are you, then ? " said the boy.

"Emma Lawrence," said the angel. "And I never heard of any angel having such a name as that."

And she laughed gently, while the boy opened his eyes and saw a bright fair lady near his bed, some thirty-five or forty years old, wearing a gay garland in her brown hair, and clothed in a blue ball-dress, gay with flowers, a white scarf hanging from her shoulders, jewels on her arms, and a smile on her face. Oh! a smile like the tender smile of—your own dear mother, boys—of your mother, when she stands so gently by your bedside in the hour of sickness or sorrow; your mother, the *real angel of the schoolboy.*

     *   *   *   *

But mine is no sensation story. I do not write for the "Halfpenny English Youngster," or whatever be the name of the last sensational print; but I humbly hope, for a better purpose; hence, you may be sure, that the lady who stood by Vivian's bedside did not turn out to be his long-lost mother, his resuscitated mother, his mysterious mother. Ah! no, she became to him *like* a mother in the days that were to come; but all that she was *now* she told Vivian in a few brief words.

"My dear," she said, "I am your schoolmaster's sister. I heard last night of your illness, and of my brother's anxiety, owing to his wife's absence; and I hurried from the dinner-party where I happened to be in this town, to see if I could be of use to him and to you. You have heard, I fancy, of a sister of Mr. Morris' who had just come to reside near Seaford?"

"But have I been dreaming?" said the boy, "for certainly I did *see* an angel last night. At least it was you whom I saw, and I—I took you for an angel."

"Well," said Emma, "I was at a grand dinner-party yesterday, where there were several gentlemen of fashion, and not one said anything half so polite as that; no one *there* took me for an angel. It was worth while coming here to hear so gallant a speech. Did you ever hear of an angel called Emma Laurence, my dear?"

"No," said the boy, a little confused; and for the first time for months he laughed.

"Was I dreaming?" said he.

"I think," said Emma, "if you took me for an angel, you must have been wide awake; at least I prefer to suppose so. You certainly were *not* dreaming when you saw me last night; though, I suspect, the moonlight and the nightlight, and your fevered fancy, and my gay costume, helped the illusion. But I fear I am far from being a real angel."

"Yet," said the boy, "you are gentler and kinder than most persons are to me. And, to speak candidly, an angel would be a most acceptable visitor to me *just at present.*"

"An angel would be an agreeable visitor to all of us, at all times," said Emma, "but why do you emphasize the words 'just at present?'"

"Because," replied Vivian, harping on his old chord, "I am the unhappiest boy in all the world; everything goes wrong with me; and, as one of my schoolfellows justly said yesterday, nothing less than an angel would set me right."

"Rather a superlative expression," said Emma. "Why do you say this?"

And while the gentle lady again smoothed his ruffled pillow, cooled his heated brow, gave him a soothing draught, and tenderly bandaged his injured

s

arm—gracious offices, which a woman's sacred hand so well accomplishes—the boy told her the story of his unhappiness.

And he told her more; he told her step by step, little by little, his whole life's story. Not the history of incidents, for of these his boyish life had known but few; but the history of his *heart*, his feelings, his hopes, his sorrows, and his doubts; and, little by little, he unfolded his inner boyish life, till it was spread like a fairly written page before her.

"Well," said she, when all was told, and when she understood all, which she did very quickly; "there are two thoughts which should influence us in such manner as to prevent us from being wholly unhappy, or, at least, comfort us in our greatest pang. One is, that our own sorrows may be of use to others. The other, that they may be of use to ourselves. And this is, it seems to me, one of the keys of the problem of life."

" But this does not always seem clear," said Vivian.

" We do not always see it at once," replied Emma; " but as we can all judge from experience, I will tell you how I found this out, from my own experiences. From them I learnt, indeed, that sorrow seems given for our own use or for the use of others. My dear," she continued, after a pause; " I was an orphan, like yourself; but, unlike you, I had a sister and a brother. A friend of my father's was our guardian, and brought us up. When I was sixteen, a cousin of ours, a man of great wealth and high social rank, came to visit my guardian. He was clever, agreeable, and attractive; he was very courteous to me, and I fancied, giddy girl as I was, that he liked me. At least, to be frank, I do

not know that I quite thought *that,* but I really did
suppose he intended to marry me.   I was quite delighted with the notion of a wedding at which I should
figure as heroine, and of a house of my own, over
which I should preside.   I think I did not lift my
notions beyond this girlish ambition.   Well, it is clear
that my *cousin* did not think me an angel, for he
married my sister.   It appears she was the object of
his visits to our house.   Ah ! my pride had a fall, and
I was fearfully disappointed, unreasonably unhappy ;
I complained, as you complain, that I was the most
wretched person on the earth.   But the sorrow that came
to me—for I felt it was a sorrow—was good to some one ;
for I learnt that my sister had long loved her husband,
for years before their engagement, and his proposal to
her had rendered her truly happy ; so my trifling
sorrow was a great source of joy to her.   Well, my
dear, what cured me was a story which my guardian
told me.   He had a brother whom he loved intensely,
and looked up to as he might have looked up to a
father ; he loved, regarded, esteemed, and admired
him.   This dear brother suddenly died.   You may
imagine my guardian's grief.   It seemed to him that
the best part of his life had gone from him.   He was
so wretched with this great sorrow that he fell ill.
But a few months after this brother died, he heard
that a great disgrace, a great shame, was attached to
his name : a disgrace so terrible that, had it been made
known in the world, a blight would have been inevit-
ably attached to his family and their reputation.   By
his brother's death this circumstance was for ever concealed and the shame for ever prevented.   It fell on
none.   It did not fall on my guardian.   He was spared

this misery, and he quite understood—ere the tears of his grief were dry—that the sorrow which came to him was good for himself.

"But when I heard of this I was myself married ; my guardian, who was always my wise adviser, had asked me to be his wife.

"I had been his happy wife one year when a great joy came to me. Oh! Vivian, a little baby lay nestling in my arms! A baby of my own! I cannot paint my pleasure in that moment of delight. Some thoughts of joy we can only tell with our tears, with the voice of our hearts—we can only tell them to heaven.

"Fifteen years ago, my dear, my baby came from heaven to me. It had been with me just three months when I had to give it back to heaven. In just three months the little life I prized passed from my loving arms—"

And here the gentle lady paused, while her tears, ah! holy tears, rained on the boy's hand.

"My dear, had my baby lived, he would have been your age. He went; but, oh! my love for my child remained—remained on earth. I do not give it now to one child alone, as I might have done if my boy had lived. No, no; I give it to all children whom I see, and most warmly to motherless children. I give it to them fully, willingly, heartily.

"It seems to me that when my baby went to heaven, my love for him remained behind, and grew greater still; for every child I see has a place in my heart; and, though I am childless, I am a mother still.

"Vivian, I did not grieve too much; at least, I did not murmur nor complain. I had learnt my lesson. I felt my trial was sent to me for good; perhaps for my own use, perhaps for the use of others. Perhaps it came to teach me to love and tend my husband even more than I had done hitherto: perhaps to teach me to think of and care for all, all other children, instead of centreing my motherly tenderness on my own; perhaps to teach me to lift my eyes from earth to heaven, and strive so to live, while still in this world, that when I went away from it, I might see my boy once more yes, and be worthy to take him to my heart.

And it may be that my boy will not be ashamed of me in a world where we must perhaps prove as pure, or as purified, as the little ones we love."

  *   *   *   *

"Ah!" said Vivian vehemently, "how wretched you must be!"

"*I* wretched," said Emma. "Ah! no! I am quite happy. I think and thank."

"You think—and you can thank?" cried the boy.

"Yes," replied the lady; "I think of how all my sorrows have turned to good. A sister made happy through my first grief; my husband saved from a wretched life by a second grief; my heart purified by my last great sorrow,—my sorrow which has made me the mother of all children within my reach who need my care on earth, and of an angel who does not need my care, in heaven."

She might have spoken more when the boy—who was crying heartily—had dried his tears; she might have taught him by precept what her story had outlined to him, had not a great cry arisen beneath the windows, and a hurrying step sped up the staircase,— which startled them both.

And Mr. Morris, breathless, pale, and trembling, rushed into the room.

"Vivian!" he cried, as soon as he could speak, which was scarcely possible to him at first. "What—what is the name of the place where the boys have gone to play cricket?"

"Cliffsend," said Vivian. "Why?"

"What train were they to go by?" asked Mr. Morris.

"The mid-day train, the only possible one for them," replied the boy.

"Ah! gracious heaven!" cried the schoolmaster, falling back on a chair. "There has been a frightful accident. It has been telegraphed to the town—an accident to the mid-day train; lives are lost—and—" He stopped, and burst into tears. "More work for poor Emma."

*   *   *   *

"Well!" said the gentle, motherly lady, when she had soothed the suffering master, and revived the fainting boy. "Ah, well, you see, Vivian, how fortunate you were. You might have been with the boys—and then! Oh, my dear, think and thank."

"No, no," answered Vivian excitedly; "Don't judge me like that! Don't think so ill of me. I am not thinking of myself; I am thinking only of them, of the boys, of my schoolfellows! Oh, my schoolfellows! Oh, dear friends! Why was I not kinder to them? Why was I not better to them? Oh, if I should never see them more! I only think of *them*. Yes, I think and thank—for I am indeed thankful that I am well enough to help, if I can yet give some help—if any help can be of avail!"

He made a great effort to rise in the bed, eager to
be of use, agitated beyond measure; and sank back, as
you may well suppose, quite insensible. He had
fainted !

*   *   *   *

She could not rouse him from his swoon. The heavy
purple eyelids still lay closed on the pale cheek; the
lips remained colourless; the cold hand motionless on
the irregularly beating heart; the lady scarcely felt
the pulsation in his wrist.

She strove with all the tender remedies which
women understand so well and use so deftly, to restore his consciousness. It seemed in vain; still the
boy lay cold, and mute and deaf; lay almost as if his
life had winged its flight for ever.

*   *   *   *

Could nothing rouse him? Nothing? Yes, yes.
He moves; he listens; he breathes; his eyes open; he
smiles! He has heard a shout—a shout of joy—a
ringing, wild, impetuous, gladdening shout! The
merry cry of boyish voices—voices he knows so well
—the dear familiar voices of the school-room and the
playground! The voices of his schoolfellows, breaking
the air with their joyous cheers, as they troop boisterously, hurriedly, almost turbulently, into the field that
lay beneath his window! And the cry that roused
him was—

" Victory for Seaford School !"

*   *   *   *

" Did you think, Vivian," cried Harry Bennett, as
he rushed into the bed-room; "that we would have
gone to Cliffsend without you? Not we? we sent
over to tell the fellows so. The cowards thought we

were frightened to meet them without Vivian Davis
for a bowler or a batter; so they hired the town
omnibus, and came over here to fight us in our own
cricket field outside the town."

"Then you were not in the train ?" cried Vivian.

"What train ?"

"The mid-day train, where the accident occurred."

"Oh, no ; and the accident was greatly exaggerated ;
only an express train ran into a luggage van. Luggage
vans always seem to be left purposely on the line for
something to run into.   Nobody killed."

Vivian nearly "went off" again; his joy and gratitude confused him, and he scarcely heard what
followed ; but perhaps you would like to hear.

It seems that the Cliffsend boys, fancying the Seaford
boys shirked the match without Davis to help them,
trooped over to "have it out."

"And it is clear," said Harry Bennett, "we had
learnt more than one notion from you, Davis.   We
have not seen you play cricket so long and so well,
without profiting by it.   We know your cool way, old
fellow !   We know your style of bowling ; and Jack
Mendel copied your cool stroke, and we beat the
Cliffsend boys to nothing !"

"And, oh ! Vivian," said Ellis, "Such good news for
me !   My father is so delighted at my having won the
Barnett prize that I am not to go abroad.   I am to
go to University College.   Barnett has promised
my father to 'look after me,' and I think I am regu-
larly in for life's promotion.   So," continued the
aggravating boy, "your grief and loss have been my
joy and gain."

"Yes," said Vivian calmly smiling ; "and I am

heartily glad of it ; my grief and loss have been my joy and gain also."

And he looked with meaning eyes—loving eyes, very full of tears—at the gentle lady who stood beside his bed.

* * * *

Vivian rose from that bed a wiser, a happier, a better boy. He did not—for life is not a fairy tale—become at once and entirely cured of his great fault. No marvellous conversion was wrought in him. It is only in chemistry and in the annals of the " Great Gull " societies, that conversions are suddenly effected. But a gentle, tender, loving influence was henceforth exerted on him ; for Emma, taking fondly to the orphan boy, became a mother to him ; she cared for him, a little for his own sake, a little from the large loving-kindness of her heart, and not a little for the sake of the baby boy who had gone away from her; the baby who, had he lived, would have been of Vivian's age.

The angel influence of her motherly heart cured the boy of his great failing ; for love has immense power. He grew up wise and good, for he learnt through her the blessed strength of a mother's love. As she herself said ; though her child was gone, her motherly love remained. And thus, in truth, it was a real angel that came to the school-boy; an angel who taught him to " think and thank."

THE EVERLASTING ROSE.

A Parable for School Boys and School Girls.

———

אֲנִי חֲבַצֶּלֶת הַשָּׁרוֹן

" I am the rose of Sharon."—Song Sol. ii. 1.

WE are bound to believe in God's Bible, even when we do not quite understand it. We must believe in His revelation, even when we cannot fully grasp its intention ; just, indeed, as we are bound to submit to His will, even when we do not comprehend His divine motives and immediate purposes. Yet it is far easier for us to believe and to obey, when we see—or think we see—the reason, motive, or intention of the heavenly scheme or divine ordinance, than when we merely yield a blind obedience.

Does it not sometimes appear singular to you, that God should have chosen one family among the many families of the earth, and should have specially manifested to that family His power and will, and should have given to it His commandments? He chose one family—the children of Jacob and their descendants ; and separated them from all other families of the earth by special institutions and observances, which rendered them a peculiar people, apart from all other people, wherever they might dwell and whatever might happen to them.

Since all the world and all its creatures are dear to their Creator, how came it that He chose one family; made it a great nation; told that nation His will; and sent it forth, armed with His Law, shielded by His promise, and girded by His institutions, into the world at large, with whose inhabitants that chosen nation might mix—*but never blend?* Now let us see if, by a simple parable, the reason can be made clear to us.

There were fifty boys in a school-room, and each boy bore in his breast a moss-rose, plucked from a tree that grew in the playground. Presently, the Master came amongst them; the Master whose voice they heard, but whom they did not always obey, nor trust, nor believe. He was a man with smiling lip but flashing eye, with a gentle but a firm voice.

He placed his hand on the shoulder of one of the boys, and said, "Pluck out the rose you have gathered, and take the one I offer. Place it in your breast. *My* rose comes not from your playground, but from a fairer and far distant garden. The other roses, the roses of the other boys, will fade and wither. They will lose their fragrance; they will droop and crumble. But *my* rose will never die. It will never lose its fragrance. It will never lose its beauty. Buds will spring from it, which you may give to your comrades. The other roses that you see around you, even if they be grafted on your own, will perish. But not my rose. Summer will fade into autumn. Autumn will grow into winter. Yet in every season—season by season—year by year

—indeed for ever—the rose I give to you shall live and bloom and blush and be ever fragrant and fair as at this hour."

The boy who had been chosen took the rose; at first according to childhood's impulse, contentedly *believing*, but, soon, as the impression of the Master's voice died away, he *doubted!* The other boys laughed when the Master left. They scoffed at the boy and at his rose.

For, as the days of the summer advanced—and they were long, light, gay days—*their* roses grew, and bloomed, and opened, and threw out bright gaudy petals. And the boys quarrelled amongst themselves because each one said that *his* rose was not alone the brightest, the largest, the fairest, and the sweetest; but that *his* was the only true rose, and all the other roses were weeds or artificial flowers.

Their roses grew and flourished, but the rose that was given to the Chosen Child never grew. It remained the same as at the moment in which it was first placed in the boy's bosom. It remained small, very small; unpretending and unchanging; fair and fragrant. The sun shone on it brilliantly; the twilight closed on it gloomily; the darkness of the night shrouded it heavily, and the storm-rains beat on it sturdily; and the dawn sent its first pale streaks on it in its humble abiding place; but the rose of the Chosen Child passed through every ordeal—the painful and the pleasant—and it remained unchanged, still fair and graceful; still bright and fragrant. And the days wore on.

Summer faded into autumn; autumn mellowed into winter. The gaudy flaunting roses which the boys carried in their bosoms, withered in their pride. They drooped; they died; they shed their blighted leaves and their over-ripe petals; they lost their perfume, their color, and their grace; "they withered on the stem." So that when the winter had well set in, the playground roses perished; they crumbled into dust. And, at last, nothing remained in the breast of each boy of the childish group, but—not even the remnant of a flower—nothing save a blighted, broken, useless, ugly, rotting stem.

Not so the rose of the Chosen Child. Summer passed into autumn, autumn hardened into winter, and the rose given by the Master from his own ground remained unblighted and unchanged. Unblighted in its freshness; unchanged in its beauty, its fragrance and its grace.

And, although when the Chosen Child held the rose aloft in his hands and shewed it to his comrades to let them know its constant loveliness and drink into their senses its undying perfume, the thorns on the stem wounded his hands somewhat roughly, "He was wounded through our transgression*"; yet he was comforted, for he held in his hands the fairest flower of all—the flower that gave pleasure by its presence and its fragrance to his comrades—the Everlasting Rose.

When the boys saw that their roses died, while this *one* rose lived on: they began to think it must be a miracle. They cast away—some angrily, others scornfully—the withered stalks that had once been surmounted by their own gay and proud flowers. They admitted that the flower of the Chosen Child was the

* Isaiah liii. 5.

only true and real rose. And they believed in the goodness, power, greatness and truth of the Master, the Master by whom the Rose was given.

Now the Master had given roses to *all* the boys; and if these roses had all remained unblighted and unfading through all the varying seasons and changes of the year, the boys would have naturally thought that this was an ordinary fashion, and that it was the nature of all roses to remain unaltered, ever fresh and fragrant in every time and change and season. They would have said, here is nothing wonderful. The Master has given us ordinary roses; garden roses. It is the custom of roses to bloom periodically. The Master differs not from ordinary gardeners. We need not believe in his wisdom or his truth: we need neither fear nor obey him.

But, when they saw their own bright roses die; and when they saw that the humble little flower the Chosen Child wore in his breast, lived on, flourished, bloomed, and gloried in its enduring beauty, grace and perfume: they recognised a MIRACLE, and they believed, and they gathered (if they were gentle); or snatched (if they were rude), buds and blossoms from the rose of the Chosen Child; and they began to believe in the Master.

And they said to the Chosen Child, "What was it that the Master whispered in your ear, when he gave you the rose? What was it that he said you were to do to keep the rose untarnished and unchanged?"

And the Child told them what had been whispered in his ear by the Master. It was this:

"The rose which I give to you was given to me by

ONE who gave me with it one command alone ;—Love ME and MINE !"

This immortal rose is God's Law! Moses is our Master. Israel the Chosen Child!

Oh, Israel! Witness of God's great truth and dear love to all thy comrades in earth's school! Thou who hast borne through all the ages, and still shalt bear, till thy mission be fulfilled, the Everlasting Rose, guard it and prize it!

Israel, the Chosen Child, has borne this rose in his breast through all the historic drama and all its varied scenes; through all the seasons, with their sunshine and their storms; through the summer of prosperity, the autumn of decay, the winter of contumely, the dawning spring of hope! through the days when his comrades feared him, and the days when his comrades oppressed him; through the days when his comrades courted him, and—gathering round him—proffered the too friendly, too hospitable, and therefore tempting hands.

May Israel guard and prize the rose with a jealous eye for the Giver's sake, and water it with the tears of contrition and affection! There was a time in the history of life's school, when, in the dark winter of trouble, it was watered with the life-blood of Israel in the sad hour of martyrdom.

Other roses grow from earthly roots. They grow, they bloom and flourish gaily; they fade and die. But the rose of the Master grew in a different soil; it sprung from heaven. Like the asphodel it cannot fade. It is indeed the tree of life which is planted in the midst of us and it cannot die!

The rose shall spread over all the earth. Its world-wide branches shall grow strong and firm ; and all the scholars, led by the Child chosen by the Giver, shall climb the stalwart boughs and pluck its rich fruits— the fruits of godliness and virtue—and thus become worthy of entering the garden whence the Rose sprung, that garden which we call Heaven !

END.

PRINTED BY WERTHEIMER, LEA AND CO., FINSBURY CIRCUS

www.ingramcontent.com/pod-product-compliance
Lightning Source LLC
Chambersburg PA
CBHW021048030726
47496CB00006B/1747